ꙮꙮꙮ Listening to the Voices

Listening

WENDY BRENNER

RITA CIRESI

HARVEY GROSSINGER

DENNIS HATHAWAY

HA JIN

CAROL LEE LORENZO

CHRISTOPHER McILROY

C. M. MAYO

ALYCE MILLER

DIANNE NELSON

ANDY PLATTNER

PAUL RAWLINS

© 1998 by the University of Georgia Press
Athens, Georgia 30602
All rights reserved
Designed by Erin Kirk New
Set in 10 on 13.5 Electra by G & S Typesetters
Printed and bound by McNaughton & Gunn, Inc.
The paper in this book meets the guidelines for
permanence and durability of the Committee on
Production Guidelines for Book Longevity of the
Council on Library Resources.

Printed in the United States of America

02 01 00 99 98 P 5 4 3 2 1

Library of Congress Cataloging in Publication Data

Listening to the voices : stories from the Flannery
O'Connor Award / selected by Charles East.
     p.   cm.
   ISBN 0-8203-1994-5 (pbk. : alk. paper)
   1. Short stories, American.   I. East, Charles.
PS648.S5L6   1998
813'.0108054—dc21   97-40051

British Library Cataloging in Publication Data available

SELECTED BY CHARLES EAST

to the Voices

Stories from the Flannery O'Connor Award

THE UNIVERSITY OF GEORGIA PRESS

Athens & London

"If you have Voices you'd
better listen to them and let
the form take care of itself."

FLANNERY O'CONNOR
LETTER TO MARYAT LEE
FEBRUARY 24, 1957

Contents

Acknowledgments

The stories in this anthology are from the following collections published by the University of Georgia Press:

Wendy Brenner, *Large Animals in Everyday Life* (1996)
Rita Ciresi, *Mother Rocket* (1993)
Harvey Grossinger, *The Quarry* (1997)
Dennis Hathaway, *The Consequences of Desire* (1992)
Ha Jin, *Under the Red Flag* (1997)
Carol Lee Lorenzo, *Nervous Dancer* (1995)
Christopher McIlroy, *All My Relations* (1994)
C. M. Mayo, *Sky Over El Nido* (1995)
Alyce Miller, *The Nature of Longing* (1994)
Dianne Nelson, *A Brief History of Male Nudes in America* (1993)
Andy Plattner, *Winter Money* (1997)
Paul Rawlins, *No Lie Like Love* (1996)

Introduction

When I was put in charge of the Flannery O'Connor Award for Short Fiction at the time the award was established in 1981, I had no idea that I would still be at it this many years later. Not that I had any doubts about the seriousness or importance of what we were doing. Like Paul Zimmer, the University of Georgia Press director who started it all, I was confident that the award would quickly find a place for itself. Most of all I felt that our commitment to publication of short fiction would be welcomed by the writers themselves, who had seen the outlets for their work diminish to the point that the likelihood of acceptance of a first book of stories by one of the New York publishers was roughly equivalent to that of being struck by lightning. When it happened, it happened not because of the publisher's high hopes for the collection (quite the contrary) but the expectation that the writer would shortly come forth with a novel.

How could a form that had produced some of the best of twentieth-century American writing—the form of choice for so many of our writers—be treated with such indifference? I didn't understand it—still don't.

Despite the far-reaching changes that have occurred in publishing over the years since then—and no one can predict what lies ahead—the situation in regard to publication of short fiction appears to have changed very little. But the short story writers are still writing. The literary magazines are still there, and still giving the writers a respectful hearing. The *New Yorker* beckons, as it always did—writers can dream, can't they? Still, if you want to make an agent or a New York publisher happy, the secret word is *novel*.

Which, as I recall, was precisely the situation when Paul Zimmer and I discussed the pros and cons of our starting a short fiction series back in 1980. Paul was in fact already thinking about the series when I came to the Press as editor that summer. From my arrival in Athens, the two of us spent lunches and drive-time to Atlanta talking about the award and the books we hoped would result from it—collections of stories that were deserving of being published but that, as a consequence of the obvious hesitation of the commercial publishers, were going unpublished.

A poet as well as a publisher, Paul shared my belief that publication of original creative work was a legitimate role for the university presses, whose primary function was, of course, publication of the fruits of scholarship. He had had experience with the poetry program at the University of Pittsburgh Press before coming to Georgia, and I had published poetry and short fiction during my years as editor and later director at the Louisiana State University Press.

We were not among the majority. Publication of original creative work by the university presses has always been in the hands of a relatively small number of people and has tended to follow them as they moved from press to press. Richard Wentworth, the LSU Press director who opened the doors to poets and short story writers in the mid-1960s, left there for the University of Illinois Press in 1970 and is still publishing poetry and fiction. But most of the presses had never published either—and were not disposed to do so. Instead they would stick to what I recall hearing some of the speakers at the annual university press meetings refer to as "the pure tobacco."

Shortly before or after my arrival at the University of Georgia Press, Paul Zimmer had the idea of naming the award for Flannery O'Connor, the Georgia writer. I should say "the writer": O'Connor would not have liked being called a Georgia writer any more than she wanted to be thought of as a southern writer. "The woods are full of regional writers," she said, "and it is the great horror of every serious southern writer that he will become one of them." Flannery O'Connor had died in 1964 at the age of thirty-nine, but her work was still being read and talked about, both on and off the college campuses.

While Paul and I went down the list of questions we had, such as whether to have one winner or two and what system of judging to use, he got a letter off to Regina Cline O'Connor, Flannery's mother, in Milledgeville, to tell her of his plans for the series and to get her blessing. To make a long story short, we got underway in 1981 with the initial round of the Flannery O'Connor Award competition—a round that produced the first of our winners, David Walton and Leigh Allison Wilson. Walton's book of stories *Evening Out* was published in the spring of 1983 and Wilson's *From the Bottom Up* in the fall of that year.

We were pleased—I might even say relieved—to see that the submissions came from across the country, about equally divided between South and East, West and Midwest. Walton was living in Pittsburgh; Wilson, then a teaching-writing fellow in the Writers' Workshop at the University of Iowa, had grown up in Tennessee. Happily, the geographical mix of the submissions continued: we were not going to be cubbyholed as regional.

Over these seventeen years we have had more winners from California, Utah, and Florida (four each) than from any other state; more from Salt Lake City (four) than any other city. The winners live in Seattle and St. Louis, in Tampa and Tucson, in Maine, West Virginia, Indiana, Maryland, Kentucky, Connecticut, North Carolina, New Mexico, Ohio. One lives in Mexico City. Another—one of the 1996 winners, Ha Jin—was born in China and served in the People's Liberation Army before coming to the United States in 1985.

Twenty-seven of the thirty-three Flannery O'Connor Award volumes published to date have been first books—or, rather, first books of fiction—though the competition is open to writers who have previously had a novel or a collection of stories (or more than one) published. The typical manuscript includes several stories that first appeared in magazines, more often than not the literary quarterlies. Many of the collections that we see include at least one and sometimes more than one story previously published in the *New Yorker*, the *Atlantic Monthly*, *Esquire*, or *Harper's*. Frequently one or more have been reprinted in *Best American Short Stories* or one of the other anthologies.

Occasionally we see a manuscript of unpublished stories, and two of these collections have ended up winners (in both cases, stories were submitted to magazines and accepted after announcement of the winners). One measure of the success of the award is that at least ten of the first-book authors have now published second or, in some cases, third books with other publishers.

This is the second anthology of Flannery O'Connor Award stories. The first, *The Flannery O'Connor Award: Selected Stories*, was published in 1992 and brought together twenty-one stories, one from each of the collections that came from the rounds held between 1981 and 1990. *Listening to the Voices* picks up at 1991 and includes twelve stories from the collections published between 1992 and 1997.

As this is being published, a new round of the competition is about to get started. Each new round brings the excitement that inevitably accompanies the arrival of the manuscripts and the beginning of the judging. Some of these will be stories we have read before, admired before (several of our winners won not the first time out but in subsequent rounds). We are always glad to see those. Most of the writers and stories will in fact be new to us, which makes the process of finding the winners the fun that it is. The next manuscript, or the next, might bring us up out of our chairs.

I have been asked what we are looking for. My answer is that we are looking for stories that surprise us, delight us, grab us and refuse to let go. We are looking for good—better than good—exceptional storytelling. In other words, stories like Christopher McIlroy's "All My Relations" and Ha Jin's "In Broad Daylight" or C. M. Mayo's "The Jaguarundi"—three altogether different stories, three widely different settings.

McIlroy's story is set amid the desert and mountains of Arizona; Ha Jin's, in the China of the Cultural Revolution; Mayo's, in a lush and exotic Mexico City. A Pima Indian whose wife and son have left him is offered a permanent job and a new life by a white rancher, but finds he is drawn back to his old life on the reservation. An adulterous wife is taken from her home by the Red Guards and paraded through the streets of the town. In the Mayo story, a writer living in Mexico spends his afternoons with another man's wife and, when she leaves for a few months in Europe, returns to her house, where the memory of her lingers in her pet jaguarundi.

We are looking for strong characters: characters that we can identify with or respond to—that give the story its force of authority. In the McIlroy story, the Indian ranch foreman, Milton Enos. Or Paul Westerly, the architect on his way to a crack-up in Dennis Hathaway's "Space and Light," who sets out to design a studio connected to his house but instead builds a cocoon for himself. Or, for another example from these stories, Jude Silverman, once

Judy Schitzman, the Jewish Chicken Little with the East Side accent in Rita Ciresi's "Mother Rocket." Whether performing as an intermediate-range ballistic missile in her avant-garde dance troupe's "World War III" or giving the polar bear in his cage in Central Park a piece of her mind, Jude Silverman demands our attention.

So, in a less insistent but no less effective way, does the former rodeo rider now on the racetrack circuit in Andy Plattner's "Winter Money." He and Amanda, a girl he met at the track in Tampa, are holed up in a motel in Tomaston, Kentucky. His Oldsmobile has quit on him, his cash is running out, and something isn't right between them. What he needs is a winning race that will bring him enough money to fix it.

Marsha, the narrator of Alyce Miller's "Tommy," and Eulene, in Carol Lee Lorenzo's "Nervous Dancer," remind us of the ties that bind and the distance that separates human beings—a recurring theme in these stories. In the Miller story, Marsha feels obliged to attend the funeral of a man she knew as a boy in junior high and high school. There they were thrown together by the color of their skin but in fact were never close, she thinks, as she recalls the points at which their lives touched and reflects on how tenuous the connection was. Lorenzo's Eulene loves her mother but does not like being around her. It has been years since she has seen her father. The closest she has "ever been able to get to anybody" is to her husband Julien. Now, ten years into their marriage, she brings him into her mother's home for the first time on a vacation that turns out to be a disaster.

We are looking for stories with a compelling voice: the writer recalling afternoons with Manette in "The Jaguarundi"; Noah, the son of a wounded POW father back from Korea in Harvey Grossinger's moving story "Home Burial"; seventeen-year-old April in Dianne Nelson's "A Brief History of Male Nudes in America," witness to the seemingly endless procession of men who wander in and out of her mother's bedroom. Listening to the sounds in the next room, she tells us, "The walls of this house aren't thick enough to keep that kind of sadness contained."

Voice is in fact one of the things that distinguish these stories, whether in dialogue or coming from the first-person narrator. "So what do you think of human blood and suffering? Ever seen any?" asks the man whose book-jacket blurb calls him "America's angriest writer" in Wendy Brenner's story "Guest Speaker." The girl to whom he addresses the question has been dispatched to the airport to drive him to his hotel, but reaches there only after some unexpected turns including a detour down a back-country road and a swim in a sinkhole.

"Now, with my wife gone, and my children with her, and my job, I start my day with eggs I buy two dozen at a time on gray cardboard sheets" begins the narrator of Paul Rawlins's "Home and Family." By the end of the story his seventeen-year-old son Ben has come to stay the night and a trim and understanding woman named Sylvia whose husband is missing in action in Vietnam has fallen asleep on the couch. "The house seems full, like it hasn't for a long time. . . ."

No faux Faulkner here, or virtual Flannery O'Connor. The latter, by the way, has been a recurring but in recent years a less frequently seen phenomenon: writers who have assumed that what we are looking for are reasonable facsimiles of Flannery O'Connor. One can only imagine what the hard-eyed and sharp-tongued Miss O'Connor would have said to that. She herself had gone her own original and solitary way. "After all, nobody wants his mule and wagon stalled on the same track the Dixie Limited is roaring down," she said—a word to the wise with Faulkner in mind. Nor was she any more anxious to have other writers follow her.

As I did in the case of the first anthology of Flannery O'Connor Award stories, I have resisted the temptation to select the "best" of the stories in the collections by these writers—which would have been a meaningless task at best. How do you choose "Home Burial" over "Dinosaurs," another of the stories in Harvey Grossinger's collection? Or "Tommy" over Alyce Miller's "A Cold Winter Light" or "Dead Women"? Perhaps "among the stories I most enjoyed" or "among the stories I have found myself coming back to" would be a more accurate description of them.

Charles East

Guest Speaker

The guest speaker flies in on the last day of July, and you are there to meet him. You watch the speck of his plane approach from behind the terminal's glass wall, which boils against the palm of your hand as though an invisible fire rages just outside. The sun is so powerful you can see through your thumb, which looks old, though you are young. The jet taxis hugely in, sending its thrilling, screaming roar up through the carpet. When you're in your windowless office, only a few miles from here, typing memos for Dr. Mime, you never, ever think about this airport, the people strolling through it, the woods and swamps spread out around it, or the enormous blue sky. A massive wooden octagon a few feet from you houses four TVs, each facing in a different direction, each showing Oprah Winfrey, whose upbeat, reproachful gaze addresses those who have not taken sufficient charge of their lives. A woman in Oprah's audience yells, "Honey, if he did it to me, he's gonna do it to you!" You put your hand on your shoulder bag, feeling the hard shape of the stolen tape recorder through the corduroy. Actually, it is not exactly stolen, but you cannot help but feel like a criminal. It is an old feeling, the feeling that you are trying to get away with something, something for which you will surely be forced to pay, eventually, though in this case you don't even have a plan, you're not even sure what you're trying to get away with.

The recorder is Dr. Mime's; he speaks into it as though he is a secret agent, holding his lips and teeth still so that you cannot make out certain words and have to type blank lines in their place, as he has instructed you to do in such an instance. *Cliff and Linda need to help me find my _____ that I misplaced the middle of last week,* you type. My garden? My bargain? My Darlene? It is impossible to tell. *To ask Williamson: Were we interested in whether anyone's been looking at the litigation papers that are filed with _____?* He uses surveillance equipment on you as well: cameras in the corridors, a computer that keeps track of your phone calls, who knows what else? He sucks Tic-Tacs all day long, keeps cartons of them in your office's file cabinet—you can even hear them clicking against his teeth on the memo tapes—but he never offers a single Tic-Tac to you or anyone. And although he owns two or three Cessnas, his hobby, he never offers to take anyone for a ride, though he makes the mailroom guy hose down the planes on days like Veterans Day, when there is work but no mail. You yourself have tutored little dyslexic Barry Mime in fractions, though you are a part-time employee, no benefits, and Nancy, a customer service operator, always takes the Mime Mercedeses in for their emissions tests. And now it's your job to chauffeur the guest speaker, who will speak at an executive function to which you are not invited.

To all employees, night custodial staff NOT *excluded,* you typed, earlier this week. *Topic: Suspicious individuals in your neighborhood making inquiries of you or your family regarding MimeCo or Dr. Mime. Last night a suspicious individual was making inquiries regarding me at the residences of my neighbors. This is possibly related to the controversial nature of our upcoming visiting guest speaker. Naturally, I followed up as appropriate. If such an individual contacts you by telephone or in person, it would be help-*

ful if you could tell them, "I don't have time to talk now, but please call me or return tomorrow at this same time." Thank you for your assistance in this matter. This is the unfortunate side of business and we are going to pursue it in a _____ fashion. Richard fashion? Bitchier fashion? Denatured fashion? Mature, that was it, you typed it in—and then, without even thinking about it, you switched off the recorder and dropped it into your bag, which sat slumped between your ankles on the floor. When Linda came to the doorway of your office a minute later, your stomach turned over.

"You are red," she said. Linda sells Mary Kay and always comments on your appearance, pushing you to let her give you a makeover, but even thinking about confronting your face matter-of-factly like that causes you shame. You purse your lips and duck your head whenever you have to look into a mirror, hanging on to certain illusions. You cry at night, sometimes, like anyone: Oh God, oh God, I'm so lonely, I'm so lonely.

"Coffee makes me flush," you told her.

She gave you a look that said, "You are crazy." Sometimes she just says it aloud to you, so you know the look. "Well, hand it over," she said then.

You just looked at her.

"Your time card," she said. "Girl, wake up! It's Friday!"

After she walked away you felt the sharp edge of the recorder with your instep, and then you cut it out of your thoughts altogether, as though Mime's clocks and cameras and computers might pick up its presence there.

Driving home you had an itchy scalp, a sign of guilt, your mother would have said, and in fact you also had the sinking sense of inevitable wrongness that you'd always felt around your mother. When you were a child your toys would disappear if you left them lying around on cleaning day; if you asked when you would get them back, she would say, "When I feel like it." Sometimes when she was out you would visit your Dawn doll in her bottom dresser drawer, but there would have been no pleasure in taking it out and playing with it. And there was a moment that came right after the first chorus of "Killing Me Softly," a record you'd won at a birthday party, that made your heart jump for years whenever you heard it, ever since the day your mother shouted your name at that moment in the song because she'd just discovered something else you'd done wrong, something you'd thought you'd gotten away with but which she had just then discovered.

But your mother was, or claimed to be, an unhappy woman, and when you complained as a teenager about how cold she had been, how cruel, she argued that it was only because she felt things so much more deeply than others. "Every morning I used to zip you into your parka and kiss you goodbye," she said, "but then one day when you were in second grade you pushed me away and told me not to kiss you, and I felt so hurt, so rejected, that I never tried to kiss you again—what else could I have done?" No warmth blossomed between the two of you after that explanation, but at least she had offered one. Mime does not seem to feel that he needs any, and perhaps he doesn't, being only a boss and not a mother.

The guest speaker pushes through the turnstile. In person he barely resembles his book jacket photo; he does not appear to be brooding or contemplating danger and loss. His head seems smaller. He wears dark woolen clothes, inappropriate in the heat, and his hand is delicate, scrubbed and vulnerable-looking on the strap of his carry-on bag. You step forward to introduce yourself and, without planning it or even knowing you're going to do it, you use a fake name. "I'm Alex Trotter," you say. Alex Trotter is a boy you slept with a few times in college, just after your mother's death—he is, actually, the last boy you slept with. That was two years ago, and his name bursts out of your mouth as though of its own volition, as though it has waited long enough.

The guest speaker smiles photogenically and says, "Alex," and you feel a little dizzied. A memory shoots back to you: when you were seven or eight, just after your father left you and your mother for his girlfriend in Norway, your mother explained to you that in real life princesses did not wear fancy gowns, were not necessarily pretty (Look at Margaret and Anne, she said, who were *homely*)—princesses looked, she said, like anyone, like everyone. The next morning, without planning it, you told the other children on the bus to school that you were a princess, explaining in the commanding, reasonable tones of your mother that there was no way of knowing a princess by her appearance alone. It was not exactly a lie; if there was no way of knowing, weren't you as much a princess as a princess nobody knew was one? And though you remember almost nothing firsthand about your father—just the outlines of his kind blond face, his low voice singing "Mares eat oats and does eat oats and little lambs eat ivy," him pressing his handkerchief to your face, saying, "You have a booby in your nose"—you remember the moment after your princess lie as perfectly as though it happened yesterday: you gazed out the smudgy bus window, changed and desperate and ordinary all at once.

"I'm all yours, Alex," the guest speaker says. His smallness suddenly seems calculated, fierce, like that of a ferret. He writes about outrages in other countries, chemical leaks and medical scams and robber barons—"America's angriest writer," a blurb on one of his book jackets says. His wife has the name of some foreign, toxic flower; you read it in the dedication of his first book and thought, *Of course, how perfect.*

In the front seat of your mother's old Fury the guest speaker asks polite questions about the town. You answer a few truthfully—"I can drive from one end to the other in eighteen minutes," you tell him—but then you begin to make things up or steal information from the lives of your friends, who are mostly secretaries or assistants like yourself. You invent and describe ordinary pets and relatives, small adventures and ambitions and defeats. You have two hamsters, Hanky and Panky, you say, and one time you found Siamese twin baby turtles in your backyard; they could only walk in a circle and you named them Yin and Yang. You tell him your mother is still alive, is in fact the most popular dentist in the county, the only female dentist, too, and you mention that you heard that in Japan it only costs fourteen dollars to get a root canal. While you talk, you notice in the rearview that the couple in the car behind yours is having an animated conversation in sign language, and for a moment it seems that you too are making shapes in the air with your words, producing and erasing commonplace things like a magician manipulating scarves and coins and wristwatches. The silver windows of the Hilton flash just off the highway, but you whiz past. "Room's not ready yet," you lie.

"That's all right," the guest speaker says. "I'm on vacation. Why don't you be my guide, show me what you do for fun?"

You smile in a measured way so that he not recognize how easily charmed you are. For fun you order Szechuan beef sometimes. You have accepted without complaint or question, though you hadn't realized you accepted it until this moment, the absence of men attempting to charm you. But *why?* you wonder now. You feel anxious, like a guest arriving at a fabulous party several hours late—what will be left for you? "There's a bar I once went to over on the Panhandle," you tell him. This happens to be the truth. It is the only excursion out of town you have taken since your mother died—you met with your mother's lawyer, signed papers, turned down his offer of dinner, and drank one gin and tonic alone at this bar. "They were so drunk and Southern there I could barely understand a word they said," you say. "This man with a sunken-in face came up to me and said something that sounded like 'Flip knot' over and over. Then he went back to his stool and said, 'If you see something you want, go for it,' until the barmaid yelled at him and kicked him out the door."

"Perfect," the guest speaker says. "Love it."

A moment later, he says, "So what do you think of human blood and suffering? Ever seen any?"

"What?" you say.

"Do you ever feel removed from it?" he says. "You know, being alive and all?"

You glance at him, but he looks like anyone, like everyone — there is no way of knowing a madman by his appearance alone. In his last book, titled *Uh-Oh*, he wrote about some children in Brazil who found glowing radioactive powder in a public dump and smeared it all over their faces, playing clowns and phantoms. How angry is he, exactly? you wonder. You think of the suspicious individuals making inquiries, you picture the guest speaker's graceful angry hands around your throat. Traffic veers off an exit behind you as you speed recklessly ahead; the deaf couple — if they even *were* deaf — have vanished. Humdrum moments from your recent life crowd you, demanding payback. *My God, you think, if I live through this, I must get busy.*

But then he is unwrapping a stick of gum for you and apologizing. "I'm uncouth," he is saying. He is charming again. You take the gum, and a deep breath. "I am highly visible," he says. "I have a wife, children. But that's all on the outside, you know what I mean?"

He is speaking again in sensible cliché, and you nod with relief, feeling your hair swing, the pretty hair of Alex Trotter. The real Alex was not kind. He asked, a day or two after your mother died, what you planned to do with your life, and when you told him that you had no idea, he said, "Well, get cracking." His tone of voice reminded you of the way your mother would stand on the porch, holding open the screen door, waiting for the cat to decide whether or not it wanted to go out, saying, "Would you make up your alleged mind?"

"I'm forty," the guest speaker says, "and I've been all over the world, but I've never been in the hospital, never been to a funeral. Have you been to a funeral?"

"Yes," you say, "but it didn't seem real. It didn't make anything seem any more real. Isn't that what funerals are supposed to do?" You borrowed eyeliner from one of your mother's friends in the funeral home's rest room after the burial. Two chigger bites on your ankle itched furiously all through the service. The next day you bought a can of apple juice from the machine in your dormitory's lobby, a can that had probably been placed in the machine before your mother's death. Everything seemed impartial, improbable. "There was no human blood," you tell the guest speaker.

He laughs. "You seem like a tough girl, Alex," he says. "Do you want to wallow with me?"

"Maybe," you say, smiling your new, offhand smile, Alex's smile. And maybe you do. Maybe this is the opportunity you've been waiting for. Go for it, you imagine your sexy blond father saying, though you know he is no longer blond, sexy, or even in Norway. You want for a moment to tell the guest speaker your real name, the real facts of your life, but, you rationalize, if what you are covering up is nothing of worth, nothing of much substance or purpose, you're not really lying, are you?

Perhaps you know the story of the hundred-year-old woman and the ice cream, your father wrote to you one summer. *The woman was asked what she would do differently if she could live her life over again, and she said, "Smell more wildflowers, and eat more ice cream." The point is that if you go through life lying to please others, you are giving nothing to them or yourself. And if you lie to please yourself, the best you will ever have to call your own is a mo-*

ment. You might as well be a ghost: you will move through the world, but you won't be living. These are important principles and you are not too young to understand them.

You were fourteen and had just come home from the beach. Your friends Tutti and Chrissy were with you, and all three of you were excited because at the beach you had met some long-haired older boys who told you they were the members of Cheap Trick. The boys had stood in the surf a little farther in than you, grinning and beckoning, flexing their skinny chests, the waves darkening their cutoffs, and you and Tutti and Chrissy had come close to them, but not too close. You high-stepped through the rising and falling water, scared of stepping on a crab, not wanting to get too wet, picking at your bikini bottom and your hair. The conversation was not about whether they were telling the truth, as it would have been if you were all boys, but about whether or not you believed them. "I would *know*," you told the boys, but you didn't want to know, and it was not required of you to decide one way or another, since of course once you decided there would be nothing to talk about. This went on for hours.

The dim beige hush of your living room afterwards was stifling, but then you saw the letter, unopened, on the floor beneath the mail slot, and your face burned as though the sun, the boys, had sneaked in after you. You bent over to pick it up and your heart rushed as though you were stealing something. Your mother was still at work. "Who do *you* know in another country?" Tutti asked, and you said, "A guy," and would tell them no more.

When your mother came home, however, you did not bother to remove the letter from the hassock on which you'd left it. She had given you permission so many times to keep secret your correspondence with your father—"or anything else you feel should be private," she often added—that there was no point. He had only sent two or three letters, total, and never one like this—seven handwritten pages from a full-sized legal pad, talking about life and your mother and happiness—but after Tutti and Chrissy left you could not escape an odd sense of letdown, and the last thing you felt like doing was rereading it, or writing a letter back. What you wanted to do, and what you did, was to lie on your bed in the dark late, late into the night and imagine again the boys on the beach.

You take one of the county road exits and angle the creaking car onto a dirt turnoff that heads into plantings of young pine. A bleached wooden sign at the road's entrance says SNACKS— 1/4 MILE; otherwise, you have no idea what to expect. You have never been out this way. A breeze through the open passenger window brings you a whiff of strong pine and the guest speaker's insidious cologne, probably purchased for him by his wife. You bump along in silence, taking little sips of the disturbing scent, until the road finally opens onto a dirt and gravel clearing containing two metal-sided sheds. One is set back in the high weeds and is the size of a doghouse or bathroom. The other has a door that looks like it's woven of chicken wire, propped open against the back of a large, napping goat. The guest speaker says, "I love that." You step over the goat, your heart pounding.

Inside are two short old women in jeans and flannel shirts and tractor caps, and, miraculously, the man with the sunken face. They are all sitting at a flimsy-looking, vinyl-topped card table, smoking cigarettes and drinking beer out of juice glasses. "You got to have that little flap, or your goddamn trowel sticks," one of the women is saying. A cartoon of a locomotive bouncing out of control down the side of a mountain flickers on a small soundless TV on the bar, and a busy munching noise comes from behind the counter, down near the cement floor. You see the black and white hoof of another goat, like something on a keychain, poking out beside the leg of the bar stool on the end. "You looking for the sink?" the old woman talking about bricklaying says, and the sunken-faced man says, "Where you from, baby?"

"The bathroom?" you say.

"The *sinkhole*," says the old woman. "Fifty yards down the path. You pay here."

"Hey, where you from?" the sunken-faced man says again.

"How much?" the guest speaker asks the woman.

"Two dollars apiece," she says.

"What's down there?" he asks.

"Well now, you got to pay to see," she says.

The sunken-faced man stands and strolls over to you. He stops when his collapsing face is just inches from yours, the yellow whites of his eyes gleaming beneath pale irises. "You know where you're from?" he says.

"Yes," you say. He can't possibly know your name; you're sure you never told it to him on the Panhandle.

"You're from your *mama*," he says. "You're from your *mama*."

"Thank you kindly," the old woman says to the guest speaker, taking his money. They are smiling at each other like friends.

Gnats fly into your mouth as you and the guest speaker follow the path through the brush. The goat from the doorway has waked up and is trotting a few feet behind you, making worried human sounds. Every time you turn to look at it, it stops and turns its long, sad face away, as though embarrassed. At the end of the path the ground dips and runs into the very round, very dark pond, which looks hundreds of feet deep. Moss hangs from the cypress, breaking up the glare and shading a line of seven sleeping turtles at the water's edge. "Ah," says the guest speaker. His small hands move down his shirt, unbuttoning.

"I'll go back and get us some beers," you say, blushing. He just laughs. You turn your back and hear, rather than see, his splash. Back in the little bar you interrupt the women again. "You can only do it two ways, honest or dishonest," one of them is saying. "You turn your hand, bring it down the line, and it's boogety, boogety, all fun and games." The other woman nods with satisfaction before they turn to you to see what you want. The sunken-faced man never looks up from his glass, just stares down into it, shaking his head as though agreeing with something.

When you return, the guest speaker is floating on his back in a patch of sun, his eyes closed. His boxer shorts balloon up around his legs like a tiny life raft. The goat is kneeling shyly beside the dozing turtles, nibbling sand. You wedge the cans of beer in the ground and roll down your panty hose, feeling ridiculous. It seems there should be a way for you to skip from dressed to un-dressed, traversing shame and fumbling and uncertainty, but there isn't. At the last moment, you reach in your bag and turn on the tape recorder, thinking, *This is the part I want to remember.* Of course, there is no way the little machine will be able to record the two of you at such a distance, through corduroy. But you do it anyway. You are naked, but there are still things he doesn't see, doesn't know.

The solid cold of the water is shocking. Treading, you feel split in two, your scalp dry and burning and exposed, your body lost in the slow, deep cold. You try to relax, but beneath the surface you feel both invisible and vulnerable, almost itchy. You are afraid of little, sinister things: worms and weeds and biting fish, all of which are down there, sensing you in ways over which you have no control. *Let me out,* your twitching body seems to say, but the guest speaker says, "Come over here." Stuck to his cheek is the wing of some large insect, a lacy oval that looks like a third eye, a ghost eye. You paddle closer, and as you do you notice for the first time how blue his real eyes are, as bright and deep as the springs. They are real, but they don't look real. "Are you wearing colored contact lenses?" you ask.

He smiles his slow, remorseless smile. "No," he says. "I'm just beautiful."

"Oh," you gasp. You cannot shake this coldness, this strange invisibility. Your body lists toward his, desire hurtling through you. But you wonder, *Will I even feel it, if he touches me in this cold? And if I can't feel it, is it really happening?*

"You know, even if your mother were still alive," Alex Trotter once remarked, "she couldn't tell you what it is you want. You'd still have to figure that out on your own." He was sitting at his computer, his back to you, programming his resumé into a mail merge. It had been ten, eleven days since the funeral. "Even your perfect daddy couldn't do that for you," he said. His fingers never stopped moving, tap-tapping the keys.

"Why are you saying these things?" you said, your face growing numb.

Alex's fingers paused and he turned his head halfway. You noticed the stack of wrinkles that formed in the back of his neck; they reminded you of TV MagicCards, the man who did the tricks in the commercial, so many years ago. "I'm only saying one thing," he said, "and I say it because I care: Whatever you're doing five years from now, you'll have no one but yourself to thank or blame. That's all I have to say."

You stood and walked down the hall to his clean kitchen and opened his cabinet and got down a package of Hydrox cookies. You ate two quickly and dropped one on the floor, crushing it to powder with your boot heel before you went out the back door. The tap-tapping went on and on. "Goodbye," you called, when you knew you were too far away for him to hear.

What kind of a favor had he thought he was doing for you? *Advice has nothing to do with reality,* your mother sometimes said. *Live your life.* But maybe that was just another way of saying what

Alex was saying; maybe she and Alex were not so far apart in their views, after all. In the hospital, even, after her heart attack, she was efficient. *Get my purse,* she said, and *You know which drawer I'm talking about, right?* The last thing she said to you was, sensibly, "Good night."

When she died, your father contacted you for the first time in years, a flowered card among other flowered cards, containing, as the others did, phone numbers. He also enclosed a photo of himself and his family: not an action shot, a team of glamorous blondes caught by the camera in the midst of their whirling pursuit of wildflowers and happiness, but four stocky, sweatered people set up against a false cornfield backdrop. On the back of the photo, in a confident, ballooning hand, was written, "Please phone us!" There has been no shortage, these past two years, of people offering you sensible solace, guidance through the real world. And, really, Alex was right: you can't blame any of them for whatever it is you are missing now. It is not as though you even thought to ask any of them—your mother, your father, Alex, Dr. Mime, Tutti, Chrissy, or anyone—why it was, in *their* opinion, that people bothered to go on living.

Monday morning you walk through the shimmering glass and leather lobby of MimeCo with the gait of a ghost or movie star. Your forearms, face, and scalp are sunburned, but the sting, disappointingly, is already gone; you keep touching the part in your hair to make sure. The chigger bites you had on your ankle at your mother's funeral continued to itch for a week—whenever you had a chance that week you examined, picked, and scratched them, dabbed them with witch hazel, pulled off their scabs. When they finally faded you had the oddest feeling, as though they had deserted you.

Two silent, newspaper-clutching men from the promotion department step into the elevator beside you. As the heavy door hisses shut, you notice the lit panel of buttons—someone has pressed them all. One of the men says, "Crap," and shakes his head. The other, who is shorter than you are and has bad acne, kicks the wall of the elevator with the toe of his loafer and says, "Whoever done that's an idiot." Neither man glances your way.

After the men get off, you go seven more floors, standing as though hypnotized through the rising and stopping, opening and shutting. You keep remembering something, playing it over and over in your head—not anything as real or definite as the guest speaker's sharp, handsome face, but just a moment, a split second in the cool, conditioned dark of his hotel room, before you changed your mind and put on your clothes and went home. All you could see was the blackness, when against your neck he said softly what he thought was your name. *Alex*. You almost said *What?* but then you caught yourself, caught your breath, because he wasn't going to tell you anything, he was simply speaking out loud what he thought was your name. And at that moment you realized you had made the leap, had swung over or past the wrong answer like a girl on a trapeze, that you were not even required to answer, but only to listen to a man who desired you speak your name in the dark. You might not have even remembered it but for the tape recorder, which picked up the word clearly, the first clear word in an hour of muffled rushing and bumping noises, faint, vaguely human sounds, like a record of poltergeists. You've erased the tape already, and the recorder's safe in your bag, ready to return, probably never missed. It may have been, as your father said, only a moment. But it is yours, yours.

Mother Rocket

So Jude Silverman was a Yiddish Chicken Little? What did it matter, when she had Rob Jones, the man who proposed to keep the sky, however gray, up above? He had promised her this years ago, in a flat in Brooklyn, when Jude poised her beat-up feet on the inside of the window ledge, clutched the drab, mud-colored curtains, and threatened to throw her 100-pound body splat into the street.

"Now Jude," Rob said. "Don't do that."

"I was born to die," Jude said.

"So do it later, when I'm not looking. Come on down now, and we'll get married."

"Well." Jude looked dubious. "Okay. All right."

The marriage license they applied for an hour later seemed to appease Jude's suicidal urge, although it whetted a desire for a hot, salty pretzel. Only a pretzel delivered from the wrinkled hands of a vendor in Central Park would do. Jude wound her hair into a knot and kissed Rob, long and lovingly, on the subway into the city. "Trains really bring out something from my cultural unconscious!" she shouted above the roar.

"Could you speak a little louder? I don't think they heard you over on Staten Island."

Jude pouted. "You never let me feel persecuted. You never let me feel guilty."

An hour later she was weeping over the polar bear—big, white, and shaggy—that paced its cage, like a madman, in Central Park. "He's been here as long as I can remember," she said. "He's so hot. He's so lonely. He probably has bad breath. He probably hates himself." Jude gave the polar bear a long, significant glance of farewell that signaled her identification with him was complete. She sniffed. "You got a Kleenex? This pretzel is so lousy, it's making me cry. I'm warning you. You'd better not marry me. The littlest thing sets me off."

As if Rob, the moment he met her, hadn't figured that out. It was what initially attracted him. He'd been a UPI photographer in Southeast Asia before his weak stomach had gotten the best of him and he returned to New York to shoot not battlefields and revolutions and riots, but movie stars and models and other such innocuous subjects. He was disappointed in his lack of heroics until the day he went to the theater to photograph Jude and broke down her explosive temper as expertly as a soldier might dismantle a grenade. "Load your guns," Jude had ordered him. "And don't make me look ugly. Make me look like Pavlova, you know? Or Isadora Duncan."

"I'm a photographer, not a plastic surgeon."

"What's that supposed to mean?"

"It means, be yourself."

Jude's forehead wrinkled. "But I don't know who I am."

Rob bit his lip in exasperation. "You can be a tightrope walker or a plumber. You can be a duck or an elephant, for all I care."

"Are you trying to call me schizophrenic?"

"I'm trying to get you to pose!" Rob shouted. "Would you pose, please, so I can get out of here and eat my dinner?"

Jude backed her body up to the wall as if preparing to be

executed. "Okay," she said penitently. "I'll cut the ishkabibble. Fire away."

She was a principal with the Future/Dance/Theater, a modern troupe committed to catering to the so-called politically aware. The week before, Rob had seen her perform her most famous solo role, "Hiroshima," a dance consisting of nothing more than an excruciatingly slow meltdown to the stage, so that at the end of seven minutes Jude lay in a heap on the floor, symbolizing the Japanese dead. The dance was a New York hit. It was supposed to be a social statement, but Rob thought it was so much sixties kitsch. The naiveté of it offended him. "What do dancers know about politics?" he challenged Jude at that photo session.

"All we need to know: Hitler killed the Jews. Hey, you want to take me out to dinner? Feel free to say no if you're married or engaged or gay."

In the restaurant, when she wasn't stealing drags off Rob's cigarette, stuffing her mouth with grilled steak, or washing her food down with beer, she complained. "It's horrible being a dancer," she said. "You can't smoke. You can't drink. You can't eat. You can't have tits or hips, you can't have a headache or a stomachache or a backache, you can't have a social life or a family or a boyfriend—"

"Why can't you have a boyfriend?"

"You should see the fruitcakes I meet." She stared at him. "You're too old not to be married."

"So my mother tells me."

"Are you sure you're not gay?"

Rob leaned across the candlelit table, gently covered Jude's hand with his hands, and looked her meaningfully in the eye. He hoped to sound tender and eloquent and romantic. "I love women," he said.

"Great," Jude answered. "Let's get laid. But first let me finish off these croutons." She dug into her salad with her fork. "I hate when they're drowning in dressing. I feel personally responsible. I need to rescue them, every survivor. I can't leave a single one behind."

Rob was amused by her zeal. Unlike his previous subjects in New York, Jude had passion, however misguided. It didn't strike him she was disturbed until she admitted it herself, back at his place. "I'm a kook," she warned. "A real nut. No analyst would touch me with a ten-foot pole."

"I'm not an analyst."

Jude Silverman pounced on him. Purring, she pressed her pelvis against his camera. "Mmm, then, photographer. Give me an F-stop I'll never forget. Fire away."

So she was famous, among the avant-garde. Her thin, birdlike face had been reproduced in all the Village rags professing allegiance to the arts, and eventually appeared in *Vogue, Elle,* and the *Times* art page. Her silhouette could be seen on Future/Dance/Theater posters tacked up on plywood construction barriers all over the city. But Jude's photographic claim to fame had come early, at age seventeen, when she had appeared on the cover of a national magazine in a performance that had absolutely nothing to do with dance. The year was 1967; the place was a Jerusalem street. Jude knelt on the cobblestones, surrounded by glass, spattered by blood. To the left of her lay the lower half of a man's body, and to the right (the viewer would be safe to presume) lay the upper half of the same man. In her arms Jude cradled the man's amputated arm, which (if the viewer examined it closely) bore the tiny blue tattoo of numbers that branded inmates of concentration camps.

The picture, taken by a rival of Rob's before Rob had ever been aware of Jude's existence, had enjoyed considerable fame. It had been reproduced in numerous newspapers, books, and magazines. Rob had always been jealous of that picture; it struck him as the perfect shot every photographer dreamed of getting. Yet something about it struck him as bogus. Such symbolic pathos seemed too good to be true; it struck so directly to the gut it seemed forced, maybe even fake.

"This pic was famous," Jude showed it to Rob. "It won all sorts of those Nobel Prize things."

"Pulitzer Prize," Rob corrected her, irritated.

Jude shrugged. She took the magazine from Rob and squinted at the picture. "That's my uncle," she said, dispassionately, pointing, "here and there. That's my uncle's arm I'm holding." Jude jabbed her finger at the picture with such vehemence that Rob was sure she was gearing up to issue a philosophical statement on the nature of peace and war, or the inhumanity of man to man. Instead, she traced her finger along the curve of her spine in the picture. "Look at that posture," she said. "Flawless."

Such a crazy girl she was, with such crazy family portraits. Oh, the crazy things she ate (boiled spinach on a bed of cottage cheese, hard-boiled eggs sunk in a pool of borscht, ice cream speckled with pastrami), the crazy things she wore (mirrored headbands and ostrich feathers, pink leotards and see-through black chiffon skirts), and the eccentric things she said (to a waiter: "Will this entree give me bad breath?" To a policeman who politely requested that she step around a barricade: "This is a free country, you fucking Nazi!"). She was paranoid and jealous. She was possessive of Rob's flesh, kneading his body in bed, sighing as she confessed she wished she could steal some of his weight. Their lovemaking was crushing, and the wind-down consisted of Jude's own crazy brand of *post-coitum triste*. She lay still for a few minutes and then hopped out of bed. Standing in front of the full-length mirror, she moaned, "Oh. Oh. She felt so good a moment ago, but now Jude Silverman has a terminal case of the uglies. Her arms are too thin, aren't they? And all those ribs. You could serve her up at a barbecue pit. You could use her as an anatomical skeleton. And her neck—Swan Lake it ain't. Nice legs, but those knees, those knees! And what about the lack of hips? Sexually unattractive, isn't it? Tell her the truth. Give it to Jude Silverman straight."

Button a lip, save a ship. Rob was not keen on playing Jude's self-destructive game, on telling her what she professed to want to know, that she looked like a skinny, shell-shocked apparition from a Ben Shahn painting, that she looked nervous and apprehensive, like those anorexic chihuahuas bejeweled women in mink stoles walked on the city streets. He loved her precisely because she made such a wonderful postwar portrait. He didn't mind the oddities of her body. What she didn't criticize about herself became his only peeve.

Jude Silverman had disgusting feet. Her big toes flattened like hammerhead sharks, and the rest of her toes, perhaps terrified of the killer big ones, cramped into tight curls and shied away. Corns spotted the knuckles, blisters broke out on her ankles, and callouses toughened the entire underside of her feet. Something about that pair suggested the abused child, the defeated soldier who had marched too long without boots. Rob refused to accompany Jude into a shoe store, afraid of what the salesmen thought. She wore nine and a half narrow, a forlorn, forsaken size. She wore, when she wasn't dancing, an anklet strung with tiny brass bells that sadly, continuously, tinkled. As she padded about the apartment Rob got the impression he was living with a little lost cat that shook its collar as it vainly searched for its home.

At first he was fascinated with those bells, but as time went by and he grew more content with the life he had chosen in New York, and more and more pleased with his paycheck, he sometimes grumbled about them. "Why don't you shed those superstitious slave chains?" he asked.

Jude stomped her foot. The very idea! "Jingle, ergo sum," she said.

The story of those bells, as it turned out, was the story behind that famous photograph. "You want to hear a good one?" Jude asked. "This is it." When she was seventeen, Judy Schitzman ("Geez, can you blame me for changing my name?") didn't want to visit Israel. She wanted to vacation in the Catskills or Atlantic City, like all the rest of the sacrilegious East Side kids. Such a curse! to have been adopted by an aunt and uncle so pious, so Old World, so anxious to talk of the hardships and narrow escapes. So committed to laying on the guilt. "Thick as cream cheese," Jude said.

Jude's own parents had met their tragic end when Ellen Schitzman knocked a plugged-in hairdryer into the bathtub, and Leo Schitzman, who found her electrocuted in the water, plunged his hand in. Even at age six, Jude was old enough to know she should be embarrassed by this farcical piece of history. When Uncle Chaim and Aunt Mina adopted her and placed her in a new school, she told her first-grade friends that her parents had been gassed in Poland. Her school chums seemed impressed.

"But you were born in 1950," Rob pointed out.

"So, was I good in math? And to a six-year-old, what's a little discrepancy in dates?"

To Chaim and Mina, it was everything. The nerve of her, making up such tales, making mockery out of one of the darkest hours in human history. So there hadn't been enough victims without Jude adding two more to the carnage? So there weren't enough horrors in the world without her fabricating more of them?

Chaim and Mina grated on Jude's nerves. "Two wet Yiddish rags," she said. They never let her tell a lie, and if you couldn't make things up, what was the point of living? Life, indeed, was boring. Jude knew if she wanted to be an artist she would have to pretend every minute was intense. She made it a point to rub everyone the wrong way. She purposefully aggravated her own sweet self. In front of a full-length mirror—Jude had always had her worst crises looking in a mirror—she hunched her shoulders and stuck her stomach out. "Judy Schitzman, you are one ugly mother," she whispered at her reflection. The next moment she gave herself a sultry smile and wink, sticking out her barely-there breasts. "Judy, dah-ling, how nice to see you! You look gohr-geous, absolutely rah-vishing, my dear."

Mina caught her in the schizophrenic act one day, and that's how Jude started ballet lessons. It was decided, in consultation with the rabbi, that Jude needed discipline. It was decided she had to get out of the house more, or Mina would have a nervous breakdown. "You'll have music lessons," Chaim told her. Jude stomped her feet. She couldn't stand still long enough to tune a violin. "French lessons," Mina suggested, and Jude howled. Bad enough she already mixed up Yiddish with English.

"I want belly-dancing lessons," she said.

"I'll teach you to dance," Chaim threatened. "I'll teach you to belly."

But in the end Jude was sent to a Russian ballet master, at quite a pretty penny. The ballet master was rude and ruthless. He spit orders in Jude's face as he turned out her arms, poked her in the gut, and practically yanked her head off her neck. He sneered at her. Curling his lip in disgust, he called her "Scheetzman." "Tuck in that belly, Scheetzman! Scheetzman, lower your chin, please! Scheetzman, I am going to snap that trunk of yours right in half!" Jude thoroughly enjoyed it. She liked the tap of his stick against the wooden floor: she liked being surrounded by mirrors. She loved throwing up, en masse, with all the other girls just before and after a lesson. She loved the Band-Aids and the Ace bandages and the injuries that made her cry. Ballet was wonderful— the music, the precision, the pain!

So Jude grew. She began to take modern dance because now

she was too old to make it in the ballet world. Chaim and Mina were skeptical. Pink tutus were fine; nude leotards were not. Chaim was less and less willing to finance what he thought was an extravagant concession to the sexual revolution. Mina was worried about Jude catching splinters dancing in bare feet. Both were worried that Jude was obsessed with dance for all the wrong reasons. When Jude turned seventeen, Chaim and Mina decided it was time to break her of her fool ideas.

Jude was dragged to the sacred homeland, where everything and everybody got on her nerves. The Holy Land Hotel? How could it stack up to the Plaza? Esther Zeitz? Give her Bloomingdale's any day. The Biblical Zoo? Jude had seen bigger and better elephants in the Bronx. Israel was a disgusting, crummy old place. What was holy about all those stupid soldiers, about a land obsessed with its military?

Jude had never thought much about God before, but now her mind drifted toward more spiritual matters. She was sure God never lived inside a tank. God—at least Jude's God—was not a gun. God was Fifth Avenue at rush hour (furs and high heels and shopping bags from Saks), Battery Park at twilight (Miss Liberty misty in the distance), and the top of the roof on Sunday morning. God was hot pastrami with a dab of horseradish on top. God was a great ballet. Jude leaned out of the hotel window in Jerusalem, dust and sweat gritted on her eyelashes. No wonder all those old guys in black were wailing at that dumb wall. Who wanted to live in the midst of a potential Armageddon, when you could live in glorious New York?

Judy Schitzman joined her aunt and uncle for breakfast in a street café. Chaim had rolls and coffee. Mina, on a perpetual diet that never seemed to work, confined herself to tea. Jude chowed down on eggs and rolls and coffee and juice, the eggs sticking suddenly in her throat when, halfway through breakfast, Chaim announced they would be making a permanent move to Israel before the year was up.

But Jude had to go back to New York. There was the dance studio. There was Central Park. There were hot dogs and pretzels and bagels. Fake suffering was great, to be sure, but she didn't want to really suffer in Israel. Jude threw down her fork on her plate. She wouldn't live in Jerusalem! She wouldn't join any old army! She looked horrible in khaki! What was she supposed to do for fun, go float in that stupid, smelly old Dead Sea? Besides, how could she dance in the middle of this cultural desert?

Chaim cursed. Jude could just lower her voice. Jude could just follow orders for once in her life. Jude could go straight to the dogs if she didn't like their plans. Mina, nervous from her tea, began to cry. Would there never be peace on earth? No, not as long as Jude was alive to fight with her uncle. Jude pushed back her chair. Where was she going? Her uncle had paid good money for that big breakfast. She had been eating them out of house and home for over ten years, and this was the thanks they should get? Besides, what about her parents? What about the past? She owed it to the past to live in Israel!

"I don't owe anybody anything," Jude said. "And you can drop dead!"

She fled the café. She stalked up a cobblestone hill, wandered down a side alley, and stumbled upon a street market. Such wonderful things for sale! Jude inspected them all, the colorful rugs and blankets, the pale yellow baskets, the sheer scarves, the heavy jewelry. In her purse she had all the money Chaim had given her before they left New York. She had planned to buy a new hot-pink leotard when she got back to the city, but now she resolved to spend every last cent on whatever would make her aunt and uncle most angry. Jude lingered before the stalls. Men eyed her. Men said things to her in languages she could not understand. She hesitated before she finally approached an Arab in long white robes. His dark face was shaded by a burnoose. His wares lay on a thick camel-colored blanket. Jude bent down. She fingered a heavy necklace, a collar that looked like something out of *Antony and*

Cleopatra, before she finally grabbed what she thought was a bracelet strung with bells. It jingled. Yes, this was it. Something that made a Christmasy, goyish kind of noise.

When she stood up and tried to fasten it around her wrist, the Arab shook his head. He took the bracelet from her, bent down to the cobblestones, and clasped it around her ankle. Jude blushed, and pressed her cotton skirt against her thighs as the Arab eyed her legs. She backed away.

She gave him all the money in her purse down to the change. As she walked off, the tinkling of the bells above her sandals distinguished her from all the others on the street. Jude was pleased. She felt like a clown. She felt like a slave. See what Chaim and Mina would have to say about that! But within a minute she began to regret her decision, as if she had betrayed the aunt and uncle who had been kind enough to care for her almost all her life—and for an Arab, no less. She wanted her money back. The sounds of the bells made her feel sick.

She was at the top of the hill when she saw Chaim and Mina walking up towards her. Aunt Mina was out of breath; Chaim's face was red with rage. "You stay there!" he yelled. "You stay right there, young lady!" Jude wanted to run away. She wanted to run towards them and throw herself at their feet, but then they would see—and hear—the bells. So for once in her life, she obeyed. Chaim and Mina puffed up the hill. As Jude bent down to yank the bracelet off her ankle, light flashed, and then came the explosion. Glass and furniture and unidentifiable objects shattered out into the street. Jude ran down the hill toward the rubble. The bells jingled.

Mina was nowhere to be found. Chaim lay in two in the middle of the street, the skin of his right arm pale against the earth-colored cobblestones, ragged and bloody where it had been severed at the shoulder. His hand was turned palm upward, as if extended toward a cashier to receive some change. Jude didn't know what to do. She stooped down to touch the hand—it no longer was Chaim's hand—and ended up cradling the arm. The tiny digits tattooed there matched the numbers Jude had often observed on the arm of her uncle when he washed his hands before dinner or opened the stubborn lid on a jar of jelly.

When Rob asked her what she was thinking at the precise moment the photographer knelt down to shoot her, Jude considered it for a few seconds before she replied. "I felt excited, as if it weren't real, as if I were an actress in a show and any minute people would start applauding. I knew I would get my face in every magazine in America. It's awful—oh, I'm an awful person!—but I remember thinking, This is what I was born for, to be famous."

So five years later, then years later, fifteen years later, Jude still had plenty to feel guilty about. "If only I were the type who wanted to live in Israel," she told Rob. "If only I had stayed at the breakfast table. If only I hadn't bought those bells. If only I had run down the hill a moment earlier. If only my parents hadn't died in the bathroom. If only I hadn't been born. If only I weren't Jewish!"

She loathed her history, and at the same time she felt superior to others because of it. "I like you," she told Rob, "and you've been lots of places and I guess you're kind of smart, but I mean, let's face it, your last name is Jones, you're so normal, so—so—adjusted" (Jude pronounced the last as if it were a dirty word), "so American. I mean, what do you people who aren't ethnic think about all day?"

"Sex and death," Rob said, "and taking a crap. Same as you, without the East Side accent."

But it was the accent that made her. Without it, who was Jude Silverman? The girl whose parents had fried in the bathtub? The girl whose aunt and uncle had been blown to pieces in an explosion? The girl who wore bells, the girl who danced "Hiroshima," the girl who was a bargain basement of neuroses, the girl who was a wholesale sack of bones, the girl in the bloody photograph, the girl in the mirror, staring sadly back? She wasn't anything, she wasn't anybody, without all that behind her. Chaim and Mina had been right. She owed something to the past, and she had known that intuitively, even way back when she had announced to her school chums that her parents had been sent to the gas chamber.

Rob, on the other hand, didn't owe anything. He lived for the here and now, for the action-filled moment. Jude was his link to the past, and Jude was his present, always responding so well to his camera. "Who'd you shoot today?" she asked when he came home, not bothering to listen to his reply. "Mmmm, photographer. Shoot me. I'm dying for it."

It was crazy. Jude was perverse. "Made for abuse," she whispered as she twisted into incredible positions Rob, except for one brief foray into pornographic photography, hardly knew existed. "Jude Silverman was built to last."

But she wasn't made to dance forever. Fifteen years after she had bought those bells, they were giving a muffled, melancholy jingle beneath the blankets every morning. "Oh God," Jude moaned, "why does anyone have to live past thirty?" Her back, once as supple as a roll of cookie dough, now felt as stiff as a cracker. Her knees creaked and complained. "Oh God, oh God, oh God," she moaned when she came home from a performance. "Oh God, rub my neck!"

Rob, with his skilled hands, filled in. "Ow!" Jude yelped when he pressed too hard. "What are you trying to do, kill me? I swear to God, everybody's out to get me. When I was waiting to cross Second this morning, a pigeon laid a number on me. When I was waiting to cross Park, a cabbie practically ran me over. So I decided the hell with this shit, I'll take the train. I went underground and the machine stole two of my tokens. I leaped over the turnstile, like a criminal on the run. Then I was waiting on the platform and this guy with a little black mustache looked like he was dying to push me on the tracks. So I walked down the platform and this punk came at me with purple hair and a T-shirt with a Nazi sign on it, you think I'm making this up? I said to myself, Jude Silverman, move those metatarsals. Run like bloody Mercury."

And now, the capper, what proved that the whole world was falling in on her: Jude Silverman, *the* Jude Silverman of "Hiroshima" fame, who had once brought down the house, was being relegated to just another member of the company corps. The Future/Dance/Theater was staging its own spectacular version of the end of the world, called, simply, "World War III," and Jude, who was hoping—expecting—to be chosen to dance the solo finale as the nuclear bomb, was doled out only a bit role as an intermediate-range ballistic missile. The nerve. It was an outrage!

Jude wailed. Rob tried his best to comfort her. "Look at it this way. If mighty empires can rise and fall and rise again, so can Jude Silverman."

"Mighty empires don't get sore feet. Mighty empires don't get arthritis. Mighty empires aren't Jewish. I'm a wash-up. There'll never be another World War III. It's over."

Jude planted her body in front of the mirror. She stuck out her tongue at herself and ran her fingers through her hair. She grabbed a pair of tweezers and went after her scalp. "I'm going to get every last gray one," she vowed. "I'm going to pull them all out. Search and destroy. This is Jude Silverman's mission."

"Pull out any more and you'll be bald," Rob warned.

Jude shrieked. "Whose head looks like a shiny pancake around here?"

"I can accept my age gracefully."

Jude stomped her feet and her bells jingled. "You were born an old man," she said. "I was born normal. I was born a baby.

Look out. I'm getting ready to have a crisis. I'm having a crisis, I tell you."

Jude Silverman detonated. Meanwhile, "World War III," drawing highly favorable reviews, took New York by storm and raged on and on. The city was seized by an apocalyptic craze. The display windows at Macy's and Lord & Taylor's took on a futuristic cast, and a famous midtown jewelry store paid a special tribute to the war by placing five solitary diamonds in a blackened display case to represent stars glittering in a postnuclear sky.

"New York has gone berserk," Rob said. "I've never seen a city that so begs to be destroyed."

Jude took it too personally to care about the broader implications. "New York didn't do diddly squat for Hiroshima."

"Now Jude. Be reasonable. The apocalypse is in vogue. Hiroshima is like the Holocaust, totally passé."

"I told you. I'm a wash-up!" Jude's eyes filled with tears. "Let's have a wee one."

"An F-stop? Now?"

"You jerk! Nobody understands me! I mean, let's have a baby."

Rob stood shell-shocked. "In the middle of a world war? Where's your sense of social responsibility?"

"I never had any." Jude grabbed Rob. "Come on, photographer. Load your guns. Fire away."

Now who felt old? Rob's guns no longer worked on such short command. Besides, he wasn't prepared for this dilemma. He had been trained to keep his objective distance. He could more easily imagine photographing a nuclear bomb than he could snapping a shot of his own baby. A bomb, after all, was a bomb, but a baby was—well, uncertainty. He tried to persuade Jude. "It wouldn't be fair to bring a child into a world so deeply committed to destruction. A world of chemical warfare, Jude. A world of mass extermination."

Jude crossed her arms and looked unconvinced.

"Okay," Rob said, "how about a world where you have to push and shove in line just to get half a pound of pastrami?"

"Since when are you such a fan of pastrami?"

"All right, then. A world where people step on your feet on the subway and don't even apologize."

"Oh, so now it's manners that are going to save the world." Jude made a la-di-da face. "If only Hitler had read his Emily Post. Just think of the marvelous effect that would have had on the twentieth century. Pass the bombs, Fraulein. Pass the U-boats, mein Herr. Pass the soap, please. I say, Goering, not to bring up anything unpleasant, but doesn't it smell like gas in here?"

"Just put a stop to that," Rob said. "Just cut that out, Jude Schitzman, I mean, Silverman. Jesus Christ. You can't even make up your mind what your own name is. How are you going to raise a baby?"

"I want a baby," Jude said. "I want the blood and guts. I want the stink and the smell and the afterbirth. I want the baby to come out the way I should have come out, with the cord around its neck. I want to bleed to death on the operating table—"

Rob slapped her. Rob slapped Jude Silverman flat across the face and left a strapping red mark on her skinny cheek. He felt good. He felt satisfied. But he wasn't prepared for that reaction. He was prepared to apologize, until Jude smiled, infuriating him even more.

"You're neurotic," he said. "You're paranoid. You want to be hit. You beg for it. You're a bitch. You're a brat. I'll bet you were the worst kid on the block. I'll bet you were the worst kid ever born, period. You drove your parents to kill themselves. You drove your aunt and uncle crazy. You think you're so persecuted, but you do nothing but persecute everyone around you. I'm sick of your moaning and whining. You're a fraud. You're a compulsive liar. You're a basket case. I'll bet you bought those bells in Brooklyn. I'll bet you cut off your own uncle's arm with a butter knife."

"So what if I did?" Jude defended herself. "So what if that schmuck photographer told me exactly how to pose for him. He won that Nobel Prize, didn't he?"

"Pulitzer Prize! He won a Pulitzer for taking a fake shot of you, and here I am, stuck with the real, honest-to-goodness neurotic thing!"

"Oh!" Jude wailed. "You don't love me. You've never loved me, you only fell in love with my picture. Why'd you marry me? Why didn't you just let me kill myself?" She began to cry. "I hate photographers. I hate cameras. I hate myself in that picture."

Rob swallowed a lump in his throat. He felt guilt slide into his stomach. The feeling wasn't altogether unpleasant. He took the tearful Jude in his arms. "I never liked that picture," he lied. "You look so much better smiling. Come on now, say *cheese*. I'm sorry. I'm saying uncle, Jude."

Jude snuggled against him. "I'd like you better if you said *Daddy*."

Two months later, backstage at the Future/Dance/Theater, a giddy Jude Silverman, a buoyant Jude Silverman, paraded about with a pillow crammed down the front of her leotard, announcing to all who would listen, "Hey guys, I'm retiring, guess what for? It's called ending your career on a big bang—ha ha, get it? God, am I pregnant with wit, or what?" She smiled demurely, young-mother-to-be-ly. "I've always wanted a pair of tits," she mused. "The big guns. Real torpedoes."

Jude couldn't decide if she wanted a son or daughter. Rob thought twins would solve the problem, but Jude wasn't having any of it. "Too schizophrenic," she said. She placed her hands on her stomach. "Big Mama to control tower," she barked. "Do you read me? Come in." She sighed and turned to Rob. "Big Mama is receiving neither masculine nor feminine vibes. Maybe it's a hermaphrodite. Maybe it's a miscarriage. Maybe it's cancer. I'm sure it's cancer, Rob."

"Jude, it's a baby, take my word for it."

"Well. Okay. Let's call it Mordecai."

"Let's not."

Jude sighed. "Poor Morey. Just think of our genes waging war within him, right at this very moment. Man, this is one time when I'm willing to lose a fight." She put her hands back on her stomach. "Big Mama to control tower," she barked again. "Do you read me? Life is easier if you have blond hair."

She was growing calmer, and slightly dreamy. She was mooning around the apartment all morning, and taking her stomach for long walks in the afternoon. She was conspicuous now, for good reason: at last, Jude Silverman was fat! Before, when people had stared at her, she used to look fearfully back, but now she simply smiled and gazed in equal wonder down at herself. "Guess what?" she told Rob. "I'm less paranoid. But it's kind of boring. Jude Silverman could use a little action."

"So take up knitting."

Jude, mildly, told him to shut up.

On her walks, she ate all the hot pretzels she wanted. She slurped orangeade and lemonade and any other syrupy tutti-frutti drink she could find. She thought, with fondness, of little Mordecai, and then she thought of all the things that could go wrong. She was convinced, for a while, that God would give her an unusual child, a deformed little duck with three eyes and twelve toes, a freak, a weirdo, or a saint. Her child would have to be different, at least from all those mediocre kids she saw on the street. She carefully inspected each one that she passed. "Dumbo," she silently pronounced a droopy-eyed toddler. "Pig," she labeled a little boy with the sticky residue of food about his mouth. "Brat," she pegged a moaning girl who stomped her feet. "If I ever had a kid like that, I'd strangle her." She smiled with superiority, then jerked her head back to the little girl, finding a vague, dissatisfying resemblance to herself. But her bad days were over now. She sighed. She knew, in her heart of hearts, that she'd have a dull, boring, well-adjusted child. It was guaranteed to be normal; with a last name like Jones, how could it miss? It would yawn at the ballet and laugh at her ostrich feathers. It would beg her to "take off those embarrassing bells, Mo-therrr." After all the love and care she would give it, it would turn on her, disown her, laugh at her, call her a kook. This, then, would be all the thanks she would get!

Jude wrinkled her forehead. She was beginning to sound like Aunt Mina. Maybe she was turning normal. Maybe she should worry. Maybe she should walk all the way down Central Park. She made a pilgrimage to Cleopatra's Needle and to the Alice in Wonderland statue. She visited the carousel, where Chaim had taken her for rides on the occasional Sunday, and where giggly, excited kids still lined up.

Jude walked away from the carousel and surfaced out of the park at Temple Emanu-El. On Fifth, she heard chanting and rumbling. Hordes of people clogged the sidewalk at 60th Street, marching straight up the park. For a moment, Jude panicked. She almost took to her heels and ran, but then she took her stomach in her hands and stood still, as if preparing to be photographed. "Sit tight, Mordecai," she said. "It's the Nazi invasion of midtown Manhattan. It's Armageddon, right in our own backyard. Jude Silverman, Hebrew warrioress, proudly stands her ground. Jude Silverman meets, with courage, her end!"

The crowd marched closer. They came upon her, bearing banners of peace, not war, and Jude smiled to see their slogans were decorated with serene little doves. *Bread, not bombs! No more Hiroshimas! No more Nagasakis! Peace is at hand!* the signs said.

The crowd thronged the sidewalk. They carried banners that said *Catholics for Pacifism* and *Muslims for Global Harmony.* They carried banners in Hebrew characters Jude was ashamed she could no longer understand. There were fresh-faced Hitler youth types carrying signs warning against the evils of *Die mutterrakete.* Jude loved the word. "Hey-hey, guys," she yelled and pointed to her stomach. "The mother rocket, that's me!"

The crowd passed by. Suddenly Jude felt overwhelmed. She felt sad. She walked back into the park and let her sense of smell lead her to the zoo. Colorful birds squawked at her, dirty farm animals bleated, and screaming monkeys put their paws over their eyes and ran away. "All right, you guys," Jude said. "I know where I'm not wanted." She jingled her way slowly to the polar bear's cage.

It was late summer, on the brink of fall. The leaves were beginning to crisp, and the wind picked up, while the sun beat down on the asphalt. It had been just this time of year when she was here with Rob, offering him a bite of that lousy pretzel that needed a dab of hot mustard on top. She'd been crying. And hadn't she, an hour before, threatened suicide? She seemed to remember a slight ruckus that afternoon. Rob had made fun of her black fishnet stockings. Rob had told her, joking around, she was the worst subject he had ever photographed—vain, stubborn, alternately belligerent as a rhinoceros and frightened as a little lamb. "Rhinoceros!" Jude said. "I don't like the smell of that, Rob Jones. What are you, some kind of closet anti-Semite?"

"I said rhinoceros because . . . Jude, what the hell are you doing, changing the curtains?"

"The whole world is out to kill Jude Silverman. Well, Jude Silverman will show the world a thing or two. Jude will kill herself!"

"Now Jude. Don't do that."

"I was born to die."

"Yes, but you can do it later."

Now it was later, and she was too tired to think of suicide. Jude finally made her way to the polar bear cage. She sat down on a park bench and watched the dirty, shaggy beast who, years after that scene with Rob, still paced his cage, like a madman, back and forth. He seemed so wild-eyed, so out of control. "Settle down now, you smelly old bear," she said. Then she smiled. "Come on out of that cage, you chicken shit. Maul me. Strangle me. Break my bells. Just don't harm my little Mordecai, is that a deal?" The polar bear panted and ignored her. Jude sleepily, deliciously, rested her hands upon her stomach and closed her eyes. The past? Just a bugaboo, compared to the future threatening to detonate inside her. It sure took a lot of strength to keep on living, Jude thought, finally feeling, kicking within her, what little energy she needed to survive.

ひひひひひひ *Harvey Grossinger*   *The dead ones are like that,*
always the last to quiet.
Louise Glück

Home Burial

For weeks I imagined I could see him coming off the plane,
carrying souvenirs. In my mind he looked the same as the day
he left—broad-shouldered, trim, deeply tanned. The picture of
him they printed in the newspaper, one of those sawtooth-edged
Brownie snapshots that always made the day appear gloomy, had
been taken years earlier, on Utah Beach, a few days after the invasion of Normandy. Behind him, on the sand, you could see the
rows of dead soldiers covered with ponchos.

My father came home from Korea when I was fourteen. Not exactly Korea, but San Francisco, where he'd spent the past four
months at Letterman Hospital recovering from pneumonia and
malnutrition. It was Election Day, 1952, and everybody in my
neighborhood had been wearing Stevenson buttons for months
while at the same time saying he didn't have a prayer against
Eisenhower. My Uncle Eli kept telling me and my mother how
Adlai would have had a fighting chance if he hadn't always looked
like he'd just emerged from a drugged sleep. I couldn't have cared
less who became the next president. Our local newspaper had a
front page story on my father; they called him a war hero. The paper said he had crawled out of his foxhole on the slope of a hill
and destroyed two enemy machine-gun nests that had pinned

down his company. Later he was captured and endured eleven months in a diarrhea-soiled toolshed as a prisoner of war. Sick from dysentery and beriberi—his belly and joints were bloated, his feet and gums swollen and bleeding—he'd been left to rot when his captors abandoned camp. A platoon of Marines out on a midnight patrol had discovered him, along with the remains of some twenty of his men.

We met him early, soon after sunrise, with the golden bars of sunlight splayed across the rusted tin freight hangar at Mitchell Field. To pass the time on the ride to the airport I'd played the game of memorizing license plates my father had taught me. There were still traces of fog out, places where the sun hadn't burned through yet. The Bronx River Parkway was full of wet leaves and the air was heavy with smoke. We drove with the windows down and the wind sounded like surf at the ocean. Above the sounds of traffic the gleaming chrome radio in my Uncle Eli's maroon teardrop DeSoto crackled with static. He moved the dial and turned the volume up when he heard Peggy Lee singing "Just One of Those Things." My mother, riding up front with Uncle Eli, could not stop coughing. She'd been hacking and wheezing for more than a month now, thanks to the ragweed and mold spores.

The whole time my father had been missing my mother would go upstairs and hide in the bathroom whenever the phone rang. She'd run water in the tub or flush the toilet three or four times— anything to drown out the sound of my voice. We'd been in the breakfast nook finishing our French toast when the phone call came informing us that my father had been found alive. She held the receiver an inch or so from her ear and her expression was pure amazement. Watching her, my mind was blank. Her mouth was open halfway, and she was taking short, urgent breaths through it. Although she never said it, I knew she'd given up hope of ever seeing him again. Her self-control was all for my sake, in order to shield me from the inevitable. To tell the truth, whenever the phone rang—this despite my knowing that the Army always sent an officer around to deliver an official account of how and where a soldier had been killed in action—I thought it would be news of his death. But my worst fear was that he would never be found at all. Relieved when the caller was my Aunt Sophie or a neighbor, I would go into the living room and salute my father's picture, which sat on top of the mantelpiece. It was a formal photograph, taken before I was born. In it he wore a dark pin-striped suit and a wide necktie, and his black hair was piled back in waves. His somber brown eyes seemed focused on something behind the camera. It was impossible to know what he was looking at, but there was an intensity in his gaze, a surge of concentration in his eyes, that I couldn't get out of my head. Before the phone call I'd been secretly hoping for, this photograph of someone I'd never known entered my dreams like a ghost and came between me and the face I remembered as my father's.

The night before we went to meet his plane, my mother took me out for supper. The Shanghai Cafe was one of those places with bad air, hazy blue light, and starched red tablecloths that smell of spilled drinks and soy sauce. It was on a narrow street across from the RKO Proctor where my father used to take me for Sunday matinees during the winter. I looked at my mother's hands as she read the menu. Her skinned knuckles were wrinkled. She put the menu down and took a pack of Old Golds out of her purse, and lit one up.

"You look tired," I said. "Anything wrong?"

She turned her face to me and smiled. "You're like your father, Noah," she said, and rubbed her wrist as if the veins inside of it were hurting her. "You shouldn't expect too much from him at the beginning."

I had a funny sensation just then, a nervous rush that made my stomach cramp. "I don't get it," I said. "When you came back

from California you said there was nothing to worry about. What
are you hiding from me? What's the big secret?"

She looked at me and smiled in a way that seemed forced and
full of something else I didn't care to find out about. A sullen
waiter wearing a black bow tie took our order of egg drop soup,
moo goo gai pan, and rainbow shrimp.

"I'm not being evasive, Noah. I thought I told you he'd be different for a while."

"All you said was that he wasn't acting like himself."

She moved the glass ashtray around with her finger. "He's *not*,"
she said, and leaned back and touched her temples. "I'm going to
need your help with him."

"Sure," I said.

Her face sank. "You know what I mean. Why are you being so
difficult? We have a situation here."

"I'm not trying to be difficult," I said.

She sipped at her gin rickey and blew jets of gray smoke out of
her nostrils. "You'll see," she said stiffly. "Sometimes there are
things a lot worse than dying."

I wondered how she could even think that, especially after what
he had gone through. "Are you saying he should've given up?"

"*Please*, eat," she said, though it was clear she had no appetite.
She crushed her cigarette out in the ashtray and fiddled with the
gold snap on her purse. We were sitting in a cramped booth encircled by panels of faded rosewood and fancy carvings of dragons
and serpents and warriors on horseback. Shreds of lo mein were
stuck in the dimpled vinyl buttons.

"What do you think *we* should do then?" I asked.

"It doesn't matter what I think," she said, her fingers searching
in her pocketbook for another cigarette.

"Don't say that," I said. "To me it does."

"I just think," she said, "that we need to take one day at a time."
She sat back and put her palms down flat on the table as if she
were going to push it away from her.

"I'm sure he'll be okay once he's back home," I said.

She shook her head. "I'm not sure about anything, Noah. It'll be a whole new beginning for us. Please don't drill me with questions I can't answer. I know I can count on you to give me a hand with him."

"You can depend on it," I said.

She hesitated when I said that, and instead of speaking reached over and slipped her hand into mine. Her fingers felt like ice. The bar up front was jammed, and the clatter of falling cutlery came from the kitchen. She flinched with each unexpected noise. "It's just not that simple, is all I mean," she said, and her whole body seemed to lift in exasperation.

I spooned into my soup and tried to be ready for whatever was coming next. I felt helpless and frightened. Watching her, I remembered how I used to sit up in bed at night after my father had tucked me in and read me a story. I'd hear his shoes scraping against the staircase as he walked downstairs, then I'd hear my parents talking in whispers through the heating register in my room. Now, she bit into her lower lip and stared reproachfully at a squabbling elderly couple in evening clothes who sat nearby. When a baby began to make a racket in the booth behind us, she seemed to shudder inside her clothes. When I asked her to please talk to me, she leaned over and streaked a finger across my forehead as if she were writing a message to herself.

On the drive out to Mitchell Field my mother and Uncle Eli argued about what my father's doctor had told them about his condition. Mostly they spoke in Yiddish so I couldn't eavesdrop. Eli was my mother's brother and he owned a Rheingold distributorship in Mamaroneck. After World War II my father had had trouble finding work, so he'd taken a number of different jobs until he could find something he could build a future on. He'd enrolled in evening accounting and business courses at Fordham University, not far from the zoo. People used to say that my father was a natural salesman, that his element was conversation. For some reason I have it in my head after all this time that he loved to work with his hands. I have a memory of him doing the grouting in our bathrooms and puttering in the garage. He managed a busy liquor store on the Grand Concourse a few blocks from Yankee Stadium before it was sold to a company that built mortuaries, and then he went to work for Eli. At the time we were living in the Bronx. With someone around he could trust, Eli was free to play golf twice a week at his country club. After a couple of years he made my father a junior partner, and we moved from the rundown apartment building on upper Broadway, a few blocks south of Van Cortlandt Park, into Westchester County.

They were discussing money now—I knew the Jewish word for it—and my mother's neck and shoulders had stiffened. She set her purse on her lap.

"What do you want from me, Irene?" Eli said in English.

"I don't want anything," she said. She opened her purse and took out a crumpled pack of cigarettes, then pushed in the lighter on the chrome dashboard with her thumb. Half of the nail was chewed away.

Eli looked at me in the rearview mirror. "Your mother thinks I want her to sign something so I can have your old man's stake in the company back. Christ, I'm simply trying to protect the both of you. Haven't I always come through?"

Her head was turned sideways and I could see that her teeth were gritted around the cigarette. "Oh, all right, Eli," she said, and cut him off with a sudden laugh. "Who asked you to protect us? Let's just get there. I've had it with these business discussions."

An egg truck with Pennsylvania tags had jackknifed across the median strip and the Southern State Parkway was strewn with yolks and shells and crushed powder-blue cartons. A large-finned police ambulance blocked traffic in our lane as the trucker was taken from the cab. He was hoisted onto a stretcher and covered with sheets, and two men in green hospital attire rolled him into the rear of the idling ambulance. The cops were still sitting in their cruisers, and Eli leaned his head out of the window and did his Milton Berle imitation that made them grin and shake their heads at him. Looking out my window, I could see that part of the trucker's head was gone.

A freckled medic with a bandaged throat wheeled my father down the cargo hold. His lap was draped in olive blankets and his gaunt face was as white as typing paper. The air smelled of gasoline and burning rubber. A heavy Army nurse with close-cropped silver hair grabbed me by the elbow and blocked my path to him. In a flat John Wayne drawl she said I'd better wait a few minutes, in order to give him a chance to adjust to the surroundings. My mother stood beside me brushing down the front of her coat. She held her other hand up like a visor to shade her eyes. "Phil," she said three or four times. "It's Irene, Phil. Irene and Noah."

Eli edged past me, breathing heavily, and I had a prickly sensation in my spine between the shoulder blades. He turned around and told me to give him some room, that he needed to ask a few questions, find out what was what. My mother had looked good when we left the house, she had made herself up for the homecoming. She was wearing a new calico dress and open-toed strapless navy pumps. Her reddish-brown hair was marcelled and pulled away from her face in a way that made her round green eyes appear even rounder. Now she was sobbing and her mascara had started to run. My father's head turned slowly, and I remember his moist eyes straining to focus on something diagonally across the runway. A helicopter with camouflage markings had landed about fifty yards from us. Suddenly he made a high, piercing moan, the grimace on his face hardening into a puzzled frown. My mother jerked as if she'd been plugged into a socket.

In a few minutes I was given permission to embrace him. He smelled funny, like burnt meat. His cheeks were a grid of healed cuts, and his sticklike arms were badly broken out in jagged patches. My mother brushed her lips across his trimmed sideburns; I could see her bowed head in the polished shine of his combat boots. The scalp around his hairline was oily and raw, and his nose was bent, as if it had been broken more than once.

I looked at my mother—standing unsteadily while Eli held her by her elbow, listening to what the nurse had to tell them about my father's care—and tried to imagine what her frame of mind was. They raised their eyebrows at each other when the nurse spoke about his bedsores. The sun glowed silently, and high passing clouds made shadows on her face. Slowly, a bit distracted I thought, she flicked her hair off her eyes. She was looking over the nurse's shoulder, making eye contact with the horizon. She didn't seem to hear anything the nurse was saying.

I listened, nodding mechanically, pretending to understand. My mother's mouth was slightly open and I could hear her teeth clicking. I wanted to ask what I was supposed to do, how I could help. I was restrained by my fear of the truth—that someone would tell me all too clearly that there was absolutely nothing I or anyone else could do. That my father's condition was final, that nothing was possible anymore. I wondered if my mother had grown suddenly astonished by the weight of that prospect.

There was a commotion when three Marines in starched battle fatigues walked over and saluted my father. He just sat there as serene as an owl. To the indifferent eye he simply looked bored, or sleepy. One of the Marines shook Eli's hand and said they were veterans of Inchon. Then he held his arms out and pretended he was a dive bomber. The other two acted as if they had pom-pom guns, flak noises coming from their throats. My mother forced a smile but I could tell she was holding something back. The Marines had tattoos of naked women on their forearms. Then they all started talking at once—brainwashing, the H-bomb, fallout shelters—things I'd heard about in school. I looked my father in the eye and made a face at him, one he used to make at me when I was little. I curled back my cheeks and slid my lips back over my upper teeth. Then I bounced around and slapped at my chest and armpits and made believe I was peeling a banana. I made screeching sounds like Cheetah in a Tarzan movie.

The Marines got a big kick out of me and one of them gave me a Three Musketeers. About a hundred feet in front of us a cargo plane had taxied to a stop and was unloading caskets. My mother wrote something on a memo pad as the Marines saluted my father once more and left. She asked the nurse about my father's eating habits; her voice was barely audible over the diminishing echo of the plane's propellers. My father hadn't budged. His eyes looked so cold I imagined you could crack ice cubes out of them.

"We'll take it from here," Eli said to the nurse, and he took hold of my father's wheelchair.

A few days before he left for Korea, we'd gone fishing for flounder and bluefish off the corrugated iron pier in New Rochelle. The dark blue-green water rippled over a sandbar, like windchimes gently tapping in a muffled breeze. Rusted oil drums drifted in the tarlike sound. I could still see the plume of copper smoke that rose from his ivory pipe when he baited my line with redfin minnows. Smiling, he stroked my hair and told me it was my job to keep things going at home. Whenever he caught something, big or small, he extracted the hook as quickly as he could and threw the squirming, bleeding fish back into the water. Now, walking behind him and Eli and my mother, I felt as if I were following his body in a funeral procession, as I had followed my grandfather's three years earlier.

Back out on the highway my mother made a throat-clearing sound and asked me how I was doing. Before I could answer, Eli said I seemed fine. "Never better," I said sharply.

Eli chewed me out for being fresh, then stopped to talk with the fork-nosed man collecting tolls. My father started shaking when we zoomed across the Triborough Bridge. It was windy out, and the water below was sudsy and black and hundreds of sea-birds seemed to hang suspended between the silver spans.

"Eli's just trying to help," my mother said without conviction. I could see her rolling her thumbs in her lap.

"Tell us what's on your mind," Eli said.

"Well, Noah?" she said. Her tone was edgy, fretful.

I glanced over at my father. He had his hands in his pockets and seemed to be watching the country glide past the window. There was something thick going over me in waves. I shrugged and told them I wasn't sure what I was thinking. I wasn't lying; he looked the same as the day he left. For a minute or so there was to-tal silence in the car, then my mother pointed to her temple and cocked her thumb and forefinger as if she were holding a pistol and squeezed the trigger. "It's in here," she said.

"His nerves are shot all to hell," Eli said, his voice choked with cigarette smoke. "Every kind of lousy thing happens to men dur-ing war, but some can't forget them. What it adds up to is that an average man can take all kinds of pressure but then—*whammo*—everything that man is just falls apart into little pieces, and his brain turns to water. Your pop is just too damn sensitive for his own good. You can't help him by moping around. You've got to put it out of your mind."

"Getting over this takes time and patience," my mother said. "Not thinking about it will help."

"I don't know," I said.

She turned around and smiled at me. Her whole face seemed compressed into that smile. "He'll be all right," she said, in a hol-low tone of voice I'd never heard her use before.

"Most men manage to shake it off and walk away from it," Eli said. "Give him time, Noah. He'll come around. I mean it."

"I hope you understand what we're saying," my mother said.

I told her I understood, but the trembling in my legs told me otherwise. I didn't believe for a second that not thinking about it would help. Instead, I told them I couldn't imagine him not being himself again. Eli then started telling a story I'd heard at least a dozen times, about how my father's infantry company had ambushed and destroyed an entire SS panzer unit in the Ardennes with bazookas and recoilless rifles. My father had won a Silver Star for that.

"I think Noah's had enough for today," my mother interrupted, ending the conversation.

We hadn't had him back with us for more than a week before I could tell they were already smoothing things over for me, getting me ready for the disappointment they were sure I couldn't handle. In their voices was the hemmed-in anger and resentment adults feel in the face of hopelessness. For the first few months my mother made me go with her to Friday night services at the synagogue, where I sat quietly and watched her pray for his recovery. I found it disconcerting that she believed God had nothing better to do than to answer her prayers, particularly when it concerned my father, a man who had had no use for religion. I asked her if all POWs had suffered the loss of their speech and memory. She must have sensed my growing despair, since she'd felt compelled to make him sound like some banished Biblical seer, one of those solitary messengers of heaven left wandering in the desert. When I told her I was bored with going to temple, she said it was important I understood that nothing could be taken for granted. Who could say for certain, she'd tell me, what he was thinking and feeling behind the immensity of his silence? Since I had no answer that would persuade her to see my side of things, I walked with her to Westchester Jewish Center and watched her close her eyes and bend her head in earnest supplication.

Things hadn't changed that much in our neighborhood, except for the TV antennas that were sprouting up by the dozen on the rooftops. Sleek-fendered Buicks and Chevys with their tinted windshields and shiny chrome grilles and humpbacked trunks were parked up and down the block, and a Daitch had recently opened around the corner from my school. Horse-drawn wagons full of iced fish stacked in tiers or fresh fruits and vegetables in wooden crates were a thing of the past. We put my father in a Polish rocker on the small porch and waited for him to recognize things. I walked him down the winding hill from our house and showed him the new telephone and power lines that stretched along the New York Central commuter tracks. My mother and Aunt Sophie, Eli's wife, wallpapered the upstairs bathroom in the refurbished attic guest room where he would embark upon his convalescence. The attic was deep, cool and musty, with glossy heartpine beams and cedar-stained wood siding and brass lamps with maps of the American Revolution for shades. It reeked of Spic and Span and shellac. The double-paned dormer window had steel bars over it. My sixth-grade class picture was on the squat fruitwood hope chest that used to be in my parents' bedroom, and my father's frayed Yankee pennant was thumbtacked to the wall alongside a framed autographed photo of Joe DiMaggio. He had an L-shaped leather sofa bed, a Philco clock-radio on the round mahogany nightstand, a tortoise-shell hooked rug, two small gilt mirrors, a burgundy hassock, and a sapphire vase full of chrysanthemums and Chinese peonies, my mother's favorite flowers.

After school, when the weather was nice, I'd take him to the playground near our house, where he sat on the chalked foul line and watched me shoot baskets or play paddle tennis. Talk to him, my mother told me every day. So I did. About school and my friends and the people in the neighborhood I knew he had liked. In an effort to revive his memory, I told him the mournful stories he had once told me: about his penniless childhood in Batavia, Illinois; about his mother, dead from septicemia a few months after they'd moved to Aurora; about his despondent father, who'd earned a measly living working for mobsters, delivering black market rum to speakeasies during Prohibition; and of his own dismal adolescence, boarding with his mother's spinster sister in New Jersey, beside the Passaic, after his father was killed by a hit-and-run driver. But he just seemed to sink deeper into himself—the folds in the skin on his neck a deepening shade of gold—a disbelieving expression on his drawn face, his pitiless blue eyes so pale they were almost white.

I tried to expand and enlarge all the meager events of our daily existence. Well, I'd say to him, what do you think? He looked desolate, as remote as a man in a coma, but for some reason I was sure a wordless part of him understood what I was saying. In January I took him tobogganing on a public golf course and watched him catch snowflakes on his tongue. Once I thought I caught him checking around for something—he looked on the verge of speaking—and I told him that his landscaper, Mr. Manicotti, had packed up his family a year ago and moved back to his parents' house in Ozone Park after his father had a stroke. He held out his fist like a boxer getting ready to jab, and I could tell from the way the muscles in his face were working that he was struggling to speak. Then he strummed his flinty knuckles with his fingertips, an involuntary gesture that could mean practically anything.

How do you help someone caged within himself? You convince yourself that nothing can be taken for granted, you tell yourself you're willing to try anything, but it's another thing entirely to believe it. Satchmo, my Angora cat, remembered him. When he wasn't nuzzling his head beneath my father's motionless hands, he slept on his belly like the Sphinx next to where my father was sitting—purring, his big front paws out in front of his face. I took my father fishing for yellow perch north of Valhalla, at Kensico Reservoir, off the sandstone dam glittering with mica. My mother packed a picnic supper of turkey club sandwiches and potato salad, and we drove to Bear Mountain State Park where I skipped stones on the duck pond beneath a rising sulphur moon as he sat on a wrought-iron bench and watched the startled birds scatter in midair. I held his arm and we pitched horseshoes in the backyard or threw darts into a rubber target against the house. I showed off my batting stances—the exaggerated crouch I'd copied from Stan Musial, deep in the batter's box, a wrist-hitter's hitch in my swing. He looked at me warily, hunched stiffly in the Morris chair, holding a Hires root beer float in his hand, and I had the notion that he was holding back a laugh. I stood him up and we stooped together in the box I'd drawn with the end of my bat in the ground. Make believe it's Carl Erskine, I said. Get ready for the overhand curve. Beneath my hands the knobs of his shoulders felt like the heads of metal screws. When I bent down to flex his knees for him he flopped over, as if he'd suddenly lost all muscle tone. What do you see? What's out there? I was shouting now, gasping for breath. Do you know who I am? Who you are? Do you? Do you?

I awoke each day with a troubling feeling that something had been settled in my family that could never be undone. Talking to my father was like taking a stranger into your confidence; he'd look at me as if he'd never seen me before. He often slept with his eyes wide open, as if he had been frightened into sleep. And as for my mother, it soon became clear that some final thread of resistance to the truth of our future had given way. Usually a smart dresser, she began to look haggard. A dimpled tic flashed in her cheekbone whenever she looked into my father's solid, unresponsive face. She started wearing clothes she'd normally have given to the Salvation Army. Her housecoats looked linty and her nylons had runs in them. She'd only do her marketing after dark, driving five miles to a small grocery store open till ten. I'd hear her come downstairs two or three times during the night, checking dead bolts and door chains and turning the oven and burners

on and off, sniffing for gas. For her supper she'd scald cans of
Campbell's soup, and while we ate, sit sideways in her chair
chain-smoking and drinking a tumbler full of straight vodka or
rye. My father sat in his chair and every few minutes I reached
across the table and straightened his terry cloth bib. At times he
seemed baffled by his food. He'd move his knife and fork around
his plate, turning over his brisket or cutlets or asparagus as if he
were searching for something. After a while she stopped shopping
and cleaning altogether, and it became my job to dust the furniture, vacuum the soiled carpets, and stock the empty refrigerator.
She used sleeping pills, and her eyes, once as bright as topaz,
looked permanently darkened, as if all the light in them had been
consumed. An old woman's eyes, she called them.

One night in February, after watching the *Cavalcade of Stars*, I
found her drinking a brandy in the darkened living room. Strings
pulsed from the phonograph console, and Satchmo snoozed on
an armrest of the brocade sofa. She stood poised on her toes, barefoot, like a ballerina, and gazed through the frosted bay window.
Icicles hung like silver pendants from the Japanese maple in our
backyard. Scattered rays of winter light pierced the curtains and
sliced across her features like razor blades. She looked stranded,
almost lofty in her isolation, and I trembled, seeing her as someone unbroken by what had happened, as someone other than my
mother. She turned and smiled at me for the first time in weeks.
"You have to stop doing this," I said.

She swayed to the lonesome cadence of a harp. "Don't I deserve a hug?" she said.

I felt snared in her beam of delusory joy. Behind her, out the
window, headlights from a snakelike string of passing cars fanned
out into the icy mist. Heavy snow was piled in our driveway. The
other houses on our street were dark. For weeks she had grown
quiet with me; it was as if her will to speak had been crippled by
despair over my father's vast silence. I struggled to find some brief

encouraging words. Her lips moved, and she motioned for me to come to her. She embraced me and hummed in my hair, and we paced the floor as if we were waltzing. An enormous dreamy mood engulfed us, and I shuddered in her arms like a small wet animal. We floated together, sustained by moonlight and dread, and I imagined what it might have been like being alive inside her. Beneath my fingers her ribs felt like piano keys. "He just needs more time," I said. "You know—day to day."

Her eyes looked weighted, numb. "It's no good," she said softly. "It won't work. I'm doing the best I can."

"Then I'll work harder," I said, taking her hands and squeezing them till I heard her murmur in pain.

There was a bit of movement in her face, as if a nerve were jumping from one cheek to the other and back again. Her eyelids stirred faintly at the sound of the wind chimes hanging from the wainscoting above the breezeway outside. A wide band of sleet had formed on the window. "I'm coming apart, Noah," she said, wrapping her arms around her chest. "I'm afraid it's too late."

"It's never too late," I insisted. "Life will be fine once we get the right breaks."

"But I have to live with him," she said, and looked around me, out the window. She hadn't had anything to drink at dinner, and I saw that her hands had started to shake.

"Why did he enlist again?" I said.

She said nothing.

"Answer me," I said.

She sighed deeply, as if something stuck inside her head suddenly loosened, and turned and faced me. "He didn't have to," she said, her voice low and thick. "He didn't have to."

The sound of waves pounded in my ears. "Why?" I repeated.

"All these questions," she said, raising her eyes to the ceiling. "These things are none of your business. I don't want to talk about any of it anymore. *Ever.*"

"All right," I said, and in that moment the feeling I had always had for her changed somehow, and I understood for the first time the void between the way things were and the way I thought they used to be.

Passover came late in April that year. It was a mistake having the *Seder* at our house. Everyone tried to act as if it were important to continue the simple family rituals we had followed before my father left for Korea. "Magical cures are not unheard of," Eli said when I expressed my skepticism. "You can never tell what might bring someone around." A shrill voice inside my head kept saying that the best intentions were rarely sufficient in making bad things turn good.

Eli was windy and gruff during the service, and both bored and starved us with one of his digressive sermons on the Diaspora. He plowed through the entire *Haggadah* like my grandfather used to, and I remembered how my father would taunt them by disputing the translation and embellishing the text with his own exotic interpretation of Exodus. When Eli spoke of the Children of Israel foraging in the wilderness, he gave my father a watery glance that upset everyone. After the meal my cousins watched *Your Hit Parade!* in the family room while I stood with my forehead pressed against the windowpane in the foyer outside the Florida room and heard my mother and Eli argue about the business and money. Something had to be done with him, she said. She couldn't go on much longer like this; things were getting worse. Then she said that she was mostly worried about my behavior; she said that *I* was acting strange. I could've been knocked cold by that remark, and I wanted to burst in on them and demand that she take back what she'd said or else I'd do something that would fill her life with sorrow. My ears were tingling, and I felt the loss of my father like a missing limb. For some reason I didn't move, and they continued their crazy bickering for the better part of an hour—more talk about insurance premiums and investing in new equipment, talk I only half heard in my growing distraction—while my father sat there silently, decked out in an embroidered Israeli *kipa* and a new Harris tweed sport coat we'd bought him for the holiday. With a sudden jerk he knocked over my mother's cup, and hot coffee ran all over his trousers. He didn't make a sound.

By the summer he would grunt for food and water and let us know when he needed the toilet by wagging his hands wildly toward his bottom and letting out a bellow. On Saturdays I strolled him around the village for exercise. Occasionally we'd stop in the park to watch the shirtless Italian men play boccie ball and argue in the sun, then we'd go have a pizza or a stromboli for lunch. We huddled together like conspirators in my room while I categorized my baseball cards according to dozens of conflicting statistical factors. I strummed the hand-carved ukulele he'd sent me from Pearl Harbor and sang made-up Hawaiian songs to him, and on the laminated card table where my mother played Mah-Jongg Wednesday nights we played Parcheesi or Chinese checkers the best we could, which always meant me playing for both of us. Most days he sat like a statue on the porch—brooding, I imagined, though he was probably just watching Satchmo, who would wash his paws and ears while perched on the lip of the limestone birdbath.

It was Flag Day and I was showing him how to play mumbletypeg, when a green, beat-up Plymouth pulled into our driveway and a man wearing an Eisenhower jacket with captain's bars and carrying a black briefcase came up our walk. "Your mother's expecting me," the man said, holding out a sleek, fluttering hand for me to shake. He made eye contact with my father and gave him an exaggerated grin. The enamel of his protruding front teeth was badly stained, and his bristly black mustache seemed to have an electric current running through it, since the hair-ends stood at attention when he spoke. "I'm Captain Glaws," he said to my father, shooting me a hangdog look. "I'm your friend."

Captain Glaws was an Army psychiatrist, and he began coming by each Monday around the same time in the late afternoon. Previously—and only intermittently—my mother would take my father to a private clinic in Ossining, not far from Sing Sing, to see someone who specialized in his type of shell shock, but he charged too much and Eli's insurance policy didn't carry that kind of coverage. Captain Glaws was long-necked and balding and had a pleased look on his face all the time. He'd greet me with his bony hand extended and then pat my father's head as if he were a playful dog. Sometimes he'd let me sit in the Plymouth and shift the gears. The car reeked of waxy chocolate milk cartons, and the rubber floor mats were always covered with sandwich rinds and cigar wrappers. He would bring me packages of Yodels or Ring Dings and then ask me to beat it for an hour or two. Sometimes—it must have been his way of establishing intimacy—he would wear khaki chinos and a polo shirt and play catch with me in the yard before he went inside. After a few minutes he'd start to look around for my mother, and a pained expression would come over his face if he didn't see her right away.

She would stand in the shadow cast by a copper lamp at the bottom of the landing, and make an entrance. He'd usually have his hands in his pockets, and he'd walk right up to her until his shirt touched her sundress. I would go behind the garage and watch him lead her by her bare elbow inside the clacking screen door. Outlined by the soft saffron glow of the citronella bulb, they moved about, circled each other, talking, smiling, arranging their gestures. She seemed to be modeling her clothes for him. He would say things to her that made her blush, and I'd see beads of spit erupt between his narrow lips.

A few times I came back from my walk to find them drinking lemon cokes or egg creams. Tommy Dorsey or Duke Ellington would be on the Victrola, and she'd be serving him wedges of rhubarb pie or strawberry *babka*. When I entered the kitchen she winked at me over his shoulder and shook her head in a way that said it was not a good idea for me to say anything now. They giggled with crumbs in their mouths and I was dizzy washing my juice glass in the sink. Something I only vaguely understood had a hold on her, and I was afraid that if I said anything at all I would only make matters worse without accomplishing anything. Like most parents, mine had worked hard to establish the kind of family they felt they'd never quite had themselves, a family that could weather all misfortunes, and now that family was gone. I knew my mother could no longer be a hostage to my father's illness, that some limit to her grief had been reached. Seeing her eyes returning to life, it was clear that I would be on my own in this, that all of us would be.

One afternoon I watched them talking outside. My father was in the backyard, napping in the hammock. Captain Glaws was leaning up against the fender of his car. He flicked her hair away from her eyes with his long, blunt-tipped fingers, and opened his mouth in a wide, imploring grin. She colored, and her whitened flesh seemed to bleed in circles beneath the surface. Smiling, she traced his mouth with her thumb. They went inside and I waited for almost an hour before following them. His jacket hung in the hall closet and his briefcase was on the ottoman. The easy chair my father always sat in had been moved to the other side of the living room. Captain Glaws was sitting in it, drinking beer from an earthenware mug, his skinny legs crossed at the ankles.

I knew it was coming, but I was stunned nevertheless when my mother told me she was putting my father in a veterans hospital. When I protested she said, "Don't be silly, it's a nice cozy place," in a tone surely meant to be consoling but that in fact sounded scornful.

"Everything's all wrong," I said.

"Oh, Noah," she said gently, smoothing her skirt. "It's all done, it's history. He'll have no decisions to make. His life'll be certain, safe. Not like ours."

I wanted to put my hands around her throat. She looked old and mean and I turned my face away.

"What am I supposed to do?" she said, her voice rising. Her eyes were riveted on me. "Go ahead, tell me."

"I want things to be the way they were," I said.

"You must think I'm a rotten mother. No one knows how to act decently anymore. Life is too short, and I need to live for myself for a change. You can have a bad conscience for both of us. Wait till you're my age, then you'll understand what I'm talking about."

"Just tell me—why did he enlist?"

She turned to leave the room. "*God*," she said, her fingers steepled over her mouth and nose, her hooded eyes alive with anguish. "Because he'd rather have been in Korea than with me."

The window was open and the air was saturated with the smell of crushed honeysuckle. I thought of a summer vacation a few years back, at Lake George. My father and I had gone hunting for arrowheads and fishing for crappie and trout; after supper we'd listen to the ball game on his shortwave radio. My mother was sulky, and she spent her days in a webbed beach lounge, reading gothic romances and drinking gin-and-tonics. It was muggy and hot and the cabin we slept in had begun to smell like buttermilk. The murky nights were charged with the fumes of ionized air. One morning I found the picnic table at our campsite covered with black ants. My parents fought all the time—about everything. I must've blocked those two weeks out, because in truth nothing had ever been the same after that. When we came home they were tentative with each other, and with me. They both simply looked exhausted most of the time, and always seemed on the verge of sleep. One evening, while I washed our mess kits and strung them on a clothesline nailed to a couple of cherry birches, I watched their shapes silhouetted against the flickering mottled light inside the cabin. Sunset's swirling dust-cloud and spotted lilac cape had dragged its ermine skirt across the peaceful lake. My parents could have been a pair of pious Jews *davening* at dusk, but their voices sounded like simmering wasps. In a few minutes my father emerged. His face was flushed—something had taken the breath out of him, he looked staggered and frail. He smoked a cigarette and ordered me to get my things together and help him pack the car. I did what he said, and didn't question him.

The night before the day of his departure, I paused in front of my mother's open bedroom door. Out the window, descending clusters of clouds were like silky pearl corollas against the sky. Her shoulders were covered with the black lace shawl my father had given her for their anniversary a few years back. My heart made odd little jumps as she stroked her wiry hair. She leaned toward the rusting dresser mirror, dragging her antique bone comb of stippled garnet against a clump of tangles. The comb wouldn't come out, and the more she pulled the more snarled her hair became. I wanted to burst into her room and say that I could help her, that we could move away to another city, another state, that everything would work out. I wanted to tell her that anything was possible, that I would make it all right, that what it all finally came down to was love and trust and endurance. But when I saw her face arrested in the dingy glass it was impenetrable, a face ragged and faded beyond recognition. I looked away and felt my pulse drumming in the roof of my mouth. When I saw her later, in the kitchen, she was unruffled, almost serene, filing her polished nails into half moons. She looked at me with eyes burned clean of any purpose or hope, and I felt like a stranger—a boarder—in her life and home. I turned away when she asked me how I was feeling, and her voice was free of bitterness when she said that it was no one's fault we couldn't make a go of it.

For more than four years I visited him regularly in his hexagon-tiled cubicle at the VA hospital on the bluffs overlooking the

Hudson. The hospital was cold and dark and always smelled of resin and mosquito repellent. It was my impression that he liked my coming, even though I knew that our time together made no ordinary sense. His ward was jammed with lonely looking men in olive pajamas who read comic books and watched game shows on a portable TV. Some had pot and whiskey and penknives smuggled into their footlockers. I brought him magazines he couldn't read, a clock-radio he never listened to, and Necco wafers and Indian nuts the other patients stole.

My mother divorced him after about a year. There were other men after Captain Glaws, good men I must admit, men recovering from divorce themselves, or from widowerhood or business failures; men, in other words, who were in the same boat she was. I don't hold any grudges toward her. After all, as she said, she had her own life to lead. She felt that her life had been quietly ebbing away from her, and she craved intimacy—who among us doesn't?—attachments that reached far beyond the transitory ones of the flesh. Heartache permeates every family in greater or lesser degrees, and I have no reason to doubt that she did the very best she could. She was distracted by her own deep needs, and who am I to judge her?

Later she eloped with a Dutchess County pharmacist—someone she'd met on an Israeli sightseeing bus in Eilat, at the southern tip of the Negev—who was still grieving over the loss of his wife and daughter ten years after their deaths in a car wreck on the Taconic State Parkway. Sidney was a shy, quiet man who reminded me of Charlie Chaplin, and my mother seemed less anxious with him, if not entirely happy. She sold the house I grew up in for a nice profit and bought a vacation bungalow in the Poconos. In a very short time she became a woman I hardly recognized. It was as if when my father left her life for good I too became someone out of another time, a time she would've rather simply buried.

As a way of escape I joined the Air Force after high school, and never saw her again. Sometimes, in places like crowded elevators or supermarket lines or movie theaters, I suffer from pangs of regret when I smell my mother's perfume on the neck of a strange woman. When she died of a pulmonary embolism a few years later, a complication of a minor operation to repair a hernia, I was an MP stationed in Thailand. I received a formal condolence note from Sidney a few weeks after her funeral.

The last time I saw my father was on his birthday, the year I was discharged from the service. I was twenty-four and ready to try college. I'd gone to Macy's and bought him one of those stuffed animals made of polyurethane pellets and cellulose fibers. It was a snowy afternoon, and I was reading the sports section of the *Daily News* to him in the steamy arboretum while he picked at the plaster on the lime-colored walls. A line of glowing freighters was anchored in the icy river beneath the Palisades. He lay on his side, facing the window, and stared at the barren trees and high-voltage lines outside. His hair was matted and his beard was rough. He was wearing the silk tea gown I'd mailed him from Bangkok and clutching the stuffed cat on his knee. I was reading him an article on the Knicks when he let loose with a groan like Satchmo did after a runaway go-cart had smashed his spine on the sidewalk in front of our house. In his hand were the toy cat's translucent green eyes. He held me in his sad gaze for more than a minute, and the feel of his whiskers and dog tags against my face and chest when I hugged him has remained with me for all these years. It was like mid-August under the pure rods of fluorescent light. Talking wildly on into the night as snow fell in sheets outside, I did not think of ever abandoning him, till some orderlies came and took him back to his room.

Space and Light

On his way to the Livingston house to mediate a dispute between Mrs. Livingston and the masons laying brick for the garden patio, Paul Westerly made a detour to look at a house designed by a man whose career had begun, one summer fifteen years before, as a draftsman in Paul's office. The house, on the side of a hill with a view of the ocean through a cluster of eucalyptus trees, was under construction, and as Paul made his way past mounds of dirt and scraps of lumber and lengths of plumbing pipe, a strange sensation overtook him, a feeling of being exposed to some unstated danger, of needing to hurry, to get out of the light. He ducked beneath a scaffold upon which a pair of workmen stood, nailing a curved strip of siding with a pneumatic gun, and as he straightened in the deeply shadowed entry one of the workmen cried, "I quit!" and the other unloosed a torrent of loud and profane abuse that felt to Paul—for a brief, irrational moment to be aimed directly at him.

He stood in a large, irregular room whose ceiling ascended to the peak of the roof. The walls were not yet covered and pink blankets of insulation imparted to the interior a rosy, slightly ethereal glow. He could not immediately grasp the function of the various planes into which the space was broken, but he could imagine the drama of light and shadow that would play out in the room. That would be Jack, who had once declared himself the enemy of understatement, who had pronounced exaggeration to be a valid principle of design. The sky, enervated by a leaden haze, constituted most of the view through a high wall of windows, and Paul overcame an urge to inspect the glazing, to uncover defects and mistakes. He listened to the rapid, successive reports of the gun and the sudden whir of an air compressor. So the man on the scaffold wasn't quitting after all. He felt relieved, as if a disaster in which he was somehow implicated had been averted.

"Paul! Good to see you. Come in, come in. What do you think?"

Dressed entirely in beige, with the exception of a red scarf loosely knotted, Jack stood above a set of blueprints unfurled upon a makeshift table in a room that appeared to be the kitchen. His clothes looked rumpled in a deliberate way. The two shook hands.

"I'll take a quick look around, Jack. Don't let me interrupt."

"No, no, no. I'll show you everything." Jack grinned disarmingly. "How is everybody? Suzanne. Your daughter."

"Well. Busy."

"You look great, Paul." Jack patted his modestly ample stomach in a gesture that looked to Paul more affectionate than rueful. "Still jogging? Eating health food?"

"Yes," said Paul, feeling again the need to find a space that was dark, enclosed, something that in this house he guessed would not exist. He followed Jack's plump finger through a chaos of lines on the blueprint.

"The contractor says this can't be done." Somewhere above their heads a loud scraping commenced—Paul looked up but Jack ignored it. His finger impaled a detail dense with arrows and numbers. "You know how these guys think. If only the damned architect would stay out of the picture, let them change whatever's different. Whatever they haven't seen before."

"It goes with the territory," said Paul, trying to sound more affable than he felt. He could still recall the first piece of design he had entrusted to Jack, how sloppy and inattentive to matters of construction it had turned out to be. He put on his glasses and began to consider solutions to Jack's problem while in the background Jack's voice outlined in a spirited tone his troubles with the plumbers and electricians.

"Look," Paul said. "If you shift this window about six inches . . ." He sketched his idea, wondering if this was the reason that Jack called him out of the blue and invited him to see the house. Jack, he imagined, believed in a world divided between those blessed with imagination and those unable to conceive of how to build what he had designed. He had seen Jack's face, sober and reflective, inside a recent issue of an important magazine. He wondered, momentarily, if this client had given Jack carte blanche.

They stood outside and the winter sunlight, diffused by the haze, made Paul think suddenly of death, his own, even though his health was fine and he'd just turned fifty. The house that shimmered deep within the fender of a Jaguar he assumed to be Jack's had startled Paul and, in some way he failed to understand, disoriented him. He conceded, without envy or enthusiasm, the possibility that Jack was a genius. He looked away from the Jaguar to his own car, a Peugeot, a car he had once admired but that suddenly seemed insipid, of no more consequence than a Toyota.

"I can't afford it," Jack was saying. "You wouldn't believe what it costs. Just the license and insurance. I don't know what I was doing."

Paul ignored the disingenuousness. He said, "I think you're doing important work, Jack."

"I'm getting a lot of commissions." Jack rummaged in a pocket and produced a ring of keys. "More than I can handle. I was wondering . . ."

As Jack's voice trailed off they both watched the progress of a boatlike leaf being prodded along the gutter by a breeze. Paul thought of Mrs. Livingston, her long, annoyed face.

"If I want clients that you've rejected?"

"No, no. That's not what I mean, Paul."

Mrs. Livingston would by now have discovered that instead of the running bond at the far edge of the patio she would prefer the brick to be laid in herringbone. The leaf skidded under the Jaguar and Paul said, "What makes you think I'm in need of charity?"

"For God's sake, Paul." Jack lifted his chin to give his scarf a second turn. "If it wasn't for you, where would I be? I'm serious. When I worked for you my head was going in twenty different directions. Remember when I wanted to hop a freighter for South America?"

Paul remembered no such thing, but instead of saying so he looked at his watch and saw that he would be late. He felt tension, a pressure to get into his car.

"Sorry," said Jack. "I didn't mean to offend you."

"Forget it."

"Let's get together." Jack unlocked the door of the Jaguar and eased his bulk into the seat. "The four of us. I mean it."

Paul nodded. They shook hands and then the Jaguar spurted away from the curb, turned the corner, and disappeared. Paul had read in the magazine an article written by Jack and had found it incomprehensible. He had fired Jack. Or if he had not fired Jack, he had at least urged him to seek some other sort of work, and with this recollection came a sensation of dread, like a column of insects, moving up his spine.

He let himself into his office through the rear, where he kept a small workshop and racks filled with various materials he intended someday to experiment with. It was eleven-thirty. His assistant, Barb, had not expected him until after lunch and now she attempted to busy herself by moving paper about the disorganized surface of her drafting table. She followed him to his desk and said without enthusiasm that Mrs. Livingston had called twice, wanting to know why he hadn't come.

"What did you tell her?"

He knew this to be unfair—she would assume that she had made a mistake, said the wrong thing. Her face wore its usual melancholy expression, a reflection, he knew, of something askew in her marriage, something depressingly common that he wanted to know as little as possible about.

"I didn't get to Mrs. Livingston's. I had other things to do."

"She sounded upset."

"Mrs. Livingston always sounds upset. It's her normal state."

Barb stared glumly at Paul. "What do I tell her if she calls again? I mean, I'm sure she's going to."

Paul gazed at his desktop, which was perfectly neat and organized. He raised his eyes to his drafting table, angled in a corner so that the window light would fall upon it in the most propitious manner. A single sheet containing the first lines of a drawing of the gazebo for Mrs. Livingston's garden was taped to the table. She had shown him the gazebo she wanted in a magazine, a magazine full of houses choked with decoration, rooms through which it would be difficult to move without bumping into furniture, antiques, objets d'art. He turned his gaze to Barb. Her expression was uncertain and defensive.

"I'm going home," he said, repressing the urge to lie and add that he was feeling ill. He picked up the single pen on his desktop and dropped it into a drawer. His mind seemed to stutter, then grip the root of an idea. "I'll write you a check." He retrieved the pen and brought from another drawer his checkbook. As he wrote her name he observed that his hand was highly legible, even florid. He felt briefly that herein might lie a clue, some sort of explication.

"I don't understand," said Barb. The quaver in her voice was so pronounced that he began to imagine an embarrassing scene. "I mean, am I fired?"

A shadow drifted into the plane of the translucent window, then moved slowly on. The street had never undergone the renaissance that realtors had predicted and promoted, and there was always the fear of someone bent upon burglary, or assault. He had moved to the office three years before, when a partnership with two other architects had dissolved. Without looking up he could see the exact contours of a water stain on the ceiling. He desperately hoped that Barb would not begin to cry.

"I'm closing the office." He clapped the checkbook shut as if to demonstrate the reality of this act. "I'm sorry. I know it's sudden. This is last week's pay plus another two. That's fair, I think. If you don't think so, I'll give you more."

He felt a little giddy. He wadded the check and reopened the checkbook. "I'll pay you for a month. That'll give you plenty of time to find something. Maybe you could take a trip, relax."

Her motion in accepting the check was wooden, uncomprehending.

The telephone rang. It was Mrs. Livingston. He listened, looking at Barb, who didn't examine the check but kept staring at Paul's desk, as if waiting for its surface to speak up with an explanation. Finally Paul said, "Mrs. Livingston, you're an idiot," and hung up the telephone. He said it for the benefit of Barb, with the foolish expectation that it would make her laugh, but of course it didn't. He turned off the lights and lowered the thermostat. He told her to get her things and waited while she silently and mechanically gathered her pencils, rulers, erasers, squares, a small framed picture of herself and her husband in happier times. He helped her with her coat and walked her to her car. He leaned over the open door and said, "Good-bye. Good luck."

She stared up at him with eyes that in the daylight looked bruised and vulnerable. "I don't understand," she said gravely. "I think you're acting crazy."

On his way home he stopped at a florist's and bought a half-dozen roses, flirting very casually with the woman who waited on him, then went into a liquor store and spent twenty minutes selecting a bottle of wine. Suzanne did not appear surprised when he gave her the roses, nor when he told her midway through dinner that he wanted to build a studio onto the rear of the house, on the corner opposite the lanai, where there would be plenty of morning light. He had been prepared to argue but she allowed him to go on without interruption, explaining that he would let the lease on his office expire and work out of the studio—he didn't need a secretary, draftspersons, the various trappings of the profession. He wouldn't be able to accept as many commissions, but on the other hand he wouldn't feel compelled to take on work that didn't interest him. The fact that her income exceeded his no longer caused him any anxiety. Their daughter, in college and, like her parents, practical and levelheaded, would soon be a burden no longer, financial or otherwise.

She's listening, Paul thought, the way she must listen to a witness in one of her trials, with utter patience, waiting for an inevitable slip, an incriminating word or phrase. He heard his voice trail off and then she spoke, in a cool and neutral tone. It was not in character, she thought, for him to act so impulsively, but she had no objection to his plan. He lifted his glass, deciding that the wine he bought for this occasion was inferior, despite its inflated price. Disappointed, he gazed at the wall beyond his wife's head and saw a faint crack between the ceiling and crown molding widen, then narrow. She seemed far away, across a landscape out of which a grainy mist arose. He watched her eat. Her fork dipped to her plate, ascended to her mouth. She's getting fat, he thought. Not really fat, but—what was the euphemism? Mature. He smiled, very slightly.

"Schmidt lied through his teeth today," she said. "He's the auditor who saw the ledgers before they conveniently disappeared." She sipped her wine and he carefully watched but couldn't detect on her face any expression of distaste. He began to feel relieved.

"I tried to catch him but he wouldn't take the bait. I only hope the jury gets the impression that he's not the paragon he pretends to be."

"I saw Jack Dow today," said Paul.

"You did?" Her tone did not convey the message that this information signified something. "How is Jack? Where did you see him?"

He hesitated. "At the office."

"We should have him for dinner. I wonder if he's still with that woman."

"Melissa."

"Yes." She smiled a smile that Paul reciprocated with relief and gratitude. "If I had your mind, darling, my life would be so much easier."

The mist had vanished and he reached across the table to touch her hand. He felt the simple, unqualified happiness that follows a narrow escape from danger. He could not remember ever having lied to her before.

At the conclusion of a chaotic dream he arose, put on shorts and sweat shirt and sneakers, and went out into the chilled pastel of dawn. He ran slowly, huffing clouds of nearly transparent vapor, up and down the low hills that in a mile culminated in a final crest and steep slant of houses built down to the edge of the ocean where only surfers would be awake, a blond-haired species of sea life bobbing in the swells. He slowly picked up speed and by the time he reached the top of the last hill he was running as if pursued, his breath coming in ragged gulps. He finally stopped and walked, looking out over a cumulus blanket of fog that entirely obscured the ocean, and suddenly, without warning, he saw the studio in his head, complete and detailed and appended to the house so cleverly that a shock of excitement tingled over his skin. He saw windows, skylights, soffits, parapets, eaves, and for a few minutes he walked with no sense of time or direction until the structure, like the final scene of an amateur movie, flickered away. He had never believed in inspiration and even distrusted those who claimed it, for his own experience had always meant hours of tedious experimentation and refinement preceding an arrival at what he could call an acceptable design. In the article Paul had attempted to read, Jack had claimed to have designed an entire public complex in a dream. He laughed aloud, for what seemed ludicrous yesterday now possessed an interesting mystique.

His usual run took him down to the sand of the beach, but now he turned at the first intersection and forced himself to run without another pause back to the house. He didn't shower but mopped his face with a towel and pulled a pair of trousers over his jogging shorts. He got the Peugeot out of the garage, trying not to draw attention, feeling a little like a thief. Suzanne had not awakened; he would call her later. He drove to his office through the first perfunctory stirrings of rush hour traffic and let himself in, half expecting to see Barb and hear her tell him that he had another call from Mrs. Livingston. He crushed the drawing of the gazebo and pitched the ball of paper toward the wastebasket. He taped a clean sheet of paper to the drafting table. At some point later the telephone rang but he didn't answer. When the ringing stopped he unplugged its cord from the wall.

Awake again at dawn, Paul was startled to realize that he could only vaguely remember what he had drawn. He got up, turned on the coffee maker, and opened the front door to see that the newspaper had not yet arrived. In the bathroom he stared at his razor and then at his face in the mirror, wondering how he would look with a beard. An exaggerated fear of waking Suzanne made him feel like an intruder, and he carried work shoes, Levis, and sweat shirt into the kitchen, where he dressed and poured himself a cup of overly strong and bitter coffee. With a burst of furious energy he had completed the drawing of the studio, down to the smallest detail, and had gotten the drawing to the printer's minutes before it closed, but the question of precisely how he had arranged the windows and placed the doors would have to wait until the copies were ready later in the afternoon. Inspiration, a college professor of his had said, does not proceed in linear fashion but consists of flashes like lightning in a black sky of ignorance. Paul wondered if those, indeed, were the professor's exact words. He heard a car in the street and the thump of the newspaper on the lawn. He had last seen lightning on a trip to the mountains, and the sky had not been black but a deep, glossy green. The power of the professor's metaphor seemed diminished by this memory, although the idea of a huge, enveloping darkness had a sudden and disconcerting appeal.

From the garage he got a sledgehammer, a crowbar, and pair of wire cutters. He propped a ladder against the back wall of the house and carefully climbed, tools in hand, to the eaves. Bracing himself with his left hand on the ladder, he swung the sledge-hammer with his right against the stucco wall and was startled by the loudness of the blow that echoed in the trees behind him. He stared at a crack, an indentation in the stucco, a sort of bruise that seemed to speak the truth that he had crossed a line and would never be able to return. He swung once more, then again, then a fourth time before the head of the sledgehammer broke into the cavity between the inside and outside walls.

He knew from watching workmen that the trick was to hammer through the perimeter of a section two or three feet square and then cut through the wire mesh beneath and pry the stucco from the wood to which the mesh was nailed and let the whole thing crash to the ground, or in this case, the flower bed, below. He tried to discover a rhythm of hammering that he could sustain. Although the air was damp and cool he felt a prickling layer of sweat beneath his shirt, and the fine powder raised by each blow of the sledgehammer burned in his throat. He felt the lurking despair of defeat as he heard a different noise and turned his head to see Suzanne, dressed for work, watching him from the open door of the lanai. He lifted his hand from the ladder and waved, then, like an employee bent upon impressing his boss, slammed the sledge hammer again and again into the stonelike hardness of the wall. When he stopped, gasping for breath, she was gone.

His arm felt like a useless weight, but he was loathe to stop for more than a moment or two because a wholly illogical voice in his head told him that any hesitation would continue to infinity, become a kind of death A throb of pain arose in his elbow and climbed through his shoulder and into his neck, but he persisted in a dogged rhythm of hammering, cutting, and prying, and by midafternoon the entire structure of the wall—the top and bottom plates, the studs, the diagonal braces, the fireblocking—was revealed. Exhausted, he collapsed on the lawn and lay on his back, staring at what he had destroyed.

He cleaned up and drove to the printer's and when he returned a brown pickup sat in the driveway. A thick man with lead-colored hair stood pondering the demolished stucco, which in its unruly pile seemed to bear no relationship to the other, undisturbed walls of the house.

"Art. I'm glad you could make it." Paul carried freshly printed drawings under his arm. "Let me get you a beer."

"You did this yourself?"

"Why not?" Art's incredulity made him feel slightly foolish. He went to the kitchen and brought two bottles of beer.

"I could have got you a couple of men," said Art. "Look at your hand there."

Paul looked and saw darkened crusts of blood from wounds inflicted by the sharp wire of the mesh. He was annoyed with Art for pointing out what he imagined to be a sign of incompetence, amateurishness, the failure to wear gloves. He unfurled the plans so new that the odor of ammonia suffused the air between them.

"This section will cantilever," he said, guiding Art around the perimeter of the imagined studio. "We'll probably have to go deeper with the foundation here."

Art grunted. The drawings apparently translated into nothing familiar and therefore he would take a dogged, resistant tack. He turned the page of elevations this way, then that, an act that set Paul's teeth on edge. Paul wasn't normally impatient, but then he could not remember a project that had felt to him so urgent. Art rubbed his chin as if prepared for hours of deliberation, and Paul's nerves felt like a dry surface over which the passing seconds slowly scratched.

"I'm going right now to order the lumber," he said. "So you can start as soon as you're ready."

Art's eyes moved slowly over the exposed frame of the wall. This deliberate and careful nature which Paul had always admired now struck him as lassitude, or at least an unnecessary stubbornness. He had once watched Art take what seemed like fifteen minutes to show a carpenter the proper way of supporting a board while making a certain type of cut. The memory nearly made him squirm.

"I don't know," Art said, finally.

"I'll pay the labor and furnish materials." Paul swallowed the last of his beer and began to crave another, although he was not in the habit of drinking at all in the middle of the day. He looked up at the gray, ambiguous sky. "But I've got to get it done before the rains." He felt a small nudge of panic. "You need to get started right away."

"I don't know," said Art again, holding a sheet of details away from his body as if it might be infectious. "I'll have to look this over. Don't know if it can be done the way you want."

Paul turned and paced the length of the yard. Undefined emotion expanded dangerously in his chest, robbing him of breath. He picked up the sledgehammer, raised it without purpose, then let it fall to the ground. All of Art's virtues, he saw, would simply infuriate him, and Art in turn would withdraw so deeply into his stolid nature that nothing would happen. Crisis, disaster, chaos would be preferable to such a state. He saw a palm-sized scab of stucco in the grass and his fastidious nature caused him to bend to pick it up.

"Thanks for coming," he said. He took the plans from Art and stuck them under his arm. "I think it might be better if I do it myself. I can hire a couple of carpenters. I'll probably need to make changes as I go." He wanted Art to hurry, to get into his pickup and drive away so that he could turn his mind to lumber, carpenters, nails. They walked together toward the driveway. Paul waved his hand, vaguely. "I may have something coming up for you to bid on. A remodel. I'll give you a call."

Art nodded. He didn't look disappointed, or annoyed, or even puzzled. He said, "What about that gazebo? At the Livingston house."

"I don't know," said Paul, rapidly discarding several fabrications. "I don't think I'll be doing it. I told the old girl where to shove it."

"Is that right?" said Art, in a flat, observational tone. He got into his pickup and rolled down the window. As Paul turned toward the house he heard him say, "You're asking for it, my friend. What you've got here is a whole lot of trouble. A whole lot. You can take my word on that."

At the lumberyard Paul was given the name of a carpenter who showed up the following morning, half an hour late, in a truck with rock music blaring from the open windows. He looked like a surfer, with bleached hair and a uniform of shorts and T-shirt with the sleeves and lower part of the body ripped away. His eyes shifted rapidly about and his agreement with everything said was so immediate that Paul distrusted him completely. He had arrived prepared to work, however, and Paul had managed to convince himself that even a single day, a single hour of delay would transform his nervousness into unbearable anxiety. All of his natural patience and restraint had expired, he realized, somewhere inside the house that Jack had designed, and with a sense of foreboding he remembered a little speech—a lecture, actually—that he had delivered long ago to Jack on the subject of the architect's ego and how it must not be allowed to dominate a design. Jack had listened, he remembered, like the carpenter listened, nodding his head, saying yes, certainly, but all the while thinking he would find a way to do whatever he wanted. For just a moment, a very brief moment, Paul felt an intense fear, a loathing, a hatred even, of Jack.

The carpenter laid out the lines of the studio while a laborer Paul picked up on the street corner dug a trench for the foundation. The carpenter built the forms and put in the various bolts and reinforcing bars. The work took three days—longer, Paul thought, than it should have. An earnest, unsmiling man from the building department inspected the formwork, and the next morning a concrete truck rumbled up the street, followed in the afternoon by another truck carrying a blonde stack of lumber. Paul inspected the sky for signs of rain, unable to shake off an illogical sense of having been singled out by the threat contained in low, smoky clouds. Distracted by her mendacious witnesses, Suzanne paid scant attention to what transpired in the back of the house, a fact for which Paul felt grateful, because he had begun to dread the moment that she would come out to look at the completed project and feel required to utter some words of approbation. He went to bed and slept—fitfully as usual—and dreamed that a terrific wind had risen and scattered the stack of lumber all up and down the street. He then dreamed that Jack had come to see the finished studio and kept walking around and around, pointing out an infinite number of defects in both the construction and the design.

The carpenter brought a friend and as Paul stood with the blueprint they bolted the sills to the foundation and laid out the floor joists while the laborer brought plywood from the stack of lumber in the driveway, one sheet at a time, for the subfloor. Paul envied the ease and banter of the two young men, bent double as they rolled nails to their fingertips and set them with two or three blows of their oversized hammers. When he was in architecture school he had worked one summer on a crew building houses in a tract, and while his memories of the work and the people had blurred with time, a feeling of exhilaration connected to the smell of sawn lumber and the echo of hammers was undiminished. As a cold drop of rain struck the back of his neck he decided, with a shiver of regret, that his life had attained some pinnacle at the moment he stood astraddle the rafters of a house he knew, even then, to be substandard, mediocre, a creation not of the mind but of economics. He wanted to pick up a hammer and dip his fingers into the box of nails, but something closed and fraternal in the way the two men worked deterred him.

A radio played, too loud, but Paul decided to ignore it. He wanted to hear a weather forecast, but the loud and jarring music was interrupted only by equally loud commercials and disc jockey repartee that was apparently supposed to amuse but struck him as inane. He decided to wait until the end of the day before speaking to the carpenters about the need to work a little faster. They dropped so many nails that Paul told the laborer to pick them up, but the man understood no English and Paul could not convey what he wanted. He bent and gathered three or four nails from the grass that was now trodden and dusty. He was gripped by a fear that the carpenters would run completely out of the nails, that the work would come to a halt, that they would get into their truck and drive away and never return. Feeling short of breath although he hadn't been exerting himself, Paul decided that he would have to drive to the lumberyard and buy another box.

The traffic flowed with a maddening lack of speed and when he returned with the nails an hour had passed. The carpenters had finished the subfloor, had raised and braced a post, and had carried a beam from the stack of lumber in the driveway to the back of the house. Now they sat. Paul wondered why they were taking a break — it was only a few minutes past two o'clock.

"I don't know," said the carpenter with the torn T-shirt. He pointed to a detail on the plans. "I can't figure it out. Where is this going to go?" There was a defensive tone in his voice, as if he felt accused of something. A very light mist had dampened the sheets of paper, making them limp. The carpenter's friend hovered nearby, shuffling his feet, acting bored.

"I'll have to change it," Paul said, after staring for a minute or two.

"I don't know," said the carpenter again. "It's starting to rain. Maybe its going to rain all afternoon."

Paul breathed slowly and deliberately, in opposition to a swell of anger. The post, jutting up, uncut, seemed to jeer at him. He shut his eyes and in darkness the rage thinned and began to feel like fatigue. He had simply made a mistake, missed a point so elementary that hardly anyone could miss it, a detail lost in the torrent of creativity, the very kind of thing for which he had faulted Jack. So he had been right all along to distrust inspiration. He smiled and opened his eyes. The gray sky cracked like an egg and rays of sunlight slanted down.

"Forget the post." The carpenter's eyes followed Paul's finger uncertainly. "We'll just straighten out this wall and then the beam can sit over here. We don't need the post. You can take it out."

"Straighten the wall?" The carpenter followed Paul's route across the paper with his own finger, the nail blackened, misshapen, apparently from a hammer blow. "The whole thing?"

"That's not a big problem, is it?"

"No." He traced the line again, as if this path led to some insight, or hidden treasure. "Well," he said, as if revealing what he knew to be a truth, but with reluctance. "That changes the whole thing, then."

"Yes," said Paul. He felt compelled against his will to answer, as if he were a witness, as if the carpenter had become Suzanne, patiently but inexorably digging after a fact. He took another deep breath. "We've got the same problem here. On the other side. We'll have to move this wall, too."

The carpenter nodded, beginning to irritate Paul by the dragging of his finger across the already smudged and marked-up surface of the drawing.

Nothing matters, Paul said to himself, nothing but getting on with the work. But he didn't want to be given time to reflect upon this conclusion. "Sun's out," he said, feeling like a sergeant. "Let's get to work."

The carpenter dipped his fingers into the leather pouch at his waist and withdrew a dozen or so nails which he began to arrange heads-up in his palm. "What you had was pretty far-out," he said. "Now it's just going to be like . . ." He shrugged his muscular shoulders.

Paul smiled what he intended to be a benevolent smile. "It's fine," he said, wanting to give the carpenter a shove, to get him moving. "It doesn't really matter. It doesn't really matter at all."

At the end of two weeks the studio was framed and the electrician had come to put in conduit and boxes for switches and lights and outlets. By the end of another week the roof was shingled, the window frames were in place, and the wire mesh that would hold the stucco was nailed to the outside walls. In Paul's first drawing there had been five separate windows, but now there were only two. The French doors leading to a deck outside had disappeared, because Paul had suddenly felt that these doors would cause him to feel exposed. A stroke of his pencil had eliminated both of the skylights, an act he explained to himself on the grounds that the studio would have gotten too hot when the sun was overhead. The carpenters finished nailing the sheetrock to the inside walls and Paul gave them checks and the three of them stood for a while drinking beer, with nothing to say to each other.

He had shown Suzanne the original drawing, but she had never been adept at inferring a finished piece of work from a maze of lines and other details. Now, when she glanced at the studio through the windows of the lanai, her silence told him that she must have expected something much different, not this appendage so purely ordinary and uninspired. At dinner she was moody and complained about the dust that the work had brought into the house.

"We'll be going to jury next week," she said. "I'd like us to get away after that. For a few days. A weekend, at least."

Paul felt unreasonably pressured by this idea. "I've got to finish the studio," he said.

"You don't have to work on it every minute."

"I'll see," said Paul, although in reality the idea of leaving before the work was completely done seemed intolerable. He waited like a fidgety child as she dawdled with her food, and when she was done he rose and went directly into the studio through the opening that the carpenters had cut into the wall between his daughter's bedroom and the lanai. Street light cast a dim glow through the pair of windows, which after a few moments came to stare at him like the overdeveloped eyes of a science fiction creature. He saw a hammer on the floor and he picked it up and struck the window frame, the sound and the shock in his arm both magnified, out of proportion to the force of the blow. He heard Suzanne's voice but he didn't answer and presently a door slammed in a distant part of the house. He struck the frame again. He stood perfectly still until the light had completely faded and the eyes had disappeared.

The crew that would put the stucco on the outside walls arrived at seven o'clock, parked their scabrous mixer in the driveway, and proceeded to unload sacks of cement from their truck. Paul walked with the foreman around the outside of the studio.

"What happened to the windows?" the foreman wanted to know.

"There aren't any windows," said Paul, eager to discourage any desire on the man's part for an explanation.

"There were windows," said the man, calmly stubborn in his belief. "I saw windows when I was here to measure."

"It's going to be a laboratory," said Paul, feeling stupid.

"Yeah?" said the man, in a tone that divulged nothing of how he felt about this statement.

"It has to be perfectly dark," Paul went on, irked by this need to fabricate. "I hadn't realized that before."

"Yeah?" The foreman gestured to one of the men lounging about the truck. "You're the boss. You don't want windows, you don't have to have windows."

"That's right," said Paul. Why can't they hurry up? he said to himself, watching a man who stood leaning upon the handle of a

shovel and another squatting beside the mixer, smoking, waiting for an order to begin whatever they were supposed to be doing. He felt so nervous that he went into the kitchen and opened
a bottle of beer. He had never drunk beer this early in the day,
and the freedom implied by such an act exhilarated him, even
while the familiar, rational part of his mind sent out a warning
of danger.

He entered the studio. The light was gloomy and the exposed
nails in the sheetrock looked so much like rivers that he imagined
himself deep inside a ship, or an industrial tank of unknown purpose. He was planning to build a wall of shelves and his own tools
were neatly arranged in a corner—his power saw, a hammer, an
electric drill, a level. He stood in the center of the room and shut
his eyes. He was beginning to feel relaxed when the sudden
scratch of a trowel and mutter of voices disrupted his solitude, and
he finished the beer and went outside. The haze had finally dissi-
pated and the sun shone powerfully from a vault of chalky blue
sky. The men were on a plank below the eaves, steadily working,
and Paul felt the pulse of his blood like the driving compulsive
rhythm of the carpenters' music in his head.

By noon the walls were covered with gray cement, mottled and
scored; the driveway had been washed down and the mixer and
truck had disappeared. Paul thought about making a sandwich,
but his hunger wasn't as urgent as the idea that licked like a flame
at the edge of his consciousness. He found three warped and dis-
carded two-by-fours on the pile of debris awaiting removal to the
dump, and he carried these into the house and dropped them in
the center of the studio floor. He felt an odd sense of detachment,
as if he were observing another person undertake these labors. He
found his tape measure with the other tools and he measured the
height of the opening cut through the wall for the door. He felt as
he had the day he went to his office to draw the studio, as if intu-
ition had wholly superseded the normal, known mechanics of his

mind. He cut the three two-by-fours to length and nailed them into the opening, breaking out in a sweat from the exertion, feeling an almost palpable rush of time, like wind on his face. From a stack of sheetrock scraps he found two pieces that would cover the opening, and these he measured and cut to fit and nailed onto the two-by-fours.

He didn't know whether he had been asleep or just deep in reverie when he became aware of sound. He was sitting on the floor, back against a wall. Light entered the room only through the joint between the two pieces of sheetrock that covered the opening, but he sat beyond this crack of slight illumination, safely in the dark. "Paul?" He now connected a clicking sound to an image of Suzanne's heels crossing the tiled foyer floor, and a dull thump to their progress over the hallway carpet. "Paul? Are you here?" She was close now, on the other side of the wall. She sounded bewildered, a tone he could not remember ever hearing before. He felt trapped. He decided to stand up, and the hammer that had for some reason been lying in his lap bounced with a thud on the floor.

"Paul!" He heard fright in her voice and then, on the far side of the sheetrock, a scraping noise that he guessed was made by her hands. "What are you doing?" The noise like fingernails on a hard surface caused him to shudder. "Where is the door? Paul!"

"I'm here." Even to himself his voice sounded distant and muffled.

"Paul." Her tone descended to a level of deliberate calm, carefully measured. "Paul, I want you to come out."

"I can't," he murmured.

"What? Paul? I can't hear you."

"I can't come out," he said.

"Paul!" He heard sounds that he could not define. Finally she went away, he heard in the distance the thump and again the click of her heels, and then the sound of a door pulled open and slammed shut. He felt relieved. She didn't interest him any longer, he realized. She was something permanently in the house, a piece of furniture whose style had once attracted him but now was out of date, a presence so familiar that it might as well be invisible. His daughter's face flickered in his mind, but the features were generalities. He allowed himself to sink slowly back to the floor. The compulsive energy of the past few weeks had run its course, leaving him with a feeling of relief, of peace. He felt very tired. His eyes closed and he drifted into sleep.

"Paul!" Something crashed against the sheetrock, causing it to bulge, raising a fine shower of dust. Another crash, then another, and the dark iron head of his sledgehammer appeared like a vision in a shaft of sudden yellow light. In a panic he scrambled to his feet, looking frantically about for a place to hide that the rational part of his mind told him did not exist. In a rain of dust and noise the remaining sheetrock shattered and he saw his wife, an apparition, her hair wild and white with bits of plaster, coming out of the light into the dusk toward him. He shut his eyes and moaned.

The psychiatrist, Dr. Nathan, short and bearded and profoundly relaxed, had asked Paul, at one of their earliest meetings, "What exactly do you believe in?" Paul had been at a loss to answer and the doctor had glimpsed something in this failure that compelled the writing of a few lines on a pad. Paul thought, in retrospect, that the question had been too large and unwieldy to answer, although he could have offered homilies such as "I believe in life" or "I believe in love" or even something clever like "I believe in clients who pay on time."

He took the medication that Dr. Nathan prescribed, faithfully, although he wondered if the pills could be responsible for the deep malaise that encumbered him through his waking hours. The doctor had not immediately asked him what he thought he was doing when he sealed himself up in the room, and when the question arrived after a dozen weekly sessions Paul was startled and could only mumble that he didn't know. It seemed unfair, after hours of exploring his feelings about matters apparently unrelated, to suddenly spring this question. It seemed like a trick. He wondered if the doctor was a charlatan, or worse, a fool.

He spent long, sluggish days inside the house, and the divisions of time—hours, days, weeks—were blurred and unimportant. For a few weeks Suzanne stayed home from her office, her legal papers spread over the dining room table, the telephone in more or less constant use as she gave directions to her various associates. Some afternoons, if he was able to overcome apathy, they walked for fifteen or twenty minutes in the neighborhood. They walked very slowly, like an elderly couple—his jogging apparel hung unused in a corner of the closet and he couldn't imagine ever having had the desire or energy to actually run through the surrounding hills.

The doctor advised against a longer trip, so they flew one weekend to San Francisco. The city for which Paul had long felt an almost evangelistic affection was on this trip so cold and gray that its beauty became yet another trick, a mirage, its inclines so cruelly exaggerated that he collapsed, exhausted, on the bed in their hotel at the end of the day. Long silences marked their time together, like ropes strung between posts to keep back a curious crowd. He thought of asking her "Do you think I'm sane?" but decided that she must, for when they spoke—of the weather, of places to eat, of the possibility of leaving on an earlier flight—they did so in a lucid, rational manner. He decided that he was neither introspective nor keenly interested in the workings of another person's mind. He decided that within this observation must reside some significance that he would share with Dr. Nathan.

He grew tired of watching rain drip onto the ledge of the hotel window, so he asked Suzanne for a sheet of paper. She looked at him, he thought, in the same attentive, judicial manner that she had always looked at their daughter when weighing even the most trivial request. She must be bored, he thought suddenly, tired of this sort of faithfulness.

"Are you all right?" He half expected her to touch his forehead, test for fever.

"Fine. I want to sketch a little. See how it feels."

"Should you discuss it?" He tried to remember, with a feeling of vague regret, when they had last made love. "With Dr. Nathan?"

"I guess so," he said. "But what am I supposed to do?"

"What do you mean?"

"About earning a living."

She let this roll around like something spicy on her tongue, and he knew that when she responded whatever she said would be in some way definitive. With effort he decided to speak first. "He said, 'Some parents never come to terms with a child's success.'"

She frowned, making herself look worn, he thought. "What's that supposed to mean?"

Paul shrugged. Had their conversations always had a quality of disconnectedness, like freeways running on different levels, in the same direction but never joining?

"I had an idea," he said.

"You don't have to rush anything," she said. "We've got enough money right now."

"It's all right," he said. "If I ask Dr. Nathan he'll just turn it into a question for me. That's how it works, you know. You ask a question and get a question in return."

And that of course is what had happened. He had said to the doctor, "How do you keep from resenting somebody else's success?" and the ensuing questions had drawn out the business of Jack and the house, which was what the studio had started out to be, before it all went haywire. And the session had ended with the statement "Some parents never come to terms with a child's success," a statement that had caused him to think, Even if it's true, what does it explain?

He got up, bent to kiss her forehead in a habitual way, then found stationery in a drawer. "How do I understand what has happened?" he had asked the doctor. He sat at the desk in the room for a long time, staring at the paper, which was something foreign in shape and texture that would take getting used to. The idea that had prompted him to ask for the paper in the first place had completely vanished. He did not possess a single idea. But he couldn't simply sit and stare at the paper after it had been the subject of so much attention. So he drew a window. The window was ordinary and in appearance opaque. He drew two more windows, identical to the first. He realized without any particular emotion that he was good at this sort of drawing. The windows lay in the flat plane of the paper. He wanted, somehow, to open them. Finally he drew some lines around the windows. Each line existed as itself and did not suggest another, but he kept drawing. It took him an hour to finish, and he had a sort of soaring structure composed of lines and angles such that individual planes could hardly be discerned. The effort had made him tired, but it was the fatigue of exertion, not the ennui that had descended like an aberrant blessing the day he had closed up the doorway to the room.

Suzanne did not comment when he placed the drawing on the bed for her to see. It probably resembled nothing to her. She did not seem to want to spend time looking at it. That evening after dinner he noticed that she was staring at him. He smiled but her expression didn't change.

"I was thinking that we should move," she said.

"Move?" Paul was startled.

"Yes. Get a different house, in a different neighborhood."

"Why?" said Paul.

"The studio. I mean, what are we going to do with it?" She grimaced. "I didn't want to bring this up, Paul."

Paul smiled again. He didn't feel agitated or depressed, whatever it was she feared. "I could put in the windows. They're still in the garage. I looked at them the other day."

"I don't mean you should do anything, Paul. We could call Art. I could speak to him."

"It's all right." He felt undisturbed, relaxed really. They were having wine again. They had been having wine more frequently. "It'll give me something to do."

"Whatever you think," she said, a little glumly, he thought. She drank more than she used to, he noticed. She had been having a cocktail after work, he could taste the alcohol on her breath when he kissed her. She had always showered and changed before dinner, but recently she had been arriving at the table in the clothes she had worn all day, looking rumpled. Paul wondered what these changes meant, but when he asked himself a question he was presented, as with the doctor, a question in return.

The morning after they returned from San Francisco he got the sledgehammer from the garage, set up the ladder, and began to break the freshly hardened stucco from the section of wall that had contained the windows. He had to frequently pause to rest and catch his breath, and when he finished it was late in the afternoon. In the dying sunlight he stared at the openings where the windows had been, awaiting the arrival of some emotion from the distant past. He waited but nothing came to dispel an odd feeling of indifference to what he had done.

In the morning he got up earlier than usual, went outside, and carried the windows from the garage to the back of the house. He poured himself a cup of coffee but instead of sitting to drink it he got out the ladder and propped it against the wall. He finished the coffee, standing beside the ladder, and finally he heard Suzanne leave for work. He climbed the ladder and nailed the window frames into the openings. He carefully leveled and shimmed the frames, but when he stood back to look he could immediately see that the placement of the windows was too symmetrical—he would have to move one of them, possibly both. All his energy had turned to fatigue, but he forced himself to pick up the hammer and strike the wall between the windows, breaking through the stucco once again. He continued to doggedly hammer. He moved slowly along the wall, getting down every few minutes to move the ladder, until the stucco was broken in a solid line from corner to corner. His damp shirt clung to his skin. He stood still for a few moments, staring, but what he had done did not seem similar or even related to his earlier act of destruction.

"Do you feel a sense of loss?" the doctor had asked. "Do you feel that something dear to you is missing?"

The next morning Paul got up even earlier, and drank three cups of coffee while waiting impatiently for Suzanne to leave. In a furious burst of exertion he continued breaking and stripping away the freshly hardened stucco, and by midafternoon all three walls of the studio were exposed, and without taking a break for food or rest he shut off the electrical breaker and began yanking the new wiring from the conduit. At five o'clock he climbed a ladder to the roof and pried off shingles with a bar. It was dusk and Suzanne was not yet home. She had been getting home later and later, he observed. With leaden arms he started to pry a rafter from the ridge board. When Suzanne's car turned into the driveway, the streetlight had begun to glow.

"I'm going," she said, after Paul had beaten dust from his pants and shirt and followed her into the kitchen, where she was drinking beer from the bottle, something he had never seen her do before. "I can't take it, Paul. I'm sorry."

"What do you mean?" said Paul, although the scene had for him an air of inevitability, of predictability even.

"I can't take it," she repeated. "I'm leaving. All this . . ." Her arm rose and fell in a gesture that seemed encompassing and final. "I'm sorry, Paul."

He felt that she was probably right, justified. He felt prepared to defend the propriety of her decision, because the rational part of his mind observed that the facts were all in her favor. She looked disheveled, slightly deranged, with her puffy face and reddish eyes, and briefly he felt pity for her.

"We'll have to tell Jennifer."

For a moment he was adrift, and then with a shock he realized who she was talking about. He realized, with a start, that what he had done was to destroy what he had invested so much of himself into designing and building. But that was all right, it wouldn't have enhanced the value of the house, not even the original design, which would have put too many people off, made them fearful. Perhaps they would sell the house and he would buy a condominium. Their daughter would come to visit father and mother, each in turn. In a moment the idea of their separation, something that had never occurred to him, appeared to be accomplished with hardly any fuss.

He decided to have a glass of wine. He asked if she wanted a glass for her beer and she shook her head abruptly, an act that drew his attention to the fact that her eyes had filled with tears which spread in tracks down over her plump, reddened cheeks. He poured wine into a glass and suddenly thought of Jack, with a little regret—they wouldn't be able to get together now, the four of them. He thought he might have an idea that would interest Jack. He thought he might sound out Jack about doing something together, a joint venture, and he began to think about how he would state this proposition. Jack could handle the design, and he would arrange the practical matters of construction, deal with the contractor, the plumbers, the electricians. He heard his wife sniffle, but he didn't look at her. He looked through the window, just catching a glimpse of the jumbled wood and debris in the nearly faded light, and he didn't feel afraid, or even nervous; he felt that the past was complete, a book he hadn't been able to put down but which, once finished, had rapidly leaked from his memory.

"Well," he said, with an ethereal, fleeting sense that the light on the ceiling was about to blink off and leave him again enclosed in darkness. "Where do we go from here?"

And in the manner of the psychiatrist, she answered his question with a question. "Why did you tell me that you saw Jack in your office?"

The light appeared to flicker, a stutter of disorientation.

"You talked to Jack?" he said.

"It was just coincidence." She sat slumped ungracefully at the table. "We're representing a developer he's involved with. When we went to look at this building he happened to be there. He said he had seen you. At a house he had designed."

Paul felt cold and naked, his life turned inside out, all of his forgotten secrets and deceptions exposed to public view. He felt a squirm of panic, and the old dormant urge to run. To run until he found another space that he could enter and then close up behind him. He opened his mouth to speak in his own defense, but his voice did not seem able to penetrate the thickness of silence between himself and his wife, who in any case appeared to have abandoned her interest in him, who sat staring like a drunk at the bottle of beer encircled by her hands.

In a voice just slightly louder than a murmur she said, "It doesn't really matter, Paul."

She had receded to the end of a long tunnel, and Paul had to blink to restore the proportions of the room, to bring her back to the place where she sat, not more than five or six feet away, close enough that he had a sudden urge to touch her, to caress her, to tug her to her feet and lead her to their bed. He was frightened momentarily, as by a loud noise or the jolt of an earthquake, but this fear was rapidly displaced by the knowledge that the space in which he stood was circumscribed and constant, that the light that banished the nearly solid darkness outside the windows was as reliable as anything in the world can be. Suzanne, Jack, Barb, Mrs. Livingston, Dr. Nathan, his daughter — they would all move in and out of the space, back and forth through light and darkness, but he would remain, alone perhaps, or with his wife, or even with someone yet to be imagined, where he had always been.

In Broad Daylight

While I was eating corn cake and jellyfish at lunch, our gate was thrown open and Bare Hips hopped in. His large wooden pistol was stuck partly inside the waist of his blue shorts. "White Cat," he called me by my nickname, "hurry, let's go. They caught Old Whore at her home. They're going to take her through the streets this afternoon."

"Really?" I put down my bowl, which was almost empty, and rushed to the inner room for my undershirt and sandals. "I'll be back in a second."

"Bare Hips, did you say they'll parade Mu Ying today?" I heard Grandma ask in her husky voice.

"Yes, all the kids on our street have left for her house. I came to tell White Cat." He paused. "Hey, White Cat, hurry up!"

"Coming," I cried, still looking for my sandals.

"Good, good!" Grandma said to Bare Hips, while flapping at flies with her large palm-leaf fan. "They should burn the bitch on Heaven Lamp like they did in the old days."

"Come, let's go," Bare Hips said to me the moment I was back. He turned to the door; I picked up my wooden scimitar and followed him.

"Put on your shoes, dear." Grandma stretched out her fan to stop me.

"No time for that, Grandma. I've got to be quick, or I'll miss something and won't be able to tell you the whole story when I get back."

We dashed into the street while Grandma was shouting behind us, "Come back. Take the rubber shoes with you."

We charged toward Mu Ying's home on Eternal Way, waving our weapons above our heads. Grandma was crippled and never came out of our small yard. That was why I had to tell her about what was going on outside. But she knew Mu Ying well, just as all the old women in our town knew Mu well and hated her. Whenever they heard she had a man in her home again, these women would say, "This time they ought to burn Old Whore on Heaven Lamp."

What they referred to was the old way of punishing an adulteress. Though they had lived in the New China for almost two decades, some ancient notions still stuck in their heads. Grandma told me about many of the executions in the old days that she had seen with her own eyes. Officials used to have the criminals of adultery executed in two different ways. They beheaded the man. He was tied to a stake on the platform at the marketplace. At the first blare of horns, a masked headsman ascended the platform holding a broad ax before his chest; at the second blare of horns, the headsman approached the criminal and raised the ax over his head; at the third blare of horns, the head was lopped off and fell to the ground. If the man's family members were waiting beneath the platform, his head would be picked up to be buried with his body; if no family member was nearby, dogs would carry the head away and chase each other around until they ate up the flesh and returned for the body.

Unlike the man, the woman involved was executed on Heaven Lamp. She was hung naked upside down above a wood fire whose flames could barely touch her scalp, and two men flogged away at her with whips made of bulls' penises. Meanwhile she screamed for help and the whole town could hear her. Since the fire merely scorched her head, it took at least half a day for her to stop shrieking and a day and a night to die completely. People used to believe that the way of punishment was justified by heaven, so the fire was called Heaven Lamp. But that was an old custom; nobody believed they would burn Mu Ying that way.

Mu's home, a small granite house with cement tiles built a year before, was next to East Wind Inn on the northern side of Eternal Way. When we entered that street, Bare Hips and I couldn't help looking around tremulously, because that area was the territory of the children living there. Two of the fiercest boys, who would kill without thinking twice, ruled that part of town. Whenever a boy from another street wandered into Eternal Way, they would capture him and beat him up. Of course we did the same thing; if we caught one of them in our territory, we would at least confiscate whatever he had with him: grasshopper cages, slingshots, bottle caps, marbles, cartridge cases, and so on. We would also make him call every one of us "Father" or "Grandfather." But today hundreds of children and grown-ups were pouring into Eternal Way; two dozen urchins on that street surely couldn't hold their ground. Besides, they had already adopted a truce, since they were more eager to see the Red Guards drag Mu Ying out of her den.

When we arrived, Mu was being brought out through a large crowd at the front gate. Inside her yard there were three rows of colorful washing hung on iron wires, and there was also a grape trellis. Seven or eight children were in there, plucking off grapes and eating them. Two Red Guards held Mu Ying by the arms, and the other Red Guards, about twenty of them, followed behind. They were all from Dalian City and wore homemade army uniforms. God knew how they came to know there was a bad woman in our town. Though people hated Mu and called her names, no one would rough her up. These Red Guards were strangers, so they wouldn't mind doing it.

Surprisingly, Mu looked rather calm; she neither protested nor said a word. The two Red Guards let go of her arms, and she followed them quietly into West Street. We all moved with them. Some children ran several paces ahead to look back at her.

Mu wore a sky-blue dress, which made her different from the other women who were always in jackets and pants suitable for honest work. In fact, even we small boys could tell that she was really handsome, perhaps the best looking woman of her age in town. Though in her fifties, she didn't have a single gray hair; she was a little plump, but because of her long legs and arms she appeared rather queenly. While most of the women had sallow faces, hers looked white and healthy like fresh milk.

Skipping in front of the crowd, Bare Hips turned around and cried out at her, "Shameless Old Whore!"

She glanced at him, her round eyes flashing; the mole beside her left nostril grew darker. Grandma had assured me that Mu's mole was not a beauty-mole but a tear-mole. This meant her life would be soaked in tears.

We knew where we were going, to White Mansion, which was our classroom building, the only two-story house in town. As we came to the end of West Street, a short man ran out from a street corner, panting for breath and holding a sickle. He was Meng Su, Mu Ying's husband, who sold bean jelly in summer and sugarcoated haws in winter at the marketplace. He paused in front of the large crowd, as though having forgotten why he had rushed over. He turned his head around to look back; there was nobody behind him. After a short moment he moved close, rather carefully.

"Please let her go," he begged. "Comrade Red Guards, it's all my fault. Please let her go." He put the sickle under his arm and held his hands together before his chest.

"Get out of the way!" commanded a tall young man, who must have been the leader.

"Please don't take her away. It's my fault. I haven't disciplined her well. Please give her a chance to be a new person. I promise, she won't do it again."

The crowd stopped to circle about. "What's your class status?" a square-faced young woman asked in a sharp voice.

"Poor Peasant," Meng said, his small eyes tearful and his cupped ears twitching a little. "Please let her go, sister. Have mercy on us! I'm kneeling down to you if you let her go." Before he was able to fall on his knees, two young men held him back. Tears were rolling down his dark fleshy cheeks, and his gray head began waving about. The sickle was taken away from him.

"Shut up," the tall leader yelled and slapped him across the face. "She's a snake. We traveled seventy kilometers to come here to wipe out poisonous snakes and worms. If you don't stop interfering, we'll parade you with her. Do you want to join her?"

Silence. Meng covered his face with his large hands as though feeling dizzy.

A man in the crowd said aloud, "If you can share the bed with her, why can't you share the street?"

Many of the grown ups laughed. "Take him, take him too," someone told the Red Guards. Meng looked scared, sobbing quietly.

His wife stared at him without a word. Her teeth were clenched; a faint smile passed the corners of her mouth. Meng seemed to wince under her stare. The two Red Guards let his arms go, and he stepped aside, watching his wife and the crowd move toward the school.

People in our town had different opinions of Meng Su. Some said he was a born cuckold who didn't mind his wife's sleeping with any man as long as she could bring money home. Some believed he was a good-tempered man who had stayed with his wife mainly for their children's sake; they forgot that the three children had grown up long before and were working in big cities far away. Some thought he didn't leave his wife because he had no choice—no woman would marry such a dwarf. Grandma, for some reason, seemed to respect Meng. She told me that Mu Ying had once been raped by a group of Russian soldiers under Northern Bridge and left on the riverbank afterwards. That night her husband sneaked there and carried her back. He looked after her for a whole winter till she recovered. "Old Whore doesn't deserve that good-hearted man," Grandma would say. "She's heartless and knows only how to sell her thighs."

We entered the school's playground where about two hundred people had already gathered. "Hey, White Cat and Bare Hips," Big Shrimp called to us, waving his claws. Many boys from our street were there too. We went to join them.

The Red Guards took Mu to the front entrance of the building. Two tables had been placed between the stone lions that crouched on each side of the entrance. On one of the tables stood a tall paper hat with the big black characters on its side: "Down with Old Bitch!"

A young man in glasses raised his bony hand and started to address us. "Folks, we've gathered here today to denounce Mu Ying, who is a demon in this town."

"Down with Bourgeois Demons!" a slim woman Red Guard shouted. We raised our fists and repeated the slogan.

"Down with Old Bitch Mu Ying," a middle-aged man cried with both hands in the air. He was an active revolutionary in our commune. Again we shouted, in louder voices.

The nearsighted man went on, "First, Mu Ying must confess her crime. We must see her attitude toward her own crime. Then we'll make the punishment fit both her crime and her attitude. All right, folks?"

"Right," some voices replied from the crowd.

"Mu Ying," he turned to the criminal, "you must confess everything. It's up to you now."

She was forced to stand on a bench. Staying below the steps, we had to raise our heads to see her face.

The questioning began. "Why do you seduce men and paralyze their revolutionary will with your bourgeois poison?" the tall leader asked solemnly.

"I've never invited any man to my home, have I?" she said rather calmly. Her husband was standing at the front of the crowd, listening to her without showing any emotion, as though having lost his mind.

"They why did they go to your house and not to others' houses?"

"They wanted to sleep with me," she said.

"Shameless!" several women hissed in the crowd.

"A true whore!"

"Scratch her!"

"Rip apart her filthy mouth!"

"Sisters," she spoke aloud. "All right, it was wrong to sleep with them. But you all know what it feels like when you want a man, don't you? Don't you once in a while have that feeling in your bones?" Contemptuously, she looked at the few withered middle-aged women standing in the front row, then closed her eyes. "Oh, you want that real man to have you in his arms and let him touch every part of your body. For that man alone you want to blossom into a woman, a real woman—"

"Take this, you Fox Spirit!" A stout young fellow struck her on the side with a fist like a sledgehammer. The heavy blow silenced her at once. She held her sides with both hands, gasping for breath.

"You're wrong, Mu Ying," Bare Hips's mother said from the front of the crowd, her forefinger pointing upward at Mu. "You have your own man, who doesn't lack an arm or a leg. It's wrong to have others' men and more wrong to pocket their money."

"I have my own man?" Mu glanced at her husband and smirked. She straightened up and said, "My man is nothing. He's no good, I mean in bed. He always comes before I feel anything."

All the adults burst out laughing. "What's that? What's so funny?" Big Shrimp asked Bare Hips.

"You didn't get it?" Bare Hips said impatiently. "You don't know anything about what happens between a man and a woman. It means that whenever she doesn't want him to come close to her he comes. Bad timing."

"It doesn't sound like that," I said.

Before we could argue, a large bottle of ink smashed on Mu's head and knocked her off the bench. Prone on the cement terrace, she broke into swearing and blubbering. "Oh, damn your ancestors! Whoever hit me will be childless!" She was rubbing her head with her left hand. "Oh Lord of Heaven, they treat their grandma like this!"

"Serves you right!"

"A cheap weasel."

"Even a knife on her throat can't stop her."

"A pig is born to eat slop!"

When they put her back up on the bench, she became another person—her shoulders covered with black stains, and a red line trickling down her left temple. The scorching sun was blazing down on her as though all the black parts on her body were about to burn up. Still moaning, she turned her eyes to the spot where her husband had been standing a few minutes before. But he was no longer there.

"Down with Old Whore!" a farmer shouted in the crowd. We all followed him in one voice. She began trembling slightly.

The tall leader said to us, "In order to get rid of her counter-revolutionary airs, first we're going to cut her hair." With a wave of his hand, he summoned the Red Guards behind him. Four men moved forward and held her down. The square-faced woman raised a large pair of scissors and thrust them into the mass of the permed hair.

"Don't, don't, please. Help, help! I'll do whatever you want me to—"

"Cut!" someone yelled.

"Shave her bald!"

The woman Red Guard applied the scissors skillfully. After four or five strokes, Mu's head looked like the tail of a molting hen. She started blubbering again, her nose running and her teeth chattering.

A breeze came and swept away the fluffy curls from the terrace and scattered them on the sandy ground. It was so hot that some people took out fans, waving them continuously. The crowd stank of sweat.

Wooooo, wooooo, woo, woo. That was the train coming from Sand County at three-thirty. It was a freight train, whose young drivers would toot the steam horn whenever they saw a young woman in a field beneath the track.

The questioning continued. "How many men have you slept with these years?" the nearsighted man asked.

"Three."

"She's lying," a woman in the crowd cried.

"I told the truth, sister." She wiped the tears from her cheeks with the back of her hand.

"Who are they?" the young man asked again. "Tell us more about them."

"An officer from the Little Dragon Mountain, and—"

"How many times did he come to your house?"

"I can't remember. Probably twenty."

"What's his name?"

"I don't know. He told me he was a big officer."

"Did you take money from him?"

"Yes."

"How much for each time?"

"Twenty yuan."

"How much altogether?"

"Probably five hundred."

"Comrades and Revolutionary Masses," the young man turned to us, "how shall we handle this parasite that sucked blood out of a revolutionary officer?"

"Quarter her with four horses!" an old woman yelled.

"Burn her on Heaven Lamp!"

"Poop on her face!" a small fat girl shouted, her hand raised like a tiny pistol with the thumb cocked up and the forefinger aimed at Mu. Some grown-ups snickered.

Then a pair of old cloth shoes, a symbol for a promiscuous woman, were passed to the front. The slim young woman took the shoes and tied them together with the laces. She climbed on a table and was about to hang the shoes around Mu's neck. Mu elbowed the woman aside and knocked the shoes to the ground. The stout young fellow picked them up and jumped twice to slap her on the cheeks with the soles. "You're so stubborn. Do you want to change yourself or not?" he asked.

"Yes, I do," she said meekly and dared not stir a bit. Meanwhile the shoes were being hung around her neck.

"Now she looks like a real whore," a woman said.

"Sing us a tune, sis," a farmer shouted.

"Comrades," the man in glasses resumed, "let us continue the denunciation." He turned to Mu and asked, "Who are the other men?"

"A farmer from Apple Village."

"How many times with him?"

"Once."

"Liar!"

"She's lying!"

"Give her one on the mouth!"

The young man raised his hands to calm the crowd down and questioned her again, "How much did you take from him?"

"Eighty yuan."

"One night?"

"Yes."

"Tell us more about it. How can you make us believe you?"

"That old fellow came to town to sell piglets. He sold a whole litter for eighty, and I got the money."

"Why did you charge him more than the officer?"

"No, I didn't. He did it four times in one night."

Some people were smiling and whispering to each other. A woman said that old man must have been a widower or never married.

"What's his name?" the young man went on.

"No idea."

"Was he rich or poor?"

"Poor."

"Comrades," the young man addressed us, "here we have a poor peasant who worked with his sow for a whole year and got only a litter of piglets. That money is the salt and oil money for his family, but this snake swallowed the money with one gulp. What shall we do with her?"

"Kill her!"

"Beat her skull!"

"Beat the piss out of her!"

A few farmers began to move forward to the steps, waving their fists or rubbing their hands.

"Hold," a woman Red Guard with a huge Chairman Mao badge on her chest spoke in a commanding voice. "The Great Leader has instructed us: 'For our struggle we need words but not force.' Comrades, we can easily wipe her out with words. Force doesn't solve ideological problems." What she said restrained those enraged farmers, who remained in the crowd.

Wooo, woo, wooo, wooooooooooo, an engine screamed in the south. It was strange, because the drivers of the four o'clock train were a bunch of old men who seldom blew the horn.

"Who is the third man?" the nearsighted man continued to question Mu.

"A Red Guard."

The crowd broke into laughter. Some women asked the Red Guards to give her another bottle of ink. "Mu Ying, you're responsible for your own words," the young man said in a serious voice.

"I told you the truth."

"What's his name?"

"I don't know. He led the propaganda team that passed here last month."

"How many times did you sleep with him?"

"Once."

"How much did you make out of him?"

"None. That stingy dog wouldn't pay a fen. He said he was the worker who should be paid."

"So you were outsmarted by him?"

Some men in the crowd guffawed. Mu wiped her nose with her thumb, and at once she wore a thick mustache. "I taught him a lesson, though," she said.

"How?"

"I tweaked his ears, gave him a bloody nose, and kicked him out. I told him to never come back."

People began talking to each other. Some said she was a strong woman who knew what was hers. Some said the Red Guard was no good; if you got something you had to pay for it. A few women declared the rascal deserved such treatment.

"Dear Revolutionary Masses," the tall leader started to speak. "We all have heard the crime Mu Ying committed. She lured one of our officers and one of our poor peasants into the evil water, and she beat a Red Guard black and blue. Shall we let her go home without punishment or shall we teach her an unforgettable lesson so that she won't do it again?"

"Teach her a lesson!" some voices cried in unison.

"Then we're going to parade her through the streets."

Two Red Guards pulled Mu off the bench, and another picked up the tall hat.

"Brothers and sisters," she begged, "please let me off just this once. Don't, don't! I promise I'll correct my fault. I'll be a new person. Help! Oh help!"

It was no use resisting; within seconds the huge hat was firmly planted on her head. They also hung a big placard between the cloth shoes lying against her chest. The words on the placard read:

I am a Broken Shoe
My Crime Deserves Death

They put a gong in her hands and ordered her to strike it when she announced the words written on the inner side of the gong.

My pals and I followed the crowd, feeling rather tired. Boys from East Street were wilder; they threw stones at Mu's back. One stone struck the back of her head and blood dropped on her neck. But they were stopped immediately by the Red Guards, because a stone missed Mu and hit a man on the face. Old people, who couldn't follow us, were standing on chairs and windowsills with pipes and towels in their hands. We were going to parade her through every street. It would take several hours to finish the whole thing, since the procession would stop for a short while at every street corner.

Bong, Mu struck the gong and declared, "I am an evil monster."

"Louder!"

Dong, bong—"I have stolen men. I stink for a thousand years."

When we were coming out of the marketplace, Squinty emerged from a narrow lane. He grasped my wrist and Bare

Hips's arm and said, "Someone is dead at the train station. Come, let's go have a look." The word "dead" at once roused us. We half a dozen boys set out running to the train station.

The dead man was Meng Su. A crowd had gathered at the railroad two hundred yards east of the station house. A few men were examining the rail that was stained with blood and studded with bits of flesh. One man paced along the darker part of the rail and announced that the train had dragged Meng at least seventy meters.

Beneath the track, Meng's headless body lay in a ditch. One of his feet was missing, and the whitish shinbone stuck out several inches long. There were so many openings on his body that he looked like a large piece of fresh meat on the counter in the butcher's. Beyond him, ten paces away, a big straw hat remained on the ground. We were told that his head was under the hat.

Bare Hips and I went down the slope to see the head. Other boys dared not take a peep. We two looked at each other, asking with our eyes who should raise the straw hat. I held out my wooden scimitar and lifted the rim of the hat a little with the sword. A swarm of bluebottles charged out, droning like provoked wasps. We bent over to peek at the head. Two long teeth pierced through the upper lip. An eyeball was missing. The gray hair was no longer perceivable, covered with mud and dirt. The open mouth was filled with purplish mucus. A tiny lizard skipped, sliding away into the grass.

"Oh!" Bare Hips began vomiting. Sorghum gruel mixed with bits of string beans splashed on a yellowish boulder. "Leave it alone, White Cat."

We lingered at the station, listening to different versions of the accident. Some people said Meng had gotten drunk and dropped asleep on the track. Some said he hadn't slept at all but laughed hysterically walking in the middle of the track toward the coming train. Some said he had not drunk a drop, because he had spoken with tears in his eyes to a few persons he had run into on his way to the station. In any case, he was dead, torn to pieces.

That evening when I was coming home, I heard Mu Ying groaning in the smoky twilight. "Take me home. Oh, help me. Who can help me? Where are you? Why don't you come and carry me home?"

She was lying at the bus stop, alone.

Nervous Dancer

We do not leave the ocean's side, but follow the thin, worn-out highway on the hard ridge of shells and sand cliffs. We see, over the swells of the ocean, night trying hard to come down. Still a crack of white light stays between the ocean and night. It is as if someone keeps reaching up and tearing night off at the bottom.

For a minute, I feel lonely in the car with Julien, my husband. We should not have come here—to my mother's house—for vacation. I am not feeling so good away from time schedules, crowds of strangers, and tight deadlines of the city that keep pushing us forward from one event into another. In the city I do not have time to ponder that I love my mother but do not like being around her.

Julien does not know my mother well. He does not know that she hates men. He knows her in the casual way of her coming to the city to visit, bringing her own washcloth, soap, and a home-made dessert, to sleep fitfully on our living room couch. Julien has never met my father, but he has spoken to him by phone. Ten years ago, when I felt desperate to marry Julien, it was then that my father chose to leave my mother's house.

The car headlights are on; it looks like Julien is following the two beams instead of the road, carefully following the color yellow.

The dog, which I hold on my lap, pants heavily, a wild taint to her breath. I crack the window as if for a heavy smoker. I feel I am inside her lungs.

We get to my mother's turnoff, a white wooden sign scarred by wind. On the turn, the empty shells slide under the tires.

I talk to Julien, his face warm and appealing in the intimate dash light, our voices brushing together feathery wings of sound. "Why have we come?" I ask him. "As a child, the two times I never liked to spend at home were holidays and Sundays."

"You have a responsibility to your parents," he says. "You have a relationship with them." But then he, too, says, "I do miss our friends. We shouldn't have come on vacation alone."

We find the cottage atilt on one of the stationary dunes, hard-packed ground shaped like swells of water.

Outside the car, I feel I have Julien's scent all over me. But it's just that we've been in the car so long together. (Perhaps we both smell like my dog.) It makes me uneasy walking toward my mother's cottage in the falling dark with Julien. I do not know the ground well. I cannot hold his hand, he is carrying our two cases. Somehow our intimacy seems flagrant now that I am bringing my marriage—actually for the first time—into my mother's house, her home base instead of ours.

My dog squats in the yard and I lift the black knocker to the front door. When my mother opens it, my dog is dancing, tethered on the end of the leash.

"You finally got here," she says for welcome.

"We never told you what time we'd come," I say. I see she is dressed like me—in odd colors—a combination not quite expected. She's in blue and copper.

"You've brought that dog," my mother says. "You're too old to always have a dog with you. Do you still sleep with them? I've tried to keep you from putting your face in theirs and to never breathe in their breaths." She pushes the door back till it catches and it's safe for us to pass through. She precedes us into her house.

Julien has been looked at but not spoken to. It is he who unsticks the door and crosses the rug to shake my mother's hand. They nod at each other.

Thinking maybe my father's in town, I look around to see if there are still signs of him in here. There are only signs of me ten years ago—which unsettles and unwelcomes me. Photographs here and there, framed on walls and tables, all from when I was a kid and pleased her by not being any different from her, not yet grown up. My dog tries to go to her; I hold on.

"Put your bags away," she says. For a second I wonder if she will let me sleep with a man in her house. "The guest room—take the hall on the left." Julien takes my case and his. I hear him clicking a couple of lights on as he goes.

"It still surprises me that you ever married," says my mother as soon as Julien leaves. She enjoys telling secrets just loud enough for the other person to overhear. "After your living through my marriage, I was disappointed that you married someone who looks just like your father."

"You used to say in front of everyone that you wished I would grow up to be an old maid or a nun, then you'd be happy. Didn't you want me to ever learn to share?"

"Do I really look like her father?" asks Julien, back quickly. He doesn't like the dark and there are no streetlights out here.

I tell my mother, "Julien is trying to figure out just what he really looks like. It's one of his hobbies."

In the tiny kitchen, my mother gives the dog water out of a pie pan. She doesn't like to touch animals, but she takes care of them.

On the counter is a huge bouquet of garden flowers, such bright colors.

"Why, Mother, you never bring flowers into the house," I say. "You treat them like yard animals."

"For you, Eulene," she says. "I know you love them by your bed."

"Do I?"

"You know," says Julien, "I'm interested in what I look like alive—other than in a mirror."

"You look like Avery, when I first fell," says my mother. "He's old now. I saw him just the other day driving in the car ahead of me."

"But since he left us," I say, "I often see him driving in the car ahead of me, no matter where I am."

"No, he's really here. He's following the Blues; the Blues are running. I got in touch for you." Her voice is bitter. "You know how important fish are to him. He loves to go fishing," she tells Julien, "but he never eats them. He can hardly get one to stay down."

She has made us a very delicate and moist cake. She offers Julien two pieces because he's a man. I'm glad when he refuses. I know my mother believes being overly generous is polite, but she will make fun of you if you accept.

"You still drink milk?" she asks, when I've poured myself some.

I never took her teasing as good humor. When you show hurt, she doesn't stop. I'm a bad sport. She tries to teach me humor by teasing me, but I'm only embarrassed.

We walk the dog together. Julien stays behind reading the same newspaper he read this morning. The dog runs, her hind legs hopping with excitement. The sea air leaves a film that draws my skin. The air catches in the young trees in my mother's garden. The trees are noisy with air, like watery waves which the ocean breaks on the beach below us and then seems to break again in the trees above us in my mother's garden.

The wind changes. My mother notices and says, "Eulene? What's the matter?"

There is a moistness between me and my clothes. "Nothing." Ocean air makes me uneasy. I feel as if everything is too loose. The curl is coming out of my long, heavy hair, which I still wear to my shoulder blades. My hair and my skirt blow forward; my hair gets in my mouth. It tends to get into everybody's mouth, Julien always says.

"How do you like having gray hair, old girl?" my mother asks.

Just this year a little white has come in at the center of my hairline. "Sometimes Julien thinks it's fascinating; sometimes I think it's nauseating," I say. "Like the beginning of the pattern in a snakeskin, I tell him."

I see her decide not to tease me about my hair. When I was little, I used to go behind the house and play pretend in the walled-in patio. It was safe and engrossing to talk to myself. This oddity of mine kept my parents from getting what I felt was too close to me. When I do it now, whisper to myself, and Julien interrupts with "Did you say something?" I tell him, "I'm talking to my dog."

We walk down long, gritty steps to the black beach, leaving the lights behind our shoulders. We are standing in just the hollow, swelling sound of the ocean. My mother has taken me some place that I am not safe. She's with me, yet I cannot reach out for her. My dog sees for me. I follow her breath beside my leg. Wet sand crusts my shoes. Back up the steps in the electric light, the sand sparkles and I knock my shoes together and the sand falls. My dog's claws hook at the wood.

I take a deep breath of salty, cold air and look up. The stars are out and look like they are riding away from us. We go inside with the dog, where it seems quieter without the surge of the sea, and my mother hugs me. My arm under her head is warm.

I think I hear a tape playing somewhere far off along the ridge.

I hope it will play over and over again until I am deeply asleep tonight.

Julien has made accordion folds out of the front page. We say good night to my mother and the dog doesn't want to go to bed yet, so I leave her in the hall and take the flowers with me, thinking my mother has done for me something she doesn't like but she knew I like.

In the guest room, the door is locked and I knock once. Julien is already undressed. "I'm so white," he says, looking surprised at himself naked. "I'm so white that I'll tan red." His naked whiteness makes him loom large. I feel his feet are as big as my head.

Sheets have been left to be spread out. Julien holds them up. "She gave us the wrong sheets." Two king-size sheets, and the beds are single, narrow, and stuck to the floor. "Who's going to tell her?" he asks.

"Well, you don't have anything on." Irritated, I put the flowers close to my bed near the edge of the table. I take the sheets, and when I get to the other end of the cottage to my mother's room, I find the tape is playing in there. Only my dog is in the room, stretched out, listening to Chopin. Just when the Chopin tape ends, she relaxes the one huge curl at the end of her tail. I take off her pearly collar, undressing her for bed. That funny little protective covering chases across her eyes, and though she looks at me she is falling asleep.

My mother is not in the other rooms that I check. It is dark inside and out, and I can't tell where the walls are. I want my mother but I will not call out for her. I want my dog to follow and I do not make her.

I pull a light cord that skins the top of my hair. My old bedroom is this unrecognizable storage room now; thank heavens she didn't keep it. I find the linen closet and in the top of it are a few boxes. Then I realize they were once presents—opened, looked at, and never used. I am repelled by my mother counting, saving, but depriving herself of presents.

My face is raw with anger at my need to avoid my mother and to have seen what she values—abstinence—and to know that I find what she values valueless.

Back in the guest room with the same sheets, Julien and I share the kinship of my stupid moment. We support each other this way. He takes one king-size and I take the other. I listen for my dog, then remember removing her thin aluminum I.D.'s. I wait till I have the bathroom to take off my dark, opaque stockings and put on my long-legged pajamas. I think the only private thing about me is my pretend and my legs. I have bad legs. I think my mother has passed them on to me, these legs in a net of fine broken veins, though I know I did it to myself. I have broken my veins from ten years of giving myself birth control pills. It strikes me suddenly that I do not even have sex so often. Yet, religiously, I continue to give myself the cycle of pills.

I don't want a child. My breasts are too small. I don't understand what size my mother's are. I have checked her bras and they are two sizes—36B and 36C. To me, her breasts seem to hang from her shoulders. I got the idea of no children from my mother. My mother doesn't like children. I am an only child.

I am addicted to wearing dark stockings and it is the way my friends remember me, I know—that I hide my legs. For my breasts, I do nothing. For my legs, I have continued my dancing lessons. I am tall and thin and taut with a consciousness of my body that I don't like. My father started me dancing when I was three. He said I was a nervous child and he believed that dancing would cure me. We both have continued to believe it even after time has proved it untrue. Instead of going to lunch at work, I take ballet; I practice though I never perform.

I take my king-size sheet to bed and roll up in it, bound and bandaged in my mother's wrong sheets. "Linens are so personal," complains Julien. He reaches out to the table lamp between us and puts the three-way down on the lowest.

The small window looks bright now. The pull and slip of the ocean is loud. The rhythm of it sets me off, rollicking and whispering through my prayers. I ride my childhood path of prayers as erratically and as slumped as I had sat astride my bicycle, always slightly to the side, ready to give up, get off, bail out. I lose my way and start my prayers over. Finally, I ask that my vacation be over soon, and that God protect my mother from herself, and from me. My father almost gets left out because he's so complicated. I gain heart and continue and ask God to give him peace, but not in the form of death. For the last, I ask slowly that I always have the strength to save myself when I need it.

My eyes keep opening during my prayers. Julien is watching. "I've been reading your lips," he says. "You are haunted by things that no one cares about but you."

The novel we've brought to read together is in Julien's hand. We read to each other the well-ordered words, running them down the delicacy of our closeness, relaxing us both.

We lean and touch lips, his sticking to mine for a second. I feel that thick peak to his lips—a thickness people generally get from sulking or playing the trumpet or nursing. Then he is lost in himself, sitting back on his bed, rubbing his eye. For all his pleasing good looks, he has a lazy muscle in one eye. It causes his eye to look stranded in his face. His fingers automatically find it and his eye slides to the side away from us, the focus floating from me in uncertainty.

"Don't mess with your eye," I say. He reaches down and touches his penis.

We turn off the light and stay quiet. Trying to get comfortable in my mother's house, my body jumps twice on the edge of sleep.

Sometime during the night, we both wake. The old moon has moved while we were sleeping and now at the window it looks like a white hole for escape. Julien makes a noise in the dark, secretly fooling with his eye, and I think I see a shadow slip out of his nose.

On the table nearest me are the flowers from my mother's garden. The flowers have opened wider. They are bigger—black, huge, primeval blooms.

"Maybe flowers do belong outside," I say.

Julien sits up in bed.

"What's the matter, love?" I ask.

"I don't know. I can't stay asleep."

I prop myself up, pillow raised against the headboard, my silky pajamas so close my breasts feel heavy, dream-filled.

"Is it your stomach?" I ask.

"I feel so different from the way I feel at home," he says. "The noise and light is different." He comes to me, bringing his own sheet. "At home we have all our stuff, all our friends. I feel so empty. I think my soul upsets my stomach." He is rubbing his chest.

"That's not your stomach. That's where your heart is," I say.

He rolls on top of me and I think that it is his weight that keeps me pinned to life. Without him, I would be right back where I came from, back home, not safe.

So many emotions, loose as live breath in the room, thrust, push, vibrations of feeling and thought. Our wedding floats through my head, sticks and stays. The reception. The raindrops, huge, pendulant, falling slowly through the trees into the groom's yard. The strong rain. Stop, start. Afterward we are all barefoot in fancy dress. Everyone on the thick, matted wet yard. Too excited. The grass felt like cold glass. And the dog barking, too excited. And the groom's father went over and hurt the dog to stop it.

One young man, younger than we, playing the sounds of ten instruments by pulling stops from an electronic keyboard. The music was vibrating, and sweet, and scary because the electronic system had gotten wet and dangerous to play.

Breathing in Julien's breath like it's his emotions, I almost hold my nose. During the thrusts from him and me, by mistake I call my mother's name. I scream it. It had rolled around in my head; he made it roll out of my mouth. I screamed for my mother who could make things happen, make this prickly adulthood disappear. Sex; what I wanted when I got it became something that terrified me, as it did her. In wanting to be so unlike, I proved to myself that I was like. My mother was powerful; she could make me like her. My mother could work magic. After all, she had made my father disappear.

Julien chased me along in sex play, I ran ahead, and he finished last. He came with his lip up and squinting like he'd gotten the seat in the sun.

I felt as if I were the winner, but was losing blood. Actually it was just transparent juice. But Julien beat me to the bathroom.

My mother has the clear voice of morning. She calls, "The sun's coming up. If you two want to see anything today, you'd better get out of that room."

My mother is looking at day coming from the other side of the island. She is in her flowered robe and the light has struck the top of her head.

I ease in, barefoot down the hall carpet. I walk in dew left from my dog's paws.

"Your dog stayed with me last night," she tells me, as if to prove what I love is easy for her to win over. "She's out now. In and out."

Over at the one windowpane in the kitchen, I look for my dog. But I can see only down the cliff, the window glass seems to be holding back the ocean. I shift to opening some cabinet doors, looking for a cup. On plates in the cabinets, fruit and tomatoes ripen. Mother always puts them away for the night—ripening fruit. She is afraid of night—and mice. I once saw a small jumping mouse, sitting, licking something on its feet, nesting in a broken conch shell on the stairs. I never told on it. I remember my mother saying she was afraid of my father only at night. It was then that he was the strongest. It seemed the dark made his nose look longer and his hairline recede, and it scared her.

"You'd better eat if you're coming with me."

My dog comes in from the yard. She is covered with pollen and doesn't want to be petted.

I decide to have a banana and a cup of coffee.

Julien calls from the hall and I go to get him. "Why didn't you wait for me?" he asks. "I've been sick this morning. I threw up a little piece of your mother's cake."

"I ate the cake. You didn't have any."

My mother has fixed Julien a huge breakfast, without asking. Julien is trying hard to be pleased. He has eaten too much on his washy stomach and is embarrassed. My dog lets out wind, and no one mentions it. I close my eyes and try not to laugh, my head aswim with glee.

Julien and I shower and talk through the warm steam and dress in our bright vacation clothes.

In the car, carrying a thermos of water for the dog, I ask, "What are we off to see?"

My mother says, "Your father."

Julien wants to go back and take another look in the mirror; we won't let him. "I never saw you so worried about your appearance," I tell him. A Polaroid camera stretches his pocket.

We sit in the back; my mother drives with the dog up front. "See how your dog takes to me when I don't even like dogs?"

We come around the elbow of land from the ocean to the mild river side. Julien practices his smile on me, and against the glass of a restaurant window we pass walking now. I haven't seen my father in so long that I'm scared.

We find him in the boathouse. He seems to be blushing, but I know it is his circulation. My mother believes that he can shut down his valves and go unconscious as you talk to him.

"Well, how-de-do," he says. He is not a conversationalist. He looks like a worn-out, hurt man who tells funny stories on himself.

My mother introduces Julien and then she asks Avery questions and he tries to guess the right answers. The water rocks in the slow slap of the tide leaving. My mother is not interested in the answers. She needs only to keep asking questions to feel in control.

Avery takes it all under the hood of a joke, but it does take its toll on him. He snaps his head around directly to me, for the first time. "How about you—are you still shaking your hands?"

"Oh," I say, extending my right hand to him to shake before I realize the intent is to hurt.

"I'm wrong," he says. "The word wasn't *shake*. It was *sling* your hands. We'd say, 'Where's she gone, off to sling her hands?'" He has caught my mother's attention and he and she are enjoying the joke.

I say to Julien, "I used to play pretend. I used to sling my hands in the walled-in patio in a little rhythm to talk to myself by. I used to play pretend till I was exhausted. Like I can dance now till I'm anemic." Now Julien laughs with me, not knowing but not wanting me to be alone.

My father makes a small face at Julien. Julien must have taken it to be friendly because he makes a small, friendly face back.

Above our heads, light reflected from the water spins and revolves on the steep arch of wood, a cradle upside down over us. My parents' voices carry up and away. The terrible smell of sea broth is running like thick rich cloth through my nostrils.

Avery leads us outside to the restaurant, politely nudging us ahead of him. "Do you still have my dog?" he asks me.

"No," I say. "I have my dog now. Our dog died. Remember?" But he has lied so much about everything, trying to guess the right answers to the right questions, that he has ruined his memory. He couldn't remember his dog was dead. I, who wanted to stop the conversation, continued it. "You remember, Daddy, you used to shout commands right after our dog did anything. If he rolled over, you'd yell, 'Roll over,' quickly. Same thing if he barked or ran. It made everyone laugh, the trick dog who did everything before he was told. That dog died years ago. You told me you took him on the front seat of the car with you to the vet's. He was so weak and cold and sick. You said, 'The vet gave him a shot, but the shot didn't make him get better.' The shot was to kill him, Daddy. You knew that." My pulse beat in my throat.

"Please, just stop your carrying on, now."

My truth made him slip farther from me.

Then he and Julien discussed all the things Julien didn't know about—boats, fish, cars, tools. Julien was a professional.

In the restaurant, at the round white table, everyone had the same Sea Platter except Avery, who had an egg-salad sandwich, though he was anxious about the mayonnaise because it goes bad so easily. My father took the rings of crust from his egg-salad sandwich; he saved the crusts.

"You still have your small appetite, Avery," said my mother. "One of the things I continue to admire about you." I felt that my vacation was going faster. My mother reminisced. I held my saliva. My father remembered what he did like; she remembered what she didn't like. He stayed safely a few sentences behind her.

My mother says, "You used to be attracted to businesses that had shut down. One night you left the car with me in it and went across the parking lot of a closed drive-in and reached for a broken metal sign and it fell on you. I was trying to protect you and as it hit you I screamed, 'Goddamn you.' And you pretended the sign hadn't hurt."

"What an odd thing for a woman to scream who is trying to protect him," I say.

"He always liked to read what was written on signs that had fallen over," says my mother.

"Why don't we get together more often?" I ask my father.

"I never think I feel good enough to see you," my father says.

"He hides," says my mother. "He doesn't want Eulene to see him lying down. He thinks he's sick when he's only drunk. He drinks as seriously as if he were taking medicine."

Julien works at a mayonnaise spot on his shirt with his napkin and drinking water.

"Physically, things are looking up," my father says. "I have a heck of a lot of possibilities." His sea-colored eyes rise to meet mine. He is ready to leave.

Outside, he stops a minute under the running clouds. "You were always pretty," he says to me. "But too picky. There were too many things you wouldn't try or do. You couldn't sing. You never learned to swim. You liked to be alone."

"That's not true," I say. "I was alone. I loved things, I loved candy. I loved you best, Daddy."

"That's not nice," he says. "I think you should love your mother best."

He detours to one of the open boat slips where huge gulls are riding the water. He scatters his crusts and says the big gray gulls are so beautiful. Then he throws the last of the crusts and hits a gull on the head.

"Why did you do that?" I ask.

"I don't know. I was just trying to figure the gulls out." He draws his shoulders together, chilly. "It's so hard for me to pee anymore," he says. "If I don't pee today, I think I'll kill myself. I wake up in the night listening for noises that would make me want to pee and trying to remember when I pee-peed last."

Julien is now taking a Polaroid shot. My mother stays at the edge of the picture. She and Avery hang around each other for a minute. Avery sucks in his cheeks and says, "Two people married and in love, but we never believed in each other."

My mother says, "You don't fool me. You're so lonely that you'd say anything—even 'I still love you.'"

Julien covers the mayonnaise spot with his left hand and gives my father his right for shaking good-bye. The Polaroid sways on a strap from his neck.

My father squints at me, I can't see in his eyes, and says, "I think you're the only one who's never hurt me. But you live in such inaccessible places."

"I live in the city. They have maps, Daddy." I feel I should have taken the luncheon napkin with me and wiped my heart.

Julien stands at my shoulder. "Come see her dog in the car," he says quietly.

"Don't want to," my father says. "My dog is dead."

Inside the car, the dog's head is hidden under the seat where it is cool. I think I hear Avery call back. I turn. He is far away. I see him bend and look intently at the ground. It is my mother's voice that says, "I hope he hasn't found anything. He keeps finding things and sending them to me in a box by mail. It's embarrassing to open the box. Sometimes it's an old watch. Sometimes a barrette. Once a broken chain."

We get in the car and the dog gets on the seat. The air is sticky. The clouds in the sky are made of wet, gray clay. My mother gives the dog water in the cap of the thermos.

Disappointment is around Julien's mouth. He shows the Polaroid. "His hair is still dark but his face has turned gray," he says as we ride away.

Then my mother is crying, her tongue clicking.

Julien sits forward, fascinated by my mother's crying. His hand is open, but there is no way to help her.

"Why would he eat mayonnaise?" says my mother, rounding a curb tear-blind, skinning the tires against concrete. "He eats mayonnaise when it could kill him. He picks up things off the ground. He never gets over a dead dog." Her throat and nose roar with tears.

"Why are you angry about that now?" I ask. "I thought you hated Daddy."

"Because," she says, "I used to care."

By the time she gets us back to the cottage she's stone-calm and talking about swimming when the weather lifts.

In the kitchen, the dog drinks from its pan. While Julien blows up a rubber float for my mother, I put beach trousers on over my bathing suit. When the float is taut, we carry it down to the water.

The approach to the beach is abrupt. We walk down ribs of sand left by wind and erosion. Now we are on planks that shift and make a kind of stairs that I had been down last night. At the bottom, I think I see my own footprints coming to meet me.

The beach is full of stones. I bend in my trousers and pick up smooth pebbles, eggs, nut-shapes, sharp tips, swirls, and curdles—shapes water has ridden into rock.

They call me, impatiently. I stand straight too fast, eyes closed against them. Light flickers red through my eyelids.

"The ocean looks dirty," my mother says. She is gazing around slit-eyed in the glare. A few kids, looking very little because they are far away, are running in circles.

"Dirty. Because of the kids," I say. "When I was little I couldn't control it either." Thinking I could have helped my chilly father. A simple little cure. It's the sudden feel of lukewarm ocean water he needs. "Feeling all that water in my bathing suit, I always peed."

"Who cares about kids?" my mother says. "I mean fish, crabs, clams, turtles—they all do their stuff in the water."

Julien must have tried to swallow a laugh. I think I see spray fly out of his mouth when my mother winks at him. Julien is getting too juicy with my mother's good nature. Mother's awakening to like Julien now simply ruins him for me.

I walk sideways to the humped water. I don't want to be with them, but I'm afraid I would get lost without them.

"Where are you going?" asks my mother.

"To look for shells."

"They're all broken."

There is little walking space between the step-off of the ocean shelf and the slipping cliffs of hot sand. I glance at the few people at the beach. Everyone seems to be at the water's edge waiting to go in.

The full trousers I wear pop with the wind. My hair rises with sea wind and makes me a sun umbrella. I find a stone with a deep crease in it. It feels so good in my hand. I keep it and will hide how much I care for it. Incoming ocean is choking the narrow beach. I walk back with one foot in the water, a sloppy, slurping sound. I am laughing until I see Julien and my mother laughing at me.

"I knew you wouldn't find any good shells," Julien says.

"I collected a stone," I say.

"You don't have to worry about finding shells. I know that you brought a seashell from the city back to the beach with you in your case. You can take it out. You don't have to hide it. You hide such simple things, Eulene, that it turns them into the grotesque."

"I remember," says my mother, "Eulene as a child trying to learn to hide emotions and endure hurts. Well, you got poison ivy and hid it. You let poison ivy go and it got all the way up into your boopsey."

"I did not," I say. "I wouldn't do it. Oh, all right, I did."

We are all smiling and laughing with each other. I give the stone in my hand a squeeze.

"You just hide things and lie to try to keep your privacy," says Julien, understanding me.

"We haven't been in the water yet," I say. "Such a large body of water."

He has our book out, using his finger for a page marker. He peeks back into it and says, "I'm at a good part," and sets it on the float. He takes my hand and a small nerve in my body runs loose.

Julien leans against me and we watch my mother slit the slick top of the water and plunge in. "I wouldn't dare get in with her," he says. She splashes so much a cluster of wet bubbles grows around her. Then she's caught the bottom with her feet and is walking back up the underwater shelf. In and out, quick as a drowning. Back on the beach, the sun turns liquid on her. Her hair looks glass.

I wait at the wet hem of the ocean.

When Julien is in the water, I shed my cotton trousers without looking down and hurry into the water. My mother calls, "Eulene? What have you done to your legs? They're worse than mine."

Salt water fills my bathing suit. The underwater rocks are so slick I almost fall. I have to swim. I sink to my neck, up to my mouth. My hair spreads out, floats around me. I look for the line of sky to hang onto. "There's no horizon," I try to say. I spit out sea water. The ocean moves in and out in respiration. I relax and float, tethered onto the very edge of relaxation.

Julien pops up floating near me. We bob together. Since neither of us can harmonize, we quote a few lines together from Woolf about colors and old glass. The vacation begins working out. I tip my face to the side. White sun lines in the water run toward my mouth.

Julien reaches for me from underneath with his legs; liquid electricity vibrates in me, a pleasing shock in water.

My mother sits up abruptly on the dry float. She shouts at us, "It's time to go do something different."

"My endless vacation," I say.

She says, "When you still think you're young, you're never satisfied. I've saved all the pictures from the time I wasn't satisfied—pictures of my boyfriends. They're dying off now, of course, but I have their pictures. I could have married a dentist when your father came chasing after me."

"Mother," I say, "I wouldn't have been born if you had married a dentist."

"Half of you would have been. My half."

I go for my mother's ride, in my bathing suit and trousers, stone in my pocket, to see the wooden churches of the island. The churches drop afternoon shadows more intricate than their architecture.

I apply brown eye shadow to tone down the burn on my lids and walk carefully in the old, boggy cemeteries. Julien reads headstones aloud as we read novels at night. Then he gets something on his shoe and has to rub it off.

We nap in the car while my mother drives. I wake with wrinkles on my face from the car velvet. The soft tissue under Julien's eyes has swollen.

At the cottage, we have a cold dinner. The dog eats from my hand. My mother comes out into the walled patio with a jug of tea, ice chiming against the glass sides. Light falls through the holes in my straw hat; it falls down into my lap and onto the pot of flowers beside my chair. Everywhere I go, the designs fly along with me on the flat flagstones, over my shoes. The ocean way below calms for sunset. Then twilight comes, a bluish airspace between each of us, as if we are close to stepping inside each other's fragments of dreams.

"I'm trying to write a letter," my mother says. She has eaten with ink stains on her fingers. "I do keep friends to write to, but I have such trouble deciding what not to tell them." The tea pitcher is between us. "I don't use sugar because it's not good for you," she says. "But I put some in for you. I don't like sweet. Is it all right?"

"You're making me feel so comfortable," says Julien.

The tea is too sweet, it drives the taste down to the root of my tongue.

I touch my dog. She kicks her hind leg convulsively and stretches her mouth into a black fur dog grin.

That night, in the bathroom, I put on a white batiste ankle-length nightgown. Nothing moves tonight, only me in my batiste gown.

"Something's happening," I say. "I don't know what."

Julien honks, "Huh?" at me as he slides down into the right-size sheets. Mother has made our beds this time. "It must be happening just to you. I don't feel it," says Julien, already searching through a book for something interesting.

I find my stone in my beach trousers pocket and slip it under my pillow. I sit beside it and say, "I need to feel better."

He turns his head from me into the sea silence of the room. A roll of deep water. Another sea silence. "I'm afraid, Eulene. If we say it out loud, we won't recover. It may be a mistake to put everything into words. Words are cruel."

Something sharp and deep is riding on my breath. "My mother never says anything out loud. She just thinks it. I believe in saying it out loud." My voice! A child's skinny, scabby, sulky one.

"If your mother told you all that she thinks," he says, "how would you be able to stand to hear it all? Would you want to know it—how could you receive it? What if you knew what makes her hate? If she gave it to you, could you carry it?"

I curl my knees toward my mouth and bow to sleep, my pillow over my smooth stone. Later, in the dark, I wake to see Julien edging around the carpet, holding his penis as if it were a banister.

"Where are you trying to go? Don't wake up my mother."

"I'm lost in this room," he says.

"Don't wake her! She's so sensitive."

"I know," he says. "All those wrinkles in her face."

"No," I say. "It was my father who wrinkled her." I am up, too.

Trying to catch him. Stop him. This is all too unreal. I touch myself to make sure my breasts are still there.

The shadows in the room are elastic. The room changes. The wind is up—it blows a small tree's shadow into the bedroom with us. I think it's laid a slippery spot on the carpet. Trying to get to Julien.

Near the door I slip and go down on the end of my white gown.

"Oh!" he cries out for me. He sees I am really down and he cries out, "Are you hurt? Are you hurt?" Then he comes down beside me and begins to hit me. He strikes me, yelling, "Get up! Get up!" On the third stroke I stand and the striking knocks the loose waist of my batiste gown up over my breasts.

My voice breaks. There are funny coatings over my vocal cords. I have two voices; another voice screams with me, "I want to go home."

Yet I cry it to him who is striking me, whose home it is, too. Because he is the closest I've ever been able to get to anybody, this man for whom I now feel hate. I am so slow. I feel tears dropping from my eyes. I try to catch them in my hand, but I can't and they fall anyway.

Three times hard he's struck me. "We should have been just good friends," he says. Now he flops down on the bed, his back bent, as domed and ancient a shape as a carapace. "I've tried hard to keep loving you," he says.

My chest aches and stretches with the blood of shock. "But it's I who don't love you! I've hidden it all this time." I raise my breasts like plumes on a bird.

In the doorway, my mother surprises us. She stands half absorbed by sleep, wearing a fancy nightgown, old white yellowed as rich as cream, saved, ripened, so old it splits as we watch—tears without a sound. My mother, in her anger at what she sees in us, has torn the front of her nightgown.

"Go to bed, Mother," I say. "Just because I'm in your house

doesn't mean I've lost the right to fight with my husband." It's as if fights are too intimate for her. My vision has one black dot jumping in each eye.

She says, "I wouldn't let either one of you be treated the way you are treating each other." She leaves with her nightgown open.

I thought I would scream or tear into the flesh of Julien's face. Instead, I sit down and put my feet up.

"Why did you marry me?" he asks.

"I am the promiscuous daughter of a promiscuous man," I say, "which is funny because I don't find sex satisfying. I don't even like it. I guess I married you to get rid of sex. When we do it great I love it, but then I always panic. Neither of us can take it all the time."

Julien looks tired. "I wonder if maybe I'm a homosexual."

"No," I say. "Homosexuals love somebody. You don't love anybody."

I listen to my dog in the other room scratching at the long nap of my mother's carpet.

"You and your dog," he says. "It sure is hard to be married to an only child."

"What are you thinking of now?" I ask.

He says, "I was thinking of aspirins."

We take bitter white aspirins together. Then we wait for the white, powdery morning to begin.

At some point, I slide into sleep. When I wake, my muscles are stiff and my eyelids tight with sun and windburn and I think I am alone. Then I find my dog is curled into the bend of my legs. I get up, dress, and find Julien in the kitchen just sitting. "I'm waiting to work up an appetite," he says.

My mother sets the table with dishes from my childhood. "I was known for never breaking things," she says. "Other people break my things, but I never break things." Today, she will not look at me.

I let my dog out for a minute. When she comes back, I leave her collar and tags on. "Want to go for a ride soon?" I say. She jumps all over me, her claws leaving white scratches down my arms.

We do not use any of the plates. I use a teacup and a spoon for honey. I do not want sugar. Because we all feel badly, and Julien has spoiled my face, I wait till no one is looking to eat directly from the honey jar—a mouthful of thick pleasure.

Minutes later, Julien puts his hand—the back of it—so softly against my marked cheek. He strains for me from his chair. He has never done anything so open and so tender before.

"I am the continuation of what's wrong," I say.

"So. You are going to sacrifice me?" He laughs.

I lean and get a spider of sun in my eye.

My mother has gone to her garden wearing ugly old clothes. She does not like sweat. She will not wear her good clothes for it.

Julien and I are alone, but for the dog biting and combing and scratching her coat with her claws. "I've put pressure on you," I tell Julien. "I've thought too much and put pressure on myself. So in the end I have to be the one to leave." Julien's eye is to the side. I rub it slowly to move it back in place.

In the room, I put my dirty things on top in the case, the city seashell still at the bottom. I do not need a souvenir of my vacation. I do not need the stone—it ends under my pillow.

Now with my case, my dog, and my pocketbook I find my mother in the yard planting leftover seeds from packets with lost labels. She will let them sprout and then see if she wants them. On her knees, she hacks away with a hand hoe at the black silk soil of her yard. "Goddamn, hell, shit, Goddamn them to hell," she says as she plants. My dog sits in a draft under the tree. My mother gets up in stiff jerks. "No reason for this," she says to me, seeing me, my case and pocketbook. "You do this to yourself. You always set yourself apart. Alone. What is so courageous about leaving?"

"I'm leaving Julien here," I say.

"Well, you always did love to play by yourself," she says.

He has come as far as the door, licking what looks like my honey spoon. "You told them at the office that you'd be back from vacation a different man," I say. "You have one more week." He lifts his head to me. This morning's shadow hangs to his side.

I thrust my case into the closed-up car; my dog sticks with the draft. The car inside is stuffy. I sneeze hot air and lower the windows to cool the car so I can get in it. I walk with Julien once around my mother's house. Near her hawthorn, we stop. "I was desperate to marry you, Julien." The starlings are overrunning the hawthorn. Julien and I make loud clapping sounds together to startle them and then we smell what they're after—crushed soft fruit fermenting on the ground under the tree. We flatten the grass with our shoes and I lead and tell him that I was wrong. "My mother doesn't hate men. She has only withdrawn from them to coddle her passion. Be careful."

"You're just angry and scared," Julien says to me, quite kindly.

I mask my glance at him, checking, thinking that I am actually leaving another Daddy with Mother again.

Next time we look at her, my mother's skin is slick. She is sweating the sweat she hates. Neither sun nor clouds move. "Julien's staying for a while to finish his vacation," I say. I move backward one step toward the car, an uneven stone shocking the bottom of my foot.

To help Julien, maybe, I ask, "Is Daddy really your failure—or your success, Mother?"

The dog climbs into the open car slowly. I start the car, it quivers with the air-conditioning. Still the dog pants. Her breath is the sharp smell of canned dog food.

I have something to say, but I cannot bear anything more. I put on my large sunglasses and think they will break the small bones of my nose. The dog beats her tail against me because she loves to ride. I catch myself in the mirror and think I must look like one dark lens to them; or maybe I'm just too small to see.

I look ahead, up the narrow road from my mother's house, and see a little boy fully clothed on a powerful motorcycle, and then a blond man bare-chested, painfully pedaling a bicycle. I am laughing and my muscles are hurting. I say, leaving Julien in my mother's garden, "I had no idea till today, Mother, that I had come here to punish you."

I swing the car into my side of the road, the wheel spinning in my hands. The dog barks and runs along the seat with pleasure. I am looking beyond us to the broken, scattered colors of the fields. It is me that's laughing and heaving in the air conditioner's air. But way below my heart, I can feel a kitten shaking in my womb. I am at the end of my vacation.

All My Relations

When Jack Oldenburg first spoke to him, Milton Enos leaned over his paper plate, scooping beans into his mouth as if he didn't hear. Breaking through the murmur of O'od-*ham* conversation, the white man's speech was sharp and harsh. But Oldenburg stood over him, waiting.

Oldenburg had just lost his ranch hand, sick. If Milton reported to the Box-J sober in the morning, he could work for a couple of weeks until the cowboy returned or Oldenburg found a permanent hand.

"O.K.," Milton said, knowing he wouldn't go. Earlier in the day his wife and son had left for California, so he had several days' drinking to do. Following his meal at the convenience mart he would hitch to the Sundowner Lounge at the edge of the reservation.

After a sleepless night Milton saddled his horse for the ride to Oldenburg's, unable to bear his empty house. As he crossed the wide, dry bed of the Gila River, leaving the outskirts of Hashan, the house ceased to exist for him and he thought he would never go back. Milton's stomach jogged over the pommel with the horse's easy gait. Two hours from Hashan, Oldenburg's Box-J was the only ranch in an area cither left desert or irrigated for cotton and sorghum. Its twenty square miles included hills, arroyos, and the eastern tip of a mountain range—gray-pink granite knobs split by ravines. The sun burned the tops of the mountains red.

Oldenburg stood beside his corral, tall and thin as one of its mesquite logs. First, he said, sections of the barbed-wire fence had broken down, which meant chopping and trimming new posts.

Milton's first swings of the axe made him dizzy and sick. He flailed wildly, waiting with horror for the bite of the axe into his foot. But soon he gained control over his stroke. Though soft, his big arms were strong. Sweat and alcohol poured out of him until he stank.

In the afternoon Milton and Oldenburg rode the fenceline.

"Hasn't been repaired in years," Oldenburg said. "My hand Jenkins is old." Oldenburg himself was well over sixty, his crew cut white and his face dried up like a dead man's. He had bright eyes, though, and fine white teeth. Where the fence was flattened to the ground, Milton saw a swatch of red and white cowhide snagged on the barbed wire. He'd lost a few head in the mountains, Oldenburg said, and after the fence was secure they'd round them up.

"One thing I'll tell you," Oldenburg said. "You can't drink while you work for me. Alcohol is poison in a business."

Milton nodded. By reputation he knew Oldenburg had a tree stump up his ass. Milton's wife C.C. had said she'd bring their son Allen back when Milton stopped drinking. For good? he'd asked. How would she know when was for good? For all anybody knew tomorrow might be the first day of for good, or 25,000 days later he might get drunk again. For a moment Milton remembered playing Monopoly with C.C. and Allen several weekends before. As usual, Milton and Allen were winning. Pretending not to be furious, C.C. smiled her big, sweet grins. Milton and the boy imitated her, stretching their mouths, until she couldn't help laughing. Milton clicked them off like a TV set and saw only mesquite, the rocky sand, sky, and the line of fence. After his two weeks, Milton thought, he'd throw a drunk like World War Ten.

At the end of the day he accepted Oldenburg's offer: $75 a week plus room and board, weekend off. Oldenburg winced apologetically proposing the wage; the ranch didn't make money, he explained.

They ate at a metal table in the dining room. Milton, whose pleasure in food went beyond filling his stomach, appreciated Oldenburg's meat loaf—laced with onion, the center concealing three hard-boiled eggs. Milton couldn't identify the seasonings except for chili. "What's in this?" he asked.

"Sage, chili, cumin, and Worcestershire sauce."

"Heyyy."

Inside his two room adobe, Milton was so tired he couldn't feel his body, and lying down felt the same as standing up. He slept without dreaming until Oldenburg rattled the door at daybreak.

Milton dug holes and planted posts. By noon his sweat had lost its salt and tasted like pure spring water. Then he didn't sweat at all. Chilled and shaking at the end of the day, he felt as if he'd been thrown by a horse. The pain gave him a secret exultation which he hoarded from Oldenburg, saying nothing. Yet he felt he was offering the man part of the ache as a secret gift. Slyly, he thumped his cup on the table and screeched his chair back with exaggerated vigor. Milton was afraid of liking Oldenburg too much. He liked people too easily, even those who were not O'odham—especially those, perhaps, because he wanted them to prove he needn't hate them.

Milton worked ten-, eleven-hour days. The soreness left his muscles, though he was as tired the fourth evening as he had been the first. Thursday night Oldenburg baked a chicken.

"You're steady," Oldenburg said. "I've seen you Pimas work hard before. What's your regular job?"

"I've worked for the government." Milton had ridden rodeo, sold wild horses he captured in the mountains, broken horses. Most often there was welfare. Recently he had completed two CETA training programs, one as a hospital orderly and the other baking cakes. But the reservation hospital wasn't hiring, and the town of Hashan had no bakeries. For centuries, Milton had heard, when the Gila flowed, the *O'odham* had been farmers. Settlements and overgrazing upstream had choked off the river only a few generations past. Sometimes he tried to envision green plots of squash, beans, and ripening grains, watered by earthen ditches, spreading from the banks. He imagined his back flexing easily in the heat as he bent to the rows, foliage swishing his legs, finally the villagers diving into the cool river, splashing delightedly.

"I don't think Jenkins is coming out of the hospital," Oldenburg said. "This job is yours if you want it." Milton was stunned. He had never held a permanent position.

In just a week of hard work, good eating, and no drinking, Milton had lost weight. Waking Friday morning, he pounded his belly with his hand; it answered him like a drum. He danced in front of the bathroom mirror, swiveling his hips, urging himself against the sink as if it were a partner. At lunch he told Oldenburg he would spend the weekend with friends in Hashan.

When he tossed the posthole digger into the shed, he felt light and strong, as if instead of sinking fence posts he'd spent the afternoon in a deep, satisfying nap. On the way to the guest house, his bowels turned over and a sharp pain set into his head. He saw the battered station wagon rolling out the drive, C.C. at the wheel, Allen's tight face in the window.

Milton threw his work clothes against the wall. After a stinging shower, he changed and mounted his horse for the ride to Vigiliano Lopez's.

Five hours later the Sundowner was closing. Instead of his customary beer, Milton had been drinking highball glasses of straight vodka. He felt paler and paler, like water, until he was water. His image peeled off him like a wet decal and he was only water in the shape of a man. He flowed onto the bar, hooking his water elbows onto the wooden ridge for support. Then he was lifted from the stool, tilted backward, floating on the pickup bed like vapor.

Milton woke feeling the pong, pong of a basketball bouncing outside. The vibration traveled along the dirt floor of Lopez's living room, up the couch he lay on. The sun was dazzling. Looking out the window, he saw six-foot-five, three-hundred-pound Bosque dribbling the ball with both hands, knocking the other players aside. As he jammed the ball into the low hoop, it hit the back of the rim, caroming high over the makeshift plywood backboard. A boy and two dogs chased it.

Seeing beer cans in the dirt, Milton went outside. He took his shirt off and sat against the house with a warm Bud. The lean young boys fired in jump shots, or when they missed, their fathers and older brothers pushed and wrestled for the rebound. Lopez grabbed a loose ball and ran with it, whirling for a turnaround fadeaway that traveled three feet. He laughed, and said to Milton, "When we took you home you started fighting us. Bosque had to pick you up and squeeze you, and when he did, everything came out like toothpaste."

"Try our new puke-flavored toothpaste," someone said, laughing.

"Looks like pizza."

"So we brought you here."

Milton said nothing. He watched the arms and broad backs collide. The young boys on the sidelines practiced lassoing the players' feet, the dogs, the ball. When he finished a beer, Milton started another. Later in the afternoon he sent boys to his house for the rest of his clothes and important belongings.

When the game broke up, some of the men joined the women in the shade of a mesquite. Saddling a half-broke wild colt, the boys took turns careening across the field. Lopez drove a truck-load to the rodeo arena, where a bronc rider from Bapchule was practicing. Compact and muscular, with silver spurs and collar tabs, he rode out the horse's bucks, smoothing the animal to a canter. Two of Milton's drunk friends tried and were thrown immediately. For a third, the horse didn't buck but instead circled the arena at a dead run, dodging the lassos and open gates. From the announcer's booth Lopez called an imaginary race as horse and rider passed the grandstand again and again — "coming down the backstretch now, whoops, there he goes for another lap, this horse is not a quitter, ladies and gentlemen."

"Go ahead, Milton," Lopez said. "You used to ride."

Milton shook his head. Allen, thirteen, recently had graduated from steers to bulls. In both classes he had finished first or second in every start, earning as much money the past months as his father and mother combined. Would there be rodeo in California? Milton wondered. In school, too, Allen was a prodigy, an eighth grader learning high school geometry. If he studied hard, the school counselor said, he could finish high school in three years and win a college scholarship. Milton didn't know where the boy's talent came from.

Tears filled Milton's eyes.

"Aaaah," Bosque said. His big hand gripped Milton's arm. They walked back to Lopez's house and split a couple of sixes under the mesquite until the men returned. Audrey Lopez and the other wives prepared chili and *cemait* dough while the men played horseshoes and drank in the dusk.

By the end of dinner everyone was drunk. Milton, face sweating, was explaining to Audrey Lopez, "Just a few weeks ago, Allen wins some kind of puzzle contest for the whole state, O.K.? And he's on TV. And C.C. and I have got our faces up to the screen so we can hear every word he's saying. And we can't believe it. He's talking on TV, and his hair's sticking up on the side like that, just like it always does.

"I can see them so real," Milton said. "When C.C. plays volleyball she's like a rubber ball, she's so little and round. She *dives* for those spikes, and her hair goes flying back."

Lopez slid his leg along Audrey's shoulder. "Good song," he said. "Let's dance." The radio was playing Top Forty.

"Wait. I'm listening to this man."

"Milton talks you into tomorrow afternoon. Come on." Lopez pulled her shoulder.

Audrey shrugged him off and laid her hand on Milton's arm. "His wife and son are gone."

"Dried up old bitch," Lopez said. "C.C.'s too old for you, man, she's way older than he is. You lost nothing."

Grabbing a barbecue fork, ramming Lopez against the wall, Milton chopped the fork into Lopez's shoulder. A woman screamed, Milton heard his own grunts as the glistening tines rose and stabbed. Lopez ducked and his knife came up. Milton deflected the lunge with his fork, the knife blade springing down its long shank. Milton shouted as the knife thudded into the wall. His little finger had bounded into the air and lay on the floor, looking like a brown pebble.

Bosque drove both men to the hospital. The doctor cauterized, stitched, and bandaged the wound, and gave Milton a tetanus shot. If Milton had brought the severed finger—the top two joints—the doctor said, he might have sewed it on. The men refused to stay overnight. When they returned to the party, couples were dancing the *choti* and *bolero* to a Mexican radio station. Gulps of vodka deadened the pain in Milton's finger. He and Lopez kept opposite corners of the living room until dawn, when Lopez pushed Audrey into Milton's arms and said, "Get some dancing, man."

Sunday Milton slept under the mesquite until evening, when he rode to the Box-J.

"That's your mistake, Milton," Oldenburg said. "Everyone's entitled to one mistake. Next time you drink you're gone. You believe me?"

Milton did. He felt like weeping. The next day he roamed the fenceline, his chest and neck clotted with the frustration of being unable to work. The horse's jouncing spurted blood through the white bandage on his finger. Finally he rode out a back gate and into the midst of the granite mountains. Past a sparkling dome broken by a slump of shattered rock, Milton trotted into a narrow cut choked with mesquite. As a boy, he would hunt wild horses for days in these ravines, alone, with only a canvas food bag tied to the saddle. He remembered sleeping on the ground without a blanket, beneath a lone sycamore that had survived years of drought. Waking as dawn lit the mountain crests, he would force through the brush, gnawing a medallion of jerked beef. Most often when he startled a horse the animal would clatter into a side gully, boxing itself in. Then roping was easy. Once when Milton flushed a stringy gray mustang, the horse charged him instead; he had no time to uncoil the rope before the gray was past. Milton wheeled, pursuing at full gallop out the canyon and onto the *bajada*. Twig-matted tail streaming behind, the mustang was outrunning him, and he had one chance with the rope. He dropped the loop around the gray's neck, jarring the animal to its haunches. It was so long ago. Today, Milton reflected, the headlong chase would have pinned him and the horse to Oldenburg's barbed-wire fence.

The sycamore held its place, older and larger. Though encountering no horses, Milton returned three stray cattle to Oldenburg's ranch. For a month, while the slightest jolt could rupture the wound, he hunted down mavericks in the miles of ravine, painted the ranch buildings, and repaired the roofs, one-handed.

Even as the finger healed, the missing segment unbalanced his grip. Swinging the pick or axe, shoveling, he would clench his right hand so tightly the entire arm would tremble. By the second month a new hand had evolved, with the musculature of the other fingers, the palm, and the wrist more pronounced. The pinky stub acted as a stabilizer against pickshaft or rope. Milton had rebuilt the fence and combed the granite mountains, rounding up another two dozen head. Oldenburg's herd had increased to 120.

In late August Milton rode beyond the granite range to the Ka kai Mountains, a low, twisted ridge of volcanic rock that he had avoided because he once saw the Devil there. Needing to piss, he had stumbled away from a beer party and followed a trail rising between the boulders. Watching the ground for snakes, he had almost collided with a man standing in the path. The stranger was a very big, ugly Indian, but Milton knew it was the Devil because his eyes were black, not human, and he spoke in a booming voice that rolled echoes off the cliff. Milton shuddered uncontrollably and shriveled to the size of a spider. Afterwards he found he had fallen and cut himself. Cholla spines were embedded in his leg. The Devil had said only: "Beware of Satan within you."

The meeting enhanced Milton's prestige, and Allen was impressed, though not C.C. "You see?" she said. "What did I always tell you?"

In daylight the mountains looked like no more than a pile of cinders. Milton chose an arroyo that cut through the scorched black rubble into red slabs, canyon walls that rose over his head, then above the mesquite. Chasing a calf until it disappeared in a side draw, Milton left the animal for later. The canyon twisted deeper into the mountains, the red cliffs now three hundred feet high. The polished rock glowed. Milton was twelve years old and his brothers were fighting.

"You took my car," Steven said.

"So what," Lee said. Milton's favorite brother, he was slim and handsome, with small ears and thick, glossy hair that fell almost into his eyes. Weekends he took Milton into Phoenix to play pool and pinball, sometimes to the shopping mall for Cokes. He always had girls, even Mexicans and whites.

"I told you if you took my car I was going to kill you." Steven always said crazy things. At breakfast, if Milton didn't pass him the milk right away—"How'd you like this knife in your eye?" About their mother—"Bitch wouldn't give me a dime. I'm going to shit on her bed." He wore a white rag around his head and hung out with gangs. Now they would call him a *cholo*.

"So what," Lee said. "Kill me." Cocking his leg, he wiped the dusty boot heel carefully against the couch. Milton was sitting on the couch.

Steven ran down the hall and came back with a .22. He pointed it at Lee's head, there was a shocking noise, a red spot appeared in Lee's forehead, and he collapsed on the rug.

"Oh my God," Steven said. Fingers clawed against his temples, he rushed out the door. Milton snatched the gun and chased him, firing on the run. Steven, bigger and faster, outdistanced him in the desert. Milton didn't come home for three days. Steven wasn't prosecuted and he moved to Denver. If he returned, Milton would kill him, even twenty years later.

Milton's horse ambled down the white sand, the dry bed curving around a red outcropping. Trapped by the canyon walls, the late summer air was hot and close. The weight of Milton's family fell on his back like a landslide—his father, driving home drunk from Casa Grande, slewing across the divider, head on into another pickup. The four children had flown like crickets from the back, landing unhurt in the dirt bank. The driver of the other truck died, and Milton's mother lost the shape of her face.

Milton felt himself turning to water. He circled his horse, routed the calf from the slit in the wall, and drove it miles to the ranch. At dinner he told Oldenburg he needed a trip to town.

"You'll lose your job," Oldenburg said.

Milton ate with his water fingers, spilling food and the orange juice that Oldenburg always served. "The lives of O'odham is a soap opera," he cried, trying to dispel his shame by insulting himself. "I love my boy, O.K.? But it's him who has to hold me when I go for C.C. He doesn't hold me with his strength. He holds me because I see him, and I stop. Sometimes I don't stop."

Oldenburg served Milton cake for dessert and told him to take the next day off if he wanted.

The following morning Milton lay on his bed, sweating. In his mind were no thoughts or images save the swirls of chill, unpleasant water that washed over him. He could transform the water, making it a cold lake that pumped his heart loudly and shrank his genitals, or a clear stream immersing him in swift currents and veins of sunlight, but he could not change the water into thoughts. The green carpeting and blue-striped drapes in his room sickened him. He could have finished a pint of vodka before he knew he was drinking.

He could not imagine losing his work.

Abruptly Milton rose. In the corral he fitted a rope bridle over the horse's head. As he rode past Oldenburg, the man looked up from a bench of tack he was fussing with, then quickly lowered his head.

"I'm going to the mountains," Milton said.

He let the horse carry him into the charred crust of the canyon. The scarlet walls rose high and sheer, closing off the black peaks beyond. Tethering the horse to a mesquite, Milton sat in the sand. The cliffs seemed almost to meet above him. Heat gathered over his head and forced down on him. A lizard skittered by his ear, up the wall. A tortoise lumbered across the wash. The water rippling through him became a shimmering on the far wall, scenes of his life. Milton racing after Steven, aiming at the zigzagging blue shirt, the crack of the gun, a palo verde trunk catching the rifle barrel and spinning Milton to his knees. His father's empty boots beside the couch where he slept. His mother in baggy gray slacks, growing fatter. C.C.'s head snapping back from Milton's open palm. The pictures flickered over the cliff. Milton sat while shadow climbed the rock, and a cool breeze funneled through the canyon, and night fell. Scooping a hole in the sand, he lay face to the stone while the canyon rustled and sighed. The wind rushed around a stone spur, scattering sand grains on his face. Several times in the night footsteps passed so near that the ground yielded beneath his head. Huddled, shivering, he thought his heart had stopped and fell asleep from terror. He dreamed of the cliffs, an unbroken glassy red.

Early in the morning Milton woke and stretched, refreshed by the cool air. The only prints beside him were his own. That evening he wrote to C.C. in care of her California aunt, telling her he'd quit drinking.

When C.C. didn't respond, Milton wrote again, asking at least for word of Allen, who would have entered high school. C.C. replied, "When I got here the doctor said I had a broken nose. Allen says he has no father."

Milton knew he must hide to avoid drinking. When he asked Oldenburg's permission to spend a day in the granite mountains, Oldenburg said he would go, too. They camped against a rock turret. The light in the sky faded and the fire leaped up. In the weeks since the former hand Jenkins's death, Oldenburg had become, if possible, more silent. Milton, meanwhile, admitted he had been a chatterbox, recalling high-school field trips to Phoenix fifteen years before, and rodeos in Tucson, Prescott, Sells, and Whiteriver. Oldenburg, fingertips joined at his chin, occasionally nodded or smiled. Tonight Milton squatted, arms around his knees, staring into the fire. About to share his most insistent emotions with the white man, he felt a giddy excitement, as if he were showing himself naked to a woman for the first time.

Milton told Oldenburg what C.C. had said.

"Your drinking has scarred them like acid. It will be time before they heal," Oldenburg said.

"There shouldn't be *O'odham* families," Milton exclaimed. "We should stop having children."

Oldenburg shook his head. After a while he said, "Milton, I hope you're not bitter because I won't let you drink. Drawing the line helps you. It's not easy living right. I've tried all my life and gained nothing—I lost both my sons in war and my wife divorced me to marry a piece of human trash. And still, in my own poor way, I try to live right." Oldenburg relaxed his shoulders and settled on his haunches.

Milton laid another mesquite limb across the fire. As the black of the sky intensified, the stars appeared as a glinting powder. Milton sipped two cups of coffee against the chill. Oldenburg, firelight sparkling off his silver tooth, wool cap pulled low over his stretched face, looked like an old grandmother. Laughing, Milton told him so. Oldenburg laughed too, rocking on his heels.

Soon after Oldenburg went to bed, Milton's mood changed. He hated the embers of the fire, the wind sweeping the rock knoll, the whirring of bats. He hated each stone and twig littering the campsite. His own fingers, spread across his knees, were like dumb, sleeping snakes. Poisonous things. He was glad one of them had been chopped off. Unrolling his blanket, he lay on his back, fists clenched. He dug hands and heels into the ground as if staked to it. After lying stiffly, eyes open, for an hour, he got up, slung his coiled rope over his shoulder, and walked down the hillside.

Brush and cactus were lit by a rising moon. Reaching a sheer drop, Milton jammed boot toes into rock fissures, seized tufts of saltbush, to let himself down. In the streambed he walked quickly until he joined the main river course. After a few miles' meandering through arroyos and over ridges, he arrived at the big sycamore and went to sleep.

Waking before dawn, Milton padded along the wash, hugging

the granite. The cold morning silence was audible, a high, pure ringing. He heard the horse's snort before he saw it tearing clumps of grass from the gully bank, head tossing, lips drawn back over its yellow teeth. Rope at his hip, Milton stalked from boulder to boulder. When he stepped forward, whirling the lariat once, the horse reared, but quieted instantly as the noose tightened around its neck. Milton tugged the rope; the animal neighed and skipped backward, but followed.

During the next two days Milton and Oldenburg captured three more spindly, wiry horses. Oldenburg would flush the mustangs toward Milton, who missed only once with the lasso. The stallions Milton kept in separate pens and later sold as rodeo broncs. Within a couple of weeks he had broken the mares.

Milton consumed himself in chores. Though the Box-J was a small ranch, labor was unremitting. In the fall, summer calves were rounded up and "worked"—branded with the Box-J, castrated, and dehorned. The previous winter's calves, now some 400 to 500 pounds each, were held in sidepens for weighing and loading onto the packer's shipping trucks. The pens were so dilapidated that Milton tore them down and built new ones. Winter, he drove daily pickup loads of sorghum hay, a supplement for the withered winter grasses, to drop spots at the water holes. Oldenburg hired extra help for spring roundup, working the new winter calves. Summer, Milton roved on horseback, troubleshooting. The fenceline would need repair. Oldenburg taught him to recognize cancer-eye, which could destroy a cow's market value. A low water tank meant Oldenburg must overhaul the windmill. Throughout the year Milton inspected the herd, groomed the horses, maintained the buildings, kept tools and equipment in working order.

Certain moments, standing high in the stirrups, surveying the herd and the land which stretched from horizon to horizon as if mirroring the sky, he could believe all belonged to him.

Every two weeks, when Oldenburg drove into Casa Grande for supplies, Milton deposited half his wages—his first savings account—and mailed the rest to C.C. These checks were like money thrown blindly over the shoulder. So thoroughly had he driven his family from his mind that he couldn't summon them back, even if he wished to. When, just before sleep, spent from the day's work, he glimpsed C.C. and Allen, the faces seemed unreal. They were like people he had met and loved profoundly one night at a party, then forgotten.

The night of the first November frost, soon after the wild horse roundup, Oldenburg had asked Milton if he played cards. Milton didn't.

"Too bad," Oldenburg said. "It gets dull evenings. Jenkins and I played gin rummy. We'd go to five thousand, take us a couple of weeks, and then start again."

"We could cook," Milton said.

On Sunday he and Oldenburg baked cakes. Milton missed the pressurized frosting cans with which he'd squirted flowers and desert scenes at the CETA bakery, but Oldenburg's cherry-chocolate layer cake was so good he ate a third of it. Oldenburg complimented him on his angel food.

Oldenburg bought a paperback *Joy of Cooking* in Casa Grande. Though he and Milton had been satisfied with their main dishes, they tried Carbonnade Flamande, Chicken Paprika, Quick Spaghetti Meat Pie. Milton liked New England Boiled Dinner. Mostly they made desserts. After experimenting with mousses and custard, they settled on cakes—banana, golden, seed, sponge, four-egg, Lady Baltimore, the Rombauer Special. Stacks of foil-wrapped cakes accumulated in the freezer. The men contributed cakes to charitable bake sales. Milton found that after his nightly slab of cake sleep came more easily and gently.

The men were serious in the kitchen. Standing side by side in white aprons tacked together from sheets, Milton whisking egg whites, Oldenburg drizzling chocolate over pound cake, they would say little. Milton might ask the whereabouts of a spice; Oldenburg's refusal to label the jars irritated him. Then they sat by the warm stove, feet propped on crates, and steamed themselves in the moist smells.

As they relaxed on a Sunday afternoon, eating fresh, hot cake, Oldenburg startled Milton by wondering aloud if his own wife were still alive. She had left him in 1963, and they'd had no contact since their second son was killed in 1969, more than ten years before.

"She wanted a Nevada divorce," Oldenburg said, "but I served papers on her first, and I got custody of the boys. I prevented a great injustice." He had sold his business in Colorado and bought the ranch. "The boys hated it," he said. "They couldn't wait to join the Army."

In Hashan, Milton said, she and her lover would have been killed.

Oldenburg shook his head impatiently. "He's deserted her, certainly. He was a basketball coach, and much younger than she was."

A Pima phrase—he knew little Pima—occurred to Milton. *Ne ha: jun*—all my relations. "Here is the opposite," Milton said. "We should call this the No-Relations Ranch."

Oldenburg sputtered with laughter. "Yes! And we'd need a new brand. Little round faces with big X's over them."

"You'd better be careful. People would start calling it the Tic-tac-toe Ranch."

"Or a manual, you know, a sex manual, for fornication. The X's doing it to the O's."

Light-headed from the rich, heavily-frosted cake, they sprayed crumbs from their mouths, laughing.

At the Pinal County Fair in May, Oldenburg entered a walnut pie and goaded Milton into baking his specialty, a jelly roll. It received honorable mention, while Oldenburg won second prize.

Milton wrote C.C., "I'm better than a restaurant."

C.C. didn't answer. When Valley Bank opened a Hashan branch in June, Milton transferred his account and began meeting his friends for the first time in a year. They needled him. "Milton, you sleeping with that old man?" His second Friday in town. Milton was writing out a deposit slip when he heard Bosque say, "Milton Oldenburg."

"Yes, Daddy just gave him his allowance," said Helene Mashad, the teller.

Bosque punched him on the shoulder and put out his hand. Milton shook it, self-conscious about his missing finger.

Bosque was cashing his unemployment check. The factory where he'd manufactured plastic tote bags for the past six months had closed. "Doesn't matter," Bosque said. "I'm living good." Before leaving, he said to come on by.

"You know what Oldenburg's doing, don't you?" Helene said, smoothing the wrinkles from Milton's check. She still wore her long, lavender Phoenix nails and a frothy perm. After years in Phoenix she'd relocated at the new branch, closer to her home in Black Butte. "Oldenburg wants to marry you. Then he'll get some kind of government money for his Indian wife. Or he'll adopt you. Same deal."

"It's not me who's the wife or child. I run that place." Nervous speaking to a woman again, Milton rambled, boasting of his authority over hired crews, what Oldenburg called his quick mind and fast hands cutting calves or constructing a corner brace, his skill with new tools. Even his baking. "He has to be the wife," Milton said. "He's a better cook." Milton leaned his hip against the counter. "Older woman. He's so old he turned white. And he lost his shape." Milton's hands made breasts. "Nothing left."

They both laughed. Elated by the success of his joke, Milton asked her to dinner. Helene said yes, pick her up at six.

Milton was uneasy in Hashan. The dusty buildings—adobes, sandwich houses of mud and board, slump-block tract homes—seemed part of the unreal life that included his family. To kill time, he rode to the trading post in Black Butte, a few miles in the direction of Oldenburg's ranch, and read magazines. When he arrived at the bank, Helene slapped her forehead: she hadn't known he was on horseback. Phew, she said, she didn't want to go out with a horse. Milton should follow her home and take a bath first.

They never left her house. She was eager for him, and Milton realized that as a man he'd been dead for a year. They made love until early morning. Milton lay propped against the headboard, his arm encircling her, her cheek resting on his chest. She briskly stroked his hand.

"Your poor finger," she said. "I hear Lopez has little circles in his shoulder like where worms have gone into a tomato."

"It was bad," Milton said, closing his hand.

"I can't stand the men in this town, the drunken pigs," Helene said. "I don't know why I came back."

Helene wasn't what Milton wanted, but he liked her well enough to visit once or twice a month. Because she lived outside Hashan, few people knew of the affair. They would eat dinner and see a movie in Casa Grande or Phoenix, and go to bed. Sometimes they simply watched TV in bed, or drove Helene's Toyota through the desert, for miles without seeing another light.

When Milton returned from his second weekend with Helene, Oldenburg was peevish. "You drink with that woman?" he said. "You going to send her picture to your wife?" Emergencies arose that kept Milton on the ranch weekends. After selling two wild colts to a stable, he took Helene to Phoenix overnight. Oldenburg berated him, "The cows don't calve on Saturday and Sunday? They don't get sick? A shed doesn't blow down on Sunday?" Still the men baked together. At the beginning of the school year they entered a fund-raising bakeoff sponsored by the PTO. Oldenburg won first with a Boston cream pie, and Milton's apple ring took second.

Helene transferred to Casa Grande, and Milton brought his account with her, relieved to avoid Hashan. Conversations with his friends were strained and dead. He worked; they didn't. They drank; he didn't. They had families. Milton nodded when he saw them, but no longer stopped to talk.

Fridays after Helene punched out, they might browse in the Casa Grande shopping center. Milton was drawn to the camera displays, neat lumps of technology embedded in towers of colorful film boxes. The Lerner shop's manikins fascinated him — bony stick figures like the bleached branches of felled cottonwood, a beautiful still arrangement. "Imagine Pimas in those," Helene said, pointing to the squares and triangles of glittering cloth. She puffed out her cheeks and spread her arms. Milton squeezed her small buttocks. Helene's legs were the slimmest of any *O'odham* woman he'd known.

During the second week of October, when Milton and a hired crew had set up shipping pens and begun culling the calves, a rare fall downpour, tail end of a Gulf hurricane, struck. For six hours thunder exploded and snarls of lightning webbed the sky. The deluge turned the ground to slop, sprang leaks in the roof, and washed out the floodgates at the edge of the granite mountains. Cattle stampeded through the openings; one died, entangled in the barbed wire. When the skies cleared, Oldenburg estimated that a quarter of the cash animals, some three hundred dollars apiece, had escaped. The shipping trucks were due in two days.

The next morning a new hired man brought further news: over the weekend a fight had broken out at the Sundowner. The fat end of a pool cue had caught Audrey Lopez across the throat, crushing her windpipe. Her funeral was to be at two in the afternoon.

Milton stood helplessly before Oldenburg. In the aftermath of the storm the sky was piercingly blue and a bracing wind stung his cheeks. Oldenburg's collar fluttered.

"You have to go," Oldenburg said. "There's no question."

"You'll lose too much money," Milton said stubbornly. "The cattle are in the mountains and I know every little canyon where they run."

"There's no question," Oldenburg repeated. "The right way is always plain, though we do our best to obscure it."

The service took place in a small, white Spanish-style church. At the cemetery the mourners stood bareheaded, the sun glinting off their hair. The cemetery was on a knoll, and in the broad afternoon light the surrounding plains, spotted by occasional cloud shadows, seemed immensely distant, like valleys at the foot of a solitary butte. Milton imagined the people at the tip of a rock spire miles in the clouds. The overcast dimmed them, and shreds of cumulus drifted past their backs and bowed heads.

Afterwards the men adjourned to the Lopez house, where Vigiliano Lopez rushed about the living room, flinging chairs aside to clear a center space. A ring of some twenty men sat on chairs or against the wall. Bosque arrived carrying three cold cases and two quarts of Crown Russe. More bottles appeared. Lopez started one Crown Russe in each direction and stalked back and forth from the kitchen, delivering beer and slapping bags of potato chips at the men's feet.

At his turn, Milton passed the bottle along.

"Drink, you goddamn Milton Oldenburg," Lopez said.

Milton said, "I'll lose my job."

"So?" Lopez shrugged distractedly. "I haven't had a job in a year. I don't need a job." Lopez had been the only Pima miner at the nearby Loma Linda pit until Anaconda shut it down. He pushed his hair repeatedly off his forehead, as if trying to remember something, then turned up the radio.

Milton sat erect in the chair, hands planted on his knees. He gobbled the potato chips. No one avoided him, nor he anyone else, yet talk was impossible. Grief surged through the party like a wave. Milton felt it in the over-loud conversation, silences, the restlessness—no one able to stay in one place for long. Laughter came in fits. Over the radio, the wailing tremolos of the Mexican ballads were oppressive and nerve-wracking. The power of feeling in the room moved Milton and frightened him, but he was outside it.

Joining the others would be as simple as claiming the vodka bottle on its next round, Milton knew. But he remembered standing tall in the stirrups, as if he could see over the edge of the yellow horizon, the end of Oldenburg's land, and he kept his hands spread on his knees. At the thought of vodka's sickly tastelessness, bile rose in his throat. Pretending to drink, tipping the bottle and plugging it with his tongue, would be foolish and shameful. Out of friendship and respect for Lopez, he could not leave. Their wounding each other, Milton realized, had bound him more closely to Lopez.

As night fell the men became drunker and louder. Bosque went out for more liquor. When he returned, he danced with the oil-drum cookstove, blackening his hands and shirt.

"Hey, not with my wife," Lopez said, grabbing the drum and humping it against the wall. "Need somebody to do you right, baby," he said. The drum clanged to the floor. The men cheered. Lopez, knees bent and hands outstretched as if waiting for something to fall into them, lurched to the middle of the room. A smile was glazed over his face. He saw Milton.

"Drink with me, you son of a bitch," he shouted.

Milton motioned for the Crown Russe, a third full. "Half for you, half for me," he said. Marking a spot on the label with his finger, Milton drank two long swallows and held out the bottle for Lopez. Lopez drank and flipped the empty over his shoulder. Side by side, arms around each other, Milton and Lopez danced the *cumbia*. Lopez's weight sagged until Milton practically carried him. The man's trailing feet hooked an extension cord, sending a lamp and the radio crashing to the floor. Lopez collapsed.

Milton ran outside and retched. Immediately he was refreshed and lucid. The stars burned like drillpoints of light. Patting the horse into an easy walk, he sat back in the saddle, reins loose in his lap, and gave himself to the brilliant stillness. As his eyes adjusted to the night, he could distinguish the black silhouettes of mountains against the lesser dark of the sky. Faint stars emerged over the ranges, bringing the peaks closer. The mountains were calm and friendly, even the jagged line of the Ka kai.

That night Milton dreamed that a chocolate-colored flood swept through Hashan. The *O'odham* bobbed on the foam; from the shore others dove backward into the torrent, arms raised symmetrically by their heads. Receding, the flood left bodies swollen in the mud—Milton's brother Lee, their mother, belly down, rising in a mound. Milton, long hair fixed in the mud, stared upward. His hands were so full of fingers they had become agaves, clusters of fleshy, spiny leaves. Peering down at him, C.C. and Allen were black against the sun, arms crooked as if for flight. Milton was glad they had escaped.

Milton woke serene and energetic, the dream forgotten. Over breakfast Oldenburg studied him intently—clear gray eyes, a slight frown—but said nothing. The penned calves were weighed and loaded onto the shipping trucks. Many remained free, and the year would be a loss.

Milton wrote C.C. of Audrey Lopez's death. "I had a big drink to keep Lopez company," he added, "but I threw it up. It was the first booze in more than a year. I didn't like it any more."

Lying beside Milton the following weekend, Helene said, "Poor finger. I'll give you another one." She laid her pinky against the stub so a new finger seemed to grow. Her lavender nail looked like the fancy gem of a ring. She lifted, lowered the finger. "And Lopez with the purple spots on his shoulder like the eyes of a potato," she said. She shifted and her small, hard nipple brushed Milton's side. "It's a wonder you two didn't fight."

"Shut up," Milton said. "His wife is dead."

"I know. It's terrible." She had worried for him, Helene said, knowing he would be at the funeral with Lopez. He should have brought her.

"I didn't want you there," Milton said. "You don't have the right feelings." He left before dawn and hadn't returned to Helene when C.C. replied.

"I was shocked to hear about Audrey," C.C. wrote. "I feel sad about it every day. Hashan is such a bad place. But it isn't any better here. At Allen's school there are gangs and not just Mexicans but black and white too."

She wrote again: "I miss you. I've been thinking about coming back. Allen says he won't but he'll come with me in the end. The money has helped. Thank you."

Milton threw up his arms and danced on the corral dirt, still moist and reddened from fluke autumn rains. Shouting, he danced on one leg and the other, dipping from side to side as if soaring, his head whirling. Oldenburg's nagging—where will they live?—worried him little. Over dinner Oldenburg suggested, "They'll live in your old place, and you can visit them on weekends. We'll have to move our baking to the middle of the week."

Milton knew he must be with the O'odham. Announcing a ride into the mountains, he saddled up and galloped toward Hashan. Because he couldn't see the faces of his family, his joy felt weirdly rootless. The past year he had killed them inside. The sudden aches for Allen, the sensation of carrying C.C.'s weight in his arms, had been like the twinges of heat, cold, and pain from his missing finger. As if straining after their elusive faces, Milton rode faster. His straw hat, blown back and held by its cord, flapped at his ear. The horse's neck was soaked with sweat.

Bosque's fat wife said he wasn't home. Milton made a plan for the Sundowner: after one draft for sociability, he would play the shuffleboard game. Tying up at a light pole, he hesitated in the lounge doorway. The familiarity of the raw wood beams criss-crossing the bare Sheetrock walls frightened him. But Bosque, sliding his rear off a barstool, called, "Milton Oldenburg."

"C.C.'s hauling her little tail home," Milton announced. "And the boy."

"All riiight." Bosque pumped his hand up and down. Milton's embarrassment at his missing finger disappeared in the vastness of Bosque's grip. Friends he hadn't spoken to in months surrounded him. "When's she coming? She going to live on the ranch? Oldenburg will have a whole Indian family now." Warmed by their celebration of his good luck, Milton ordered pitchers. His glass of draft was deep gold and sweeter than he had remembered, though flat. Others treated him in return. Someone told a story of Bosque building a scrap wood raft to sail the shallow lake left by the rains. Halfway across, the raft had broken apart and sunk. "Bosque was all mud up to his eyes," the storyteller said. "He looked like a bull rolling in cow flop." Everyone laughed.

Fuzzy after a half dozen beers, Milton felt his heart pound, and his blood. He saw them then—C.C., wings of hair, white teeth, dimpled round cheeks. Allen's straight bangs and small, unsmiling mouth. Their eyes were black with ripples of light, reflections on a pool. Milton was drawn into that pool, lost. Terror washed over him like a cold liquid, and he ordered a vodka.

"I'm a drunk," he told the neighbor on his right.

"Could be. Let's check that out, Milton," the man said.

"I never worked."

"No way," the man said, shaking his head.

"I didn't make a living for them."

"Not even a little bitty bit," the man agreed.

"Not even this much," Milton said, holding his thumb and forefinger almost closed, momentarily diverted by the game. "I hurt them."

Holding up his hands, the man yelled, "Not me."

"I tortured them. They don't belong to me. I don't have a family," Milton mumbled. Quickly he drank three double vodkas. The jukebox streamed colors, and he floated on its garbled music.

Shoving against the men's room door, Milton splashed into the urinal, wavering against the stall. He groped for the Sundowner's rear exit. The cold bit through his jacket. He pitched against a stack of bricks.

Waking in the dark, Milton jumped to his feet. C.C. was coming, and his job was in danger. He was foreman of a white man's ranch. Allen and C.C. would be amazed at his spread. With a bigger bank account than three-quarters of Hashan, he could support them for a year on savings alone. The night before was an ugly blur. But his tongue was bitter, his head thudded, he had the shakes. Cursing, Milton mounted and kicked the horse into a canter. To deceive Oldenburg he must work like a crazy man and sweat out his hangover. The fits of nausea made him moan with frustration. He kicked the horse and struck his own head.

Milton arrived an hour after sunup. Shooing the horse into the corral with a smack to the rump, he stood foggily at the gate, unable to remember his chore from the previous day. A ladder leaning against the barn reminded him: patching. He lugged a roll of asphalt roofing up the ladder. Scrambling over the steep pitch didn't frighten him, even when he slipped and tore his hands. He smeared tar, pressed the material into place, drove the nails. Every stroke was true, two per nail. Milton had laid half a new roof when Oldenburg called him.

"Come down." Oldenburg was pointing to the corral. The gate was still ajar. Milton's horse, head drooping, dozed against the rail, but the other three were gone.

Milton stood before him, wobbly from exertion, blood draining from his head.

"You lied," Oldenburg said. "You abandoned your job. The week is *my* time. You've been drunk. I'm going to have to let you go, Milton."

Milton couldn't speak.

"You understand, don't you?" Oldenburg said more rapidly. His eyes flicked down, back to Milton. "Do you see what happens?" His arms extended toward the empty corral.

"So I lose a day running them down."

Smiling slightly, Oldenburg shook his head. "You miss the point. It would be wrong for me to break my word. You'd have no cause to believe me again and our agreement would be meaningless."

"Once a year I get drunk," Milton burst out. "We'll put a name on it, November Something Milton's Holiday."

Oldenburg smiled again. "Once a month . . . once a week . . . I'm sorry. I'll give you two weeks' pay but you can leave any time." He turned.

"I've worked hard for you!" Milton's throat felt as if it were closing up.

Oldenburg stopped, brow furrowed. "It's sad," he said. "You've managed the Box-J better than I could. I'm going to miss our baking." He paused. "But we have to go on, Milton, don't you see? My family leaves me, Jenkins leaves me, you leave me. But *I* go on." He walked away.

Two long steps, a knee in the back, arms around the neck, and he could break the man in half—Milton's arms dropped. He had lost the urge for violence. Long after Oldenburg had disappeared into the open green range where the horses were, he stood by the corral. Then, arms over his head as if escaping a cloudburst, he ran into the adobe, packed his belongings in a sheet, and that afternoon rode the exhausted horse back to his old home.

To C.C., Milton wrote, "I don't have my job any more but there's plenty of money in the bank." Weeks later she replied, "Milton, I know what's going on. I can't come home to this." But she would continue to write him, she said. Milton saw no one. Pacing the house, he talked to the portraits over the TV—Allen's eighth-grade class picture, a computer-drawn black-dot composition of C.C. from the O'odham Tash carnival. He disturbed nothing, not even the year-and-a-half-old pile of dishes in the sink.

For several weeks he laid fence for a Highway Maintenance heavy equipment yard. Working with a new type of fence, chain link topped with barbed wire, cheered him. The foreman was lax, married to one of Milton's cousins, so when Milton requested the leftover spools of barbed wire, he said, "Sure. It's paid for."

Milton dug holes around his house and cut posts from the warped, gnarled mesquite growing in the vacant land. As he worked, the blue sky poured through chinks in the posts, reminding him pleasantly of the timeless first days repairing the line on Oldenburg's range. When he had finished stringing the wire, Milton's house was enclosed in a neat box—two thorned strands, glinting silver. Sunlight jumped off the metal in zigzag bolts. In Hashan, where fences were unknown and the beige ground was broken only by houses, cactus, and drab shrubs, the effect was as startling as if Milton had wrapped his home in Christmas lights.

Milton sat on the back doorstep, drinking beer. Discouraged by the fence, no one visited at first. But dogs still ran through the yard, as did children, who preferred scaling the fence to slithering under it. Their legs waggled precariously on the stiffly swaying wire; then they hopped down, dashed to the opposite side, and climbed out, awkward as spiders. Milton's fence became a community joke, which made him popular. Instead of walking through the gap behind the house, friends would crawl between the strands or try to vault them. Or they would lean on the posts, passing a beer back and forth while they chatted.

Keeping her promise, C.C. wrote that Allen had shot up tall. Even running track he wore his Walkman, she said. But he smoked, and she had to yell at him. Last term he'd made nearly all A's.

Milton grew extremely fat, seldom leaving the house except to shop or work the odd jobs his new skills brought him. Through spring and summer he drowsed on the doorstep. In November, almost a year after he'd left Oldenburg's, he fell asleep on the concrete slab and spent the night without jacket or blanket. The next day he was very sick, and Bosque and Lopez drove him to the hospital. The doctor said he had pneumonia.

Milton's first day in ICU, Bosque and Lopez shot craps with him during visiting hours. But as his lungs continued to fill with fluids, his heart, invaded by fatty tissues from his years of drinking, weakened. Four days after entering the hospital, he suffered a heart attack.

In the coronary ward, restricted to ten-minute visits, Milton dreamed, feeling as if the fluids had leaked into his skull and his brain was sodden. In one dream the agaves again sprouted from his wrists, their stalks reaching into the sky. He gave the name *ne ha: jun*—all my relations—to his agave hands.

The next morning C.C. and Allen appeared in the doorway. Huge, billowing, formless as smoke, they approached the bed in a peculiar rolling motion. Milton was afraid. From the dreams he realized that his deepest love was drawn from a lake far beneath him, and that lake was death. But understanding, he lost his fear. He held out his arms to them.

ᘰᘰᘰᘰᘰᘰ C. M. Mayo

mirror, mirror, on the page
have you known a happier age?
and deliver us from rage
and keep tigers in their cage
Carlos Fuentes

The Jaguarundi

I was sitting on Manette's faded chintz sofa when the jaguarundi rubbed its flank against my calf. I paid it no notice,
thinking it was a house cat. Later, when I was leaving, I saw it
curled up atop one of Uwe's music boxes. Its head was as long and
flat as a weasel's, and its coat was a dusty black, like an otter's.

"That's my jaguarundi," Manette said as she passed me my umbrella. It flicked open its eyes at the sound of her voice. They were
larger than a cat's, coffee-colored, with round pupils.

"Uwe bought her for me from a rancher in Chiapas," Manette
was saying. "I'm painting her into my 'jungle pastiche.' Uwe's
written a poem about her, '*Gibt es einen Zoo in der Nähe?*'"

"You know I can't understand a word of German," I said and I
kissed her on the mouth.

This was in Coyoacán, an old neighborhood of Mexico City.
This was 1982, when we all had dollars in the Mexican banks and
we all felt rich, or rich enough anyway. Uwe was importing music
boxes from Austria and Denmark, brought in on some politician's
private plane to avoid paying duty. Manette had begun to sell her
jungle paintings through a gallery in the Zona Rosa. I had most of
my money parked with my father's stockbroker in New York; in

Mexico I lived simply, in work shirts and blue jeans, no furniture, a portable typewriter. If I needed a tie, I didn't go.

I began to go to Manette's house nearly every afternoon. We drank shot glasses of prickly pear brandy, or tequila with a spritz of lime; once, we drank a finger of Uwe's peppermint schnapps and smoked a joint. Manette's jaguarundi lolled on the apricot kilim at our feet, its purr deep and rough. The rains started by about four, and they made the jaguarundi restless. It would leap from music box to music box, to the ledge over the sofa where it set Uwe's Zapotecan bowls wobbling and spinning. Sometimes I caught a glimpse of its tail, much longer, more slender than a cat's, among the forest of antique silver frames on the baby grand piano. When it came near the sofa again, Manette would rake her hand along its back, then lightly, with one finger, along its tail.

"Precious," she always said.

The garden was chill and lush. Manette had hung wind chimes made of abalone shells from the eaves, and it is this that I remember, more than her voice, although that too was soft and flute-like. And I remember the faint smell of ferns and of wet geraniums, the cool lightness of her eiderdown duvet thrown over my back; teak, waxed rosewood, and the jaguarundi that smelled like Manette, tart and sugary, like bramble, or hazelnuts.

Uwe was German. There were a lot of Germans in Mexico, people whose great-grandfathers had confused Galveston with Veracruz, most of them engineers or chicken farmers or accountants. Uwe wrote poetry and sold music boxes. I met him a few weeks after I'd begun to see Manette, at one of his and Manette's Thursday night "open houses."

"So you are a writer," he said. He wasn't really looking at me; he was watching Manette. She had the jaguarundi in her arms and was going around the room, allowing people to pet it. Somehow, Uwe got it out of me that I had lived in Nairobi, and Fez, and a village of exactly seven souls and a flock of bandy-legged sheep on the northwest coast of Skye, and that I had published two chapbooks of poetry, and recently, a collection of travel essays I'd written for a Canadian magazine.

"You are busy, busy, busy," Uwe said. He had jet-black hair, dyed I suspected, and a broken nose. "For you," he said, taking a swallow of his cognac, "'The Flight of the Bumble Bee.'" He led me to a dark corner in the foyer. Next to the hat stand was a stone pedestal, and on it, an oval-shaped box made of mahogany and polished burlwood; there was a bee the size of my hand on each of its sides, inlaid with obsidian and yellow jade. Uwe wound it up with an iron key.

"I travel light," I laughed. "I don't have a car, I don't even own a tie."

"Does not matter," he said. He knew who my father was. "If you can have a beautiful thing, why not have it?"

The music sounded like the abalone shell chimes in a storm.

"Rimsky-Korsakoff," he said, stroking his chin and smiling tightly, as if in ecstasy. "I will give you a good price."

"No thanks," I said. "But thanks."

"Uwe's a lousy poet," Manette told me once. We had stepped out of the shower and toweled each other off. She was pulling a tortoiseshell comb through her waist-length blonde hair. "Do you know, he's never published anything?" she said fiercely. "Uwe only knows how to collect things. Things and people."

I had seen the music boxes, the ones Uwe kept for himself; the antique beer steins lined up on a shelf near the living room ceiling, the Zapotecan bowls, the filigreed silver frames, black and white photographs, a basket full of fingernail-sized gold coins stamped with the profile of the Archduke Maximilian.

"God," she said, her eyes glistening. "Even here, in the bathroom." She tapped her comb against the glass on a print. "Uxmal," she said with disgust. She pointed to the print next to the sink. "That one's Chichén." They covered the walls, Sayil, Labná, Dzibilchaltún, Mayan ruins under a hand-colored dawn.

She'd slicked her hair into a rope and was leaning forward, twisting the towel around her head. When she stood up, it was as if she had on a fantastic headdress. Water drops sparkled in the wells of her collarbone.

"Tortoiseshell combs!" she said, grabbing a fistful from a Talavera bowl. "Tin soldiers, politicians, Agustín Lara recordings, poets—"

I ran my hands down her shoulder blades and buried my face in her neck.

I thought I would see another jaguarundi. But I never have, not once in my life.

Manette never finished what she called her "jungle pastiche" painting. Near the end of the rainy season the president gave a speech everyone who had a television watched. I didn't have a television, but Manette called me that night to tell me that the president had begun to shout, towards the end, about plunder, conspiracies; tears welled in his eyes, he shook his fist at the cameras. He said he would nationalize the banks, and no one was allowed to change pesos for dollars, or dollars for pesos. Uwe hurled one of his beer steins at the screen. The beer stein had been worth a lot of money, Manette said, enough to buy a small car.

Uwe had decided they would go to Vienna, for several months.

"Uwe's taking me to the operas," she mumbled, and began to cry.

"Don't forget your opera glasses," I said.

"Look in on my jaguarundi," she said.

I hung up on her.

I couldn't work for days. I sat on the mattress in my bare apartment, balancing the typewriter on my knees. I drank weak *té de tila*, I smoked stale Marlboros and chewed my nails. I tried to finish a travel piece about the Pacific Coast, but instead I wrote a series of poems I titled "Manette in the Morning," because, I realized, I had never seen her in the morning. Later, when I left Mexico, I would tear them to shreds and flush them down the toilet.

I toured every single church and museum in the city limits, I walked through the Alameda, and Chapultepec Park, looking each woman I saw full in the face. I went to the Chapultepec zoo and threw a hot dog to the tiger. I took the metro to Coyoacán, thinking I might look in on the jaguarundi, but my feet wouldn't take me to Manette's cobblestone lane. I kept walking down Francisco Sosa, past Las Lupitas, through the plaza to El Parnaso where I bought a chapbook by a Mexican poet I'd met on one of those Thursday nights, a short mousy-haired woman I didn't really respect. I stared at her words as I drank a coffee I didn't really want. I left the book face down next to the tip.

Then I did look in on the jaguarundi. The maid let me in, saying she'd been expecting me. She asked me if I wanted a brandy, or a shot glass of tequila. I asked where the jaguarundi was, and she clapped her hands and called its name. But it didn't come.

"It is sad," she said, "now that Señora Manette is gone." Her red and white checked apron was soiled. "It broke one of Señor Uwe's Zapotecan bowls. I had to punish it." She stared at the floor and twisted her braid.

We began to search for the jaguarundi, behind the chintz sofa, around the music boxes, behind the plumería in clay pots painted with the faces of the sun and moon. And in the laundry patio, the garden, the dining room. I went upstairs, to Manette's and Uwe's bedroom. The drapes were closed and Manette's jewelry box was gone, but everything else was the same. There were dusky black hairs shed all over the eiderdown duvet, and a small oval indentation where the jaguarundi had slept on her pillow. I could hear the maid downstairs, still clapping her hands and calling for it. I opened the drapes and pushed out the window. The abalone shells tinkled in the breeze.

Manette's closet door was ajar. I walked in, and I thought I might sink to my knees, drown in the smell of laundered cotton, grassy linen, the oranges she'd stuck with cloves. I grabbed an armful of her blouses and held them to my cheek. The jaguarundi began to purr and to weave between my legs.

It let me pick it up and carry it downstairs to the sofa. I sat with it on my lap for a while, nuzzling it, burying my face in its scruff. Everything was the same, as if Manette and Uwe might be coming home for cocktails any minute. I poured myself a schnapps and wound up the nearest music box, a large dust-covered chest. It played too slowly, missing the A and the F sharp, "Dance des Mirlitons," from *The Nutcracker Suite*. I sat on the sofa for a long time, smoothing the jaguarundi's fur with the flat of my hand, listening for the faint rush of the city's arteries, to the jaguarundi's shallow breath and my own. When I got up to leave, the jaguarundi cocked its head, staring at me.

Outside, the sun was a harsh white, everything was dry.

The maid had been giving the jaguarundi cat food and it looked a little thin, so I returned the next afternoon with a fish wrapped in butcher paper. The jaguarundi came dashing up to me when I called it from the foyer, and it put its front paws on my knees, sniffing for the fish. I could feel its claws through my blue jeans, and its eyes shone, even in the dim.

I stood in the kitchen, watching the maid fry the fish in a teaspoon of corn oil, then pick the bones out, then spoon it into the jaguarundi's dish on the tile floor.

"This fish is very expensive," the maid said, wiping her hands on her apron.

"Yes," I said.

I went home and wrote a poem about brambles and hazelnuts, bumblebees, the gossamer blue cast to the winter morning. I started to write Manette a letter, something about the economic recovery program the new president called the PIRE. "Your maid would call it the 'pyre,'" I wrote. Ha ha. I crumpled that one up and tossed it in the trash. I started another letter, about how Francisco Sosa, the main street in Coyoacán, had been cleaned up now that the president's family had their house there, near the bridge over the river and the terra-cotta-colored eighteenth-century chapel. Armed soldiers patrolled the street outside, looking bored, smoking cigarettes. Inflation was more than 200 percent, I wrote her in another letter. There was no sugar or flour in the supermarket. There were campesinos, I told her on the back of a postcard (a garish view of Acapulco by night), who came to the city and drank gasoline and then lit a match and breathed fire. The people in their cars at stoplights gave them coins. I saw this from the window of a public bus. I thought I might go to Chang Mai after Christmas, I wrote, or Marrakesh, or Cairo.

I kept the letters I wrote to Manette in my jacket pocket; the poems I wrote about her, by my bedside table. All through that winter I came to see the jaguarundi in the afternoons; yet somehow, I always forgot to ask the maid for their address.

Manette had left her paints, her brushes, canvases, everything. I couldn't imagine what she was doing in Vienna. Manette didn't read much, or watch television. The opera didn't go on all day. I'd been to Vienna, but still I imagined it as a closed, black damp place where old people huddled in unheated apartments, playing violoncellos.

Her studio was in a padlocked shed at the back of the garden, overgrown with ragged bougainvillea. Through a tiny window I could see the corner of her "jungle pastiche" painting where she had left it on the easel. Pinned on the walls were pencil sketches of the jaguarundi: its head, from different angles, with its eyes shut, opened, its ears sleek against its skull; one hind leg, its rosebud nose, lolling on its back, pouncing on a shard of pottery. With the dry season, though, the bougainvillea blossomed and spread, purple, brilliant orange, and the small room darkened.

I drank all the schnapps and most of the tequila. I smoked the marijuana I found stashed in the bathroom, and I wound up and listened to every single music box. I shuffled through Uwe's black and white photographs: of Indian women in headdresses made of live iguanas; the volcanoes ringed with clouds, like scarves; a snapshot of B. Traven in his library on the Calle Mississippi.

I brought the jaguarundi tuna and huachinango, and once a bit of catnip a friend drove down from Laredo. Soon I didn't have to clap or to call for the jaguarundi; it was waiting for me in the shadows of the foyer at the same hour every afternoon. After it ate, the jaguarundi would pad into the living room and jump up to lie next to me on the sofa. It would lick its whiskers or the pads of its paws; it would purr loudly and flick its tail with contentment. Sometimes the jaguarundi rubbed its chin against my leg, asking me to tickle its ears.

The days passed like this, one after the other, and another. I wrote an article about mariachis for the Canadian magazine, and a sort of philosophical essay on the floating gardens at Xochimilco. I reviewed the galleys for another chapbook. I read travel guides, to India, North Africa; I considered living in a settlement on the edge of Hudson Bay. And then the rainy season began again, suddenly, with a violent downpour.

"I am sitting in your living room," I scribbled to Manette. I crumpled the paper in my fist.

"I was fucking your wife," I wrote to Uwe.

I asked the maid for their address.

The next afternoon I brought the jaguarundi a stingray. The maid wrinkled her nose at it, but I told her not to worry, the meat was like tuna, only with a slightly sharper, salty taste. Go ahead and boil it, I said, and I went into the living room. I opened the liquor cabinet and lined up what was left: a finger of tequila, anise liqueur, Campari, gin, a shot of the prickly pear brandy. I poured them all into a tumbler. The liquor filled a little more than half the glass. The mixture was a reddish brown, like coagulated blood. I drank it all. Then I sat on the sofa.

When the jaguarundi jumped up, I skidded my hand along its back. I began to kiss it on the scruff, between its eyes, and I hugged it until it cried, until it clawed at me, spat at me and hissed. It wriggled away finally and I staggered into the bathroom and threw up.

"You are singing Oaxaca?" the maid shouted through the bathroom door. Maids would speak this way to foreigners. "You ate some stingray?"

"No!" I shouted, my knuckles white on the edge of the toilet bowl. "I'll be all right," I said. I lost my balance and fell to the floor.

The light was a pale rosy gray when I woke up, with a sour taste in my mouth and a blinding headache. I touched my fingertips to my face: it was crusted with fresh scabs. There was a musty smell, from the eiderdown duvet, I realized, on Manette's bed. I heard the jaguarundi's raspy purr: it was curled at the foot of the bed, watching me carefully. When I sat up, it scampered into the closet, its long tail swishing behind it.

I remembered then that I hadn't yet affixed the postage to those letters. I clapped my hands, once, weakly. I sank back into the pillow and slept until late afternoon.

When I left the clouds were a fretwork, spent and drifting. The cobblestones were slick and the air smelled of earth and gasoline.

Some days later I came back with a pair of plastic earrings for the maid, and a huachinango.

"Ah," the maid said, her eyes very round, as she took the packages. She had on a clean apron. I asked for the jaguarundi. She called out its name, but the jaguarundi did not come. She shrugged. "Would you like a tequila?" she asked.

"But aren't we out of liquor?" I tried to approximate a sheepish look. I had my hands in my pockets.

"Oh," she murmured. She knit her brow, as if she suddenly recognized something large and obvious. She crossed her arms over her chest. "The Señor Uwe is home," she blurted. She seemed to intuit what she needed to say from my expression. "He went to the store," she said, "to buy lightbulbs."

"Thank you," I said, and I left.

The next day I came home to find an enormous canvas wrapped in brown paper standing up against my bed. It was Manette's unfinished "jungle pastiche." Henri Rousseau's lion peeped out from the long grasses; there were myna birds and banana trees, vermilion hawaiianas, and a spider monkey swinging from a vine. Picasso's harlequin sprawled in the ferns, smoking a joint. Manette had painted me and the Venus de Milo waltzing through a blank sky.

I looked for the jaguarundi; she said she'd painted it in, but I couldn't find it.

The next afternoon I flew to Cairo with my duffel bag and my typewriter. I left the landlady my styrofoam coffee cups, a half empty box of laundry detergent, and the painting. I was going to write a series of articles about the River Nile, but I ended up doing something on belly dancers, and the oud, and Anwar Sadat's novel. I ended up spending a winter in Alexandria, writing sonnets; then a couple of years in Tangiers in an apartment behind the souk, with a view of the straits, the swallows, the biscuit-white shores of Spain.

I didn't think much about Mexico. It seemed exotic, the farther away I was from it, like Cairo itself, the wildly colored turbans the women wore in Nairobi, like an emerald twilight. Every once in a while the *International Herald Tribune* would print a few column inches about Mexico with a photograph of a high-rise beach hotel or a woman picking through a mountain of garbage. I read that there were earthquakes in Mexico City in 1985. I was worried, and I considered calling, but then I met someone on a plane who told me most of the damage was in the Colonia Centro, where cheap hotels and rotting palaces and *vecindades* were built over the ancient lake bed. The earthquakes hadn't affected Coyoacán, which was on volcanic rock. The price of crude oil fell, drastically, the president was booed and heckled at the World Cup Soccer matches. The fans trashed the Sanborn's where I used to go to buy American magazines. A team of fresh-faced economists with names like Téllez Kuenzler and Carstens was renegotiating the foreign debt.

I suppose I could say the flat-headed North African cats reminded me of the jaguarundi, or that I had some kind of epiphany when I went out to see, dutifully (but without a camera), the Sphinx. Or that I once spent an afternoon in a village near Luxor drinking cheap white wine with a Dutch girl who had a laugh, and hair, exactly like Manette's. Or that I went with her to her hotel room and ran my hands down her shoulder blades, drew my fingers along the rim of her collarbone, like a fan of feathers skimming smooth bark. And that afterwards I listened to her tell me about Uxmal and Chichén, as if I'd never been there, I'd never heard of them, and everything she said, she did, even the way she smelled, was new and surprising.

I don't know if I could say all that; if it would be true, really.

I did see Manette again, once, briefly. I met her for breakfast at a Sanborn's near my hotel in the Colonia Centro. This was in 1992, when most of the earthquake damage had been repaired, although there were still a few empty lots here and there, boarded up with plywood. Another president was privatizing the banks; everyone was talking about a free trade agreement with the U.S. and Canada. The stock market had sailed up like a skyrocket, and my father had been calling me, telling me I should buy Telmex, Cifra, Cemex.

She wore a red suit that looked tight at the hips. Her hair was cut short, pulled back with a plastic headband. No, she hadn't painted anything in ages, there wasn't room in her apartment. Uwe had gone back to his first wife in Vienna. She had thought about moving to Houston, she said, but she was offered a job translating reports for the American Chamber of Commerce. It was fun, she said. It was nearby.

We ate hotcakes and drank coffee. She took out her compact and put on her lipstick. I lit a Marlboro. She'd been doing tai chi, on Saturdays, at the Casa de Cultura in Coyoacán. She'd been going to the Beverly Hills Workout at the Plaza Inn mall. The jaguarundi was in the zoo.

We split the bill. When I pushed back my chair, she touched my hand. "Where will you be going?" she said. She had fine lines around her eyes now.

"Chiapas," I said.

"You are?" Her voice was very soft. "Will you be back?"

"I don't know," I said.

It crossed my mind, as we said goodbye in the street, that she expected me to kiss her. But she was wearing heavy makeup and I didn't want to smudge it.

I was back in Mexico City the following week, and I went, to pass a few hours before my plane left, for old-time's sake, or for some reason I don't really want to admit to myself, to the Chapultepec zoo. I bought a hot dog and an orange soda and I walked along the winding paths shaded by eucalyptus and ancient *ahuehuetes*. The tiger I had fed so many years ago had died. The panda was on loan to a zoo in Washington, D.C., a little plaque said. I saw a gorilla with its tiny baby, a family of gibbons, a frantic chinchilla in a small cage. The zoo was nearly empty, but for a noisy group of schoolchildren in their navy blue uniforms. An old man sat on a bench, tossing popcorn to the pigeons.

I found the jaguarundi in a glassed-in cage, in a pavilion near the exit. It was sleeping, its head in its paws. Its fur was speckled with white. It looked thin. The cage had a backdrop painted to look like a jungle, with sloppy olive-green banana trees and a cloudless turquoise sky. I clapped my hands, but the jaguarundi didn't move. Its food dish was covered with flies. I clapped my hands again, louder this time, and its eyes flicked open. The jaguarundi looked at me without moving. Then it yawned and rolled over on its side.

I thought I might tap on the glass, call out its name. But for the life of me I couldn't remember what it was.

Tommy

There are people who remain connected to us throughout our lives, who seem to follow a similar trajectory, more often through accident than design. It was that way with Tommy Pendleton and me: all those years since we'd both left Fields, Ohio, right up until last week when I got the call from his sister Betty. Strange how quickly I placed her: regal brown Betty Pendleton, four grades ahead, the school's first black homecoming queen. I hadn't seen her in over twenty years. Now, Betty's tone was pleasant and matter-of-fact, with the familiar flattened vowels and slow drawl of our hometown. She'd just flown in to San Francisco, she started off in a chatty way. I knew better than to think this was just a social call.

Her voice softened ever so slightly as she asked if I'd heard about Tommy. That he'd died—this past Wednesday—and his funeral service was going to be held day after tomorrow in Oakland. Did I think I could make it? When I recovered myself, Betty said sweetly, "I'm so sorry, Marsha," as if she'd done something wrong.

My "yes" got lost in my throat. I jotted down the address of the chapel in someone else's shaky handwriting.

"I'm glad you can come," Betty said. "You were one of his best friends. The Lord bless you."

When I hung up, I realized that when I'd asked, "How?" Betty had avoided the word "AIDS." Instead, she said, "Pneumonia." I cursed myself for not having figured out that Tommy was sick. Of course he wouldn't have told me, not the way he was about these things, always so clever about protecting himself. But it would explain his conversion to religion, the final wedge between us that made it so difficult to communicate much at all the last couple of years. "Best friend," I thought bitterly. Tommy and I were never best friends. I don't cry often, but I let myself go on this one.

Back in Fields, all through junior high and high school there were only three of us in the advanced classes. Me, Diane McGee, and Tommy, a regular triumvirate of color, toting around our accelerated literature anthologies and advanced trig textbooks, along with the other college placement kids.

The Tarbaby Triplets, Diane used to joke, loud-talking in her more audacious moods, just to make the white kids turn red. In that snowy dominion, we did manage to quietly flourish, three dark snowflakes alighting on the ivory pile like bits of ash. We ran the spectrum from light to dark — Tommy the color of a biscuit, me cinnamon brown, and Diane bittersweet dark chocolate — handpicked from our 40 percent of the population there in Fields and carefully interspersed among the white kids for that slow-fizzling illusion known in our liberal town as racial harmony. Other than that, we had little to do with one another. Me, Diane, and Tommy, someone's proof of something, all going our separate ways, Diane with the black kids, Tommy with the white, and me floundering somewhere in between.

It was in junior high that Diane indignantly informed our stunned English class that we were no longer "colored," nor "Negro," but "black." She spat out the word with proud anger that reverberated distantly within a part of an as-of-yet undiscovered me. I quickly seconded her outburst, conscious of the puzzled looks of my white classmates. Hadn't they guessed, I thought, sitting there year after year, tolerating us and taking their own privilege for granted? Hadn't it ever occurred to them that beneath our agreeable demeanors there was more than just a faint rumble of discontent? Diane held out one long, thin ebony arm. "Can't you see?" she demanded. "I'm not colored. Everybody's *colored*. I'm *black*."

The whole time she talked, her voice trembling and passionate, Tommy Pendleton sat stiffly in his seat, never saying a word. I didn't have the nerve, but Diane did. "You too, Tommy Pendleton," she needled. "You too, *brother*." There was a barely perceptible flutter of movement in his left jaw.

The Pendletons owned a small horse farm on Lincoln Street not far from Mt. Zion Baptist Church. There were four boys and Betty, Tommy being the youngest. Mr. Pendleton was a cripple, his body hunched and crumpled like an aluminum can. Years before, he'd been the victim of a horrible riding accident. Everyone said the crippling had affected his mind, as if twisted limbs could spawn a meanness of spirit. You could catch him out back in his icy field in the most inclement weather, staggering among his horses, as if daring another one to kick him.

Tommy's mother was known as "the invisible woman." She was a Jehovah's Witness, spent all her time inside praying. Rumor had it that Mrs. Pendleton was so weak she let Tommy's father padlock the refrigerator so Tommy and his brothers wouldn't eat him out of house and home.

"That man is downright stingy and hateful," Diane informed me once. She lived just down the street from the Pendletons. "He treats those boys something awful. Beats them—those grown boys, too. That's why Tommy's *that way*, you know."

Back then, I hadn't a clue what she meant. Diane knew so much, but I was too caught up in myself to understand.

Tommy never seemed troubled. Every morning he sauntered good-naturedly up the school's circular walkway with the boys in our advanced classes, or goofed off with white girls at their lockers.

Tommy, never pretending one thing while being another, eventually slipped through the cracks of rebuke and after a while the black kids seemed to forgive him for his betrayal and left him in peace. He was so determined in his position that people quit linking him to the Toms and Oreos who faked it on both sides. It was as if, at least in our minds, Tommy had ceased to be black, or even white. He was just Tommy, handsome Tommy Pendleton ("Mr. *Too* Fine Tommy Pendleton, some of us girls used to concede enviously), even in his downright square clothes: long-sleeve cotton button-down shirts, pressed slacks, and lace-up Hush Puppies from J.C. Penney's in Elyria. When the other black kids were growing their hair, Tommy kept his short and cropped like a newly mowed lawn. You wouldn't have caught him dead with a cheesecutter in his pocket or a braid in his head.

Instead, he walked off with the highest test scores and model essays, posing solemnly for yearbook photos of the Speech, Drama, and Chess Clubs, the only poppyseed in the bunch. His best friend was a white egghead named Paul Malloy.

"The Pendletons must be so proud," my mother used to say wistfully of Tommy's top grades. "Watch, that boy ends up at Harvard."

Big deal Harvard, I grumbled to myself, let him go ahead off with a bunch of peckerwoods and see if anybody cared. Tommy aroused in me all my own uncertainty, about myself, about my awkward friendship with a shy white girl named Mary, about militant Diane acting like everyone's conscience, about my goody-twoshoes boyfriend Phil Willis, and the accompanying push and pull of contradictions. I used Tommy as proof that I was more acceptable.

Though we saw each other daily all through grade school and junior high, we rarely spoke. High school was no different. Even now I can remember only little incidents, like the time he broke a piece off the black frames of his glasses during silent reading and

I wordlessly took them from him and repaired them with a piece of masking tape from my bookbag. As the weeks wore on, he never bothered to have his glasses fixed. I derived an odd and private satisfaction from seeing the piece of masking tape there. Too bad, I used to think, too bad he's so fine and so peculiar.

Social divisions run all latitudes and longitudes, and we were all mostly too busy worrying about black and white and on which side of the racial borders romance was flowering to give much attention to what Tommy Pendleton might actually be.

After high school, turned upside down by racial tensions and old pains, I went off to college in the rolling hills of southern Ohio; Tommy predictably left for Harvard on a scholarship, though his father had loudly protested. But our lives, oddly enough, remained entangled long after Diane McGee turned to drugs, my old boyfriend Phil Willis married a white girl named Ellen, and I had moved as far away from Ohio as I could get.

The morning of Tommy's funeral service I canceled my classes in San Francisco and drove over the East Bay Bridge to the Chapel of the Chimes where Tommy's body lay. I took a seat on a wooden pew in the very back of the chapel. It was an odd bunch, to say the least—mourners taken from someone else's life, I couldn't help thinking. Half the pews were filled with formally dressed Japanese business people from a company Tommy had done legal work for. The other half were occupied by mostly well-scrubbed white couples who looked as if they might want to sell me insurance. There was a sprinkling of single men, what Tommy used to in his rare candid moments jokingly refer to as "friends of Dorothy." The front row was packed with a conspicuous group of black women in silk dresses and oversized hats, obviously relatives. There were a couple of men as well, portly and graying. All I could see were the backs of their heads, but I had a feeling Betty and Mrs. Pendleton were among them.

Viewing the corpse was a shock. I had never looked at the dead body of someone my own age, pasted and glued together with heavy makeup, worn out from the ravages of a devastating disease. It didn't look like Tommy at all, too pale, too thin. I turned away, ignoring the woman next to me who was murmuring, "Doesn't he look just wonderful?"

I was both stunned and angered by the simplistic explanation of Tommy's death which, according to the minister, was "part of God's wonderful plan to call his son Tommy home, because Tommy had special business with God." Still no mention of AIDS. It was as if Tommy's "special business" was the reassurance we all needed to pacify us against the senselessness of his death. Easier to believe God chose Tommy than to believe Tommy had slept with many men. I thought about one of the last conversations I'd had with him. I'd accused him of choosing this religion as a way of turning his back on himself. He was smart enough to know what I meant, and he looked pained. Now I wanted to yell, "It's not true!" Somehow, deep inside, I think Tommy might almost have approved.

I kept waiting for someone else to object. I looked to the front row; not so much as a feather on those wide-brimmed hats trembled. As the minister talked on about Tommy's talents (he'd directed the church youth choir), I wondered which one, if any, of those starchy looking white men present had caused him to grow sick and die. I studied the bowed heads, the impassive faces, the soft "Praise the Lord's," and I knew that no one here, except maybe me, was really part of Tommy's past.

The gravesite was three blocks away up a green hill. I parked my car and stood on the periphery, feeling anxious. An overly polite white couple in shades of gray and black and moussed hair accosted me. "We're Bill and Cynthia, friends of Tommy's from church. Are you a *relative*?"

I shook my head. "We grew up together, back in Ohio."

"Oh!" they cooed, "isn't that nice?" I was suddenly being introduced around to strangers. "This is Marsha. She grew up with Tommy in Ohio."

In a way it was true, I thought, truer than anyone could imagine, the growing-up part, I mean. The words rebounded unexpectedly like a heavy fist. I moved back along the edges of the mourners. As the preacher prayed over Tommy's casket, I wandered a ways up the cemetery hillside and looked out over the Bay, the stunning view from Tommy's gravesite, which he would never see, now that he would soon be six feet underground.

The Christmas dance of 1969—such a silly thing, but a turning point of sorts. Tommy and I had never talked about it. Not when we ran into each other one summer on Harvard Square, not when we stumbled on each other in the Cleveland Art Museum one wintry afternoon during Christmas break. And not even when Tommy moved to San Francisco and shared my apartment for six months, shortly after I'd finished graduate school and he was studying for the California bar exam. I knew better than to think Tommy had actually forgotten. Perhaps it was why he felt comfortable inviting me as his "date" to subsequent law office parties and events, even holding my hand sometimes when we were among strangers.

Tommy could be so peculiar about his private life. I mean, one minute he and I would be laughing about the baths and red rooms and glory holes and the games boys used to play, and the next he'd draw back, like a crab in its shell, and say disapprovingly, "MAR-sha," as if I'd said something too personal for him.

Even when Tommy shared my apartment and I'd go to tease him about one of his occasional tricks I'd passed that morning in the hallway, he'd tell me sternly, "It isn't what you think."

"Then what is it?" I'd ask him.

"It's too complicated," he answered. "Don't try to figure it out."

Actually, one night I did broach the subject of the 1969 Christmas dance. Tommy and I were sitting around the kitchen table eating fried egg sandwiches and laughing about the old days in Ohio. We were laughing about Fields, about Diane McGee, about the time gay Terence Lords put on makeup and ran down the school hallway shouting, "I'm ready for my close-up, Mr. De-Mille!"

"Tommy . . ." I began, still convulsed with laughter. "Tommy, do you remember that stupid dance we went to?" It slipped out before I knew it.

He looked up at me in such a way that the laughter died on my lips. And then the phone rang. Tommy went to answer it, and from the other room I heard him say cheerfully, "Hi, Jeff." A pause, followed by a low soft chuckle, and then the door of his bedroom closed. A terrible pang cut through me. I had underestimated, as I often did with Tommy, the ways I could offend him.

The 1969 Christmas dance happened like this. In tenth grade I broke up with Phil Willis because, in my teen arrogance, I decided he was a nobody. His only future was to inherit his father's bakery, one of two black-owned businesses in town, and I couldn't picture myself behind the counter for the rest of my life wearing a white baker's apron and serving up dozens of oatmeal cookies to local kids. His parents were what we used to call "siddity." They were extremely fair people, with pink skin and curly sandy hair, the kind of "good Negro that, oh, if only the others could be like, we wouldn't have such problems." Mrs. Willis headed the Boy Scout troop, composed mostly of little white boys, Phil being the exception. Oh, how people like the Willises kidded themselves! Black is black, no matter how white.

I myself had found this out the hard way when, the summer after tenth grade, my friend Mary's family became "concerned." They thought Mary ought to be relating more to her own "peers," and stopped finding it convenient to have me over. Finally, when confronted, Mary's mother informed us gently that we were too old now to continue our friendship, that there would be too many problems. I knew exactly what Mary's parents believed to be in store for Mary: tall, jet-black friends of my boyfriends with hair like tumbleweed sidling up to their front porch asking for porcelain Mary in silky whispers; parties on the east side of town where Mary might dance a hairsbreadth from dark-skinned boys in Ban-Lon shirts and smelling of hair oil.

I started hanging out with other black girls, Camille Hubbard and Monica Pease, who lived on streets named for presidents. We'd meet after school for our singing group and practice in the choir room, and then accompany one another home. I now bypassed the streets named for trees, avoiding the route Mary and I used to take.

Just after Halloween, Camille and Monica and I sneaked into a college dance on borrowed ID's. It was that night I fell in love with Calvin Schumate, a student majoring in political science. Calvin was the kind of boy who gets under your skin and keeps you restless every second of the day. He was, in the opinions of Camille and Monica, just about the *finest, toughest, bossest* thing that ever set foot on the college campus, *ooooh, girl.* Tall and chocolate brown. His hair was thick and wild, and added softness to his angular face. He was a full three years older than I, an abyss I leaped with pure frenzy.

That first night I danced every record with Calvin. He danced New York, I danced Detroit. "You've got some moves there," he said admiringly. Afterwards, dripping sweat, we wandered into the moonlight, fanning ourselves with paper napkins. I suffered from that delicious exhaustion when one is beyond caring. Calvin clasped my hand in his, walked me out to the square, and kissed me so deeply I thought he'd sucked my heart out.

I accepted his ring. My parents heard about this through the grapevine and confronted me immediately.

"He's a full-grown man," said my father, "and you're still a young girl. He's much too old for you."

"He'll pressure you," worried my mother. "He'll expect things of you. I don't understand for the life of me why you broke up with Phil. Now those were nice people, the Willises, whatever could you be thinking?"

I could explain it: Calvin came from the mean streets of Harlem, which was about as exotic as you could get for a sheltered middle-class black girl from a tiny Ohio college town. And he was brilliant and tough. He had grown up in a neighborhood where streets were numbered, where everybody had a hustle, and junkies shot dope in the alleys. He'd shot it himself, he told me, and gambled, and hung around prostitutes until his fed-up father finally dragged him around to the nuns at a Catholic boarding school and insisted they and their God "do something with my wild boy before he gets himself killed."

I thrilled to these stories of the precocious street hood turned scholar, wise and sassy beyond his years, full of himself, and not fooled for one minute by me and what he called my "bourgeois thinking."

My parents and I fought terribly about Calvin. Raised voices and slammed doors were not acceptable at our house, yet the subject of Calvin provoked both.

"He's not even Catholic," my mother fretted.

"He went to Catholic school."

"Not the same," said my mother. "Phil's Catholic."

"I don't love Phil!"

"You don't love this boy either. You're too young. You'll thank us later," my mother went on. "We have only your welfare in mind."

My father warned me, "I want to see you go on to college and get a good education. A boy like Calvin could get you involved in things . . ." His voice trailed off at that intersection of truth where what he really wanted to say lay well beyond what a man can comfortably say to his own daughter.

Little did my parents know that their cryptic, anxious warnings came too late. I did not mean to be careless, but Calvin had a man's ways and a man's ideas. He told me the most compelling things a man can tell a woman, and I was a foolish, lovesick girl with my nose open a mile wide.

We pursued a ritual of clandestine meetings in his dorm room, dangerous and heated congresses, where under sagging fishnets suspended from the ceiling a red strobe light whipped over our bodies with the force of fireworks and stern-faced posters of Malcolm X and Huey Newton observed our tussles grimly. Jasmine incense burned ceremonially in a small ceramic holder by the bed. Now, I was still cautious about certain things and refused Calvin the final token of romantic commitment, but we played at everything else, tumbling around in his sheets, even showering together after in his yellow-tiled shower stall, with me soaping up his thick gorgeous hair. He'd lie naked in bed and read me Harlem Renaissance poetry and essays by Baldwin. We listened over and over to the Last Poets, memorizing together the rhythms of our own lives and talking about "the struggle," Calvin explaining to me earnestly what it meant to be part of a revolution. When he was out on the town square, megaphone in hand, railing against "the Man," I stood on the edge of the crowd, reading his passionate appeals as a secret message directed to me.

At Calvin's urging I took the straightener out of my hair and grew a curly 'fro. I talked more and more about the Revolution, and took to wearing dashikis and brass bangles and the African elephant-hair bracelet Calvin gave me. In my sophomore speech class I expounded on such subjects as "The Role of the New Black Womyn" and the necessity for black students to bear arms. I was Calvin's mouthpiece, his right hand. I was frightening even to myself, uncovering decades of rage my parents had covered over with their prosperity.

"Girl, where the hell do your folks think you are all the time?" Camille wanted to know as she waited for me outside Calvin's dorm room one afternoon.

"Aren't you afraid of . . . *you* know . . . ?" Monica asked.

"Calvin and I don't do that," I informed them self-righteously. Virginity was still a big deal back then, and I wore mine like a badge. "I love Calvin and he loves me, but *that* is out of the question."

I believed what I offered Calvin was enough for any man. I believed Calvin when he said we were two lost halves who'd made a whole, destined to leave our mark on the world together, and that our grapplings in the dark were a natural extension of the sublime communion that passed between us as two exceptional lovers.

And so the Christmas dance approached. I was crazy with wanting to bring Calvin, just long enough to stroll through the door with him and let everyone who'd ever snubbed me, black and white, see me with my fine college brother on my arm. I wanted to set their ignorant tongues to wagging.

It was out of the question.

My mother began pestering me about making up with Phil. She even went so far as to drop hints about having seen Mrs. Willis at Sparkle Market and letting me know that Phil had looked longingly at her when she stopped in the bakery to buy a pie. "You need a date for the dance," she pressed.

And that's when I seized on the idea. In a moment of pure inspiration I became the architect of a crafty plan: I couldn't stand Phil, but I could, yes, I would, invite Tommy Pendleton. The perfect camouflage. My parents, content to think I was finally out with a "nice boy," would extend my curfew, and after I'd pleaded the flu and rid myself of the unsuspecting Tommy, the remaining hours would be spent in rapture with Calvin.

Camille's only comment, when I told her, was "You might as well invite a white boy as invite Tommy Pendleton."

Frostily I approached Tommy outside of English class a day or two later. It felt more like a business proposition than a party invitation, but I said my piece in a casual, upbeat tone I had rehearsed in front of the bathroom mirror.

Tommy studied me a moment, fingering the masking tape on his black-framed glasses. For a moment I thought he might say no, a possibility that had not occurred to me. "Okay," he said simply, as if it were about time a black girl like me showed interest. Perhaps it was relief I saw in his face, more than expectation. "Thank you," he added. I walked off feeling strangely sad.

I bought a new orange minidress and matching fishnet stockings and T-strap, sling-back heels. I even roamed the lingerie department and selected a silk bra-and-panty set, with Calvin and Calvin alone in mind. This would be the night, I thought, my entire body radiating the heat of anticipation. I would be sixteen in the spring; it was time.

"Why doesn't Tommy pick you up?" my mother asked over an early dinner.

"He doesn't drive," I explained, which was conveniently true. "You know how weird and strict the Pendletons are, with that crippled dad and all their crazy religion that's gone to their heads."

"Now that's no way to talk about folks," said my mother, the devout Catholic. "Make sure you two stop by here so your father and I can get a peek."

They were suspicious of my sudden interest in Tommy Pendleton, but I could read the one word in their minds: *Harvard*.

I drove my father's blue Buick LeSabre across Main Street to Tommy's house. When I pulled into the dark driveway and honked, the headlights picked up Mr. Pendleton's twisted silhouette out near the small barn behind the house. He might have been a crooked, leafless tree. A shiver ran through me as though I'd had a premonition. Then the porch light flashed on and Tommy's father vanished into wintry darkness. Mrs. Pendleton stood foregrounded on the porch, her arms clasped across her chest to ward off the chilly December night. She motioned me to come in. Reluctantly, I cut off the motor and got out of the car.

It was the first time I'd ever seen Mrs. Pendleton up close. She was a plain woman, but not severe. She wore her hair pulled back in a loose bun, and a long, brown flowered housedress. She had been pretty once.

"Hello, Marsha," she greeted me with warmth and drew me by my arm into the stale house. "I've heard so much about you. Tommy says you're in all his classes."

"Except P.E.," I clarified nervously. The house was overheated and the smell of cooking grease hung in the air.

Mrs. Pendleton offered to take my coat and insisted I join her for a cup of tea. I had no choice. The house was uncannily silent. Tommy was nowhere in sight. I took a tentative seat on the sofa under a triple portrait of Martin Luther King and the Kennedy brothers. Just knowing they hovered above disturbed my conscience.

"So, Tommy tells me your father teaches at the college." She seated herself across from me, her eyes bright in that smooth, serene face.

"Administration," I corrected her. "He works in administration."

"Isn't that wonderful!" She asked me all about my mother, my brothers, and the exact location of our house. "Of course," she said, "that lovely big white one on the corner of Pine. And I know who your mother is too. Pretty woman, has all that nice thick hair."

She prattled on, appraising me with her eyes as if I were an article of clothing she was assessing for a good fit. Guilt made me overcompensate. I had what folks call good home training, and I didn't hold back. Each courtesy seemed to please her more, until I realized my politeness would be my own undoing.

Her smile was broad now. "I'm just so pleased you two are

going to this dance. I don't normally let Tommy go to such things, but I know what a nice girl you are."

I glanced nervously at my watch. When I looked up, Tommy was standing in the doorway in a dark brown suit, his hair parted on one side. We exchanged cautious hellos.

Mrs. Pendleton had a camera ready and she insisted we pose before the fireplace. "Turn this way, you two," she cooed. "Now, give me a big smile. I can't see your eyes, Tommy."

Tommy removed his glasses and held them behind his back as he squeezed awkwardly beside me. We stared dutifully into the blinding flash.

"Oh, the flowers!" Mrs. Pendleton disappeared into the kitchen and I heard the refrigerator door open and close. Too quickly, I thought, for her to have undone a padlock.

She'd seen to it I had a corsage, something frilly and white, with perfume and ribbons, which she pulled from the chilled box. She handed the corsage to Tommy and then photographed him pinning it to my chest ("Oh, I wish I'd known you were going to wear orange!"), cautioning him when he came too close to my breasts ("Careful now, you don't want to stick your little girl-friend!"). I could see how hard she was trying, how important this moment was to her. She wanted to make things right.

Tommy was flustered under the pressure. Beads of sweat broke out over his forehead.

"Now put your arm around Marsha's waist," insisted Mrs. Pendleton. "There, now don't you make a lovely looking two-some? Praise the Lord."

The flash went off three or four more times. I finally pleaded sensitivity to bright lights.

"Look at me keeping you all to myself. I wish the others were around. I'm so sorry Tommy's father wasn't here tonight to see you two off."

I was still at an age when a lie from an adult startled me. Mrs. Pendleton followed us to the door, her eyes bright as a child's: her son Tommy was off to a dance with a girl, and a black one at that, and now she had the pictures to prove it. She stood on the porch clutching the camera as if she'd just photographed Our Lady of Lourdes.

"My parents want us to stop by," I explained dully to Tommy as we came down the driveway.

"*Quid pro quo*," he said agreeably, but I had no idea what he meant.

Fortunately my parents seemed satisfied just to have us stand in the living room and be viewed. Tommy was not Phil, but my mother made over him just the same. Coatless, she and my father braved the cold and followed us onto our front porch.

"So, will it be Harvard or Princeton?" my father asked Tommy, already joining the two of us in his mind's eye.

"Let them go, Ralph. Have a nice time," said my mother. "Don't worry about hurrying home. Take your time."

We piled back into the LeSabre, and I backed out of the snowy drive. By now it was almost nine, and I was frantic. Calvin's face loomed before me; I felt the irresistible pull of his soft lips on my neck.

"I need to stop by the college for a minute," I said on impulse. "I have to drop something off to a friend."

Tommy didn't object. Instead, he sat stiffly in the passenger seat, staring out the window.

We drove the few blocks to Calvin's dorm. I left the engine running and my maxi coat flung across the back seat: a promise that I would return quickly.

Adrenaline swelled my pulses. Every joint in my body throbbed as if badly bruised. I scampered quickly in my thin-soled T-straps through the darkness, feeling the cold on my half-naked feet and in my bones. Calvin was a hot fire in my brain.

I took the stairs two at a time, coming up through the propped-open fire-exit door. I was Cinderella from the ball. I tapped at his door. No answer. I tapped again. Then again.

"Who're you looking for?" asked a boy poking his head out from the room next door.

"Calvin." My tone implied privilege.

"He's gone."

I should have left it at that and headed for the dance with Tommy. I should have realized that the fever and chills alternately coursing through me signaled danger. But I couldn't resist one more knock, and then the knob was in my hand, turning much too easily, and the sudden chill of my own body startled me in the wake of damp heat that poured toward the open door.

It was like entering a sauna. First the dimness, then the steam rising from Isaac Hayes's brooding *Hot Buttered Soul* album and mingling with the essence of jasmine incense. The air was thick and moody, the candlelit walls alive with ambiguous shadows.

A motion from the corner of the room caught my eye, and then it became two separate motions I saw: one was Calvin rising up from the sheets, with nothing but his medallion around his neck; the other was the silhouette of a long dark body with large tubular breasts and a huge halo of black hair unfolding itself with knowing insolence.

Someone exclaimed, "Oh, my God!" There was a sudden flurry of sheets and pillows and brown limbs, then a woman's voice cried out, "Calvin, what the hell is going on here?" and I realized it was me speaking, using the tone of voice I had imagined only a woman capable of.

"Marsha!"

I didn't recognize my own name. I yelled, "Bastard!" and ran out, twisting my ankle when one of my heels caught on the carpet.

I was too stunned to cry. My chest threatened to cave in on itself. As I ran back out the fire exit, I found I could not catch my breath. Panic set in. It took several minutes of standing in the outside stairwell below, pulling in the frosty air with lungs so tight I thought they would explode.

I had never suspected, because I lacked the experience to suspect.

I stuffed my fist in my mouth and bit down hard until I tasted salt. I shook my hand free and thrust it into a thin layer of snow to stop the pain. And then there was nothing to do except walk back around to the other side of the dorm and get into my father's car next to Tommy Pendleton as if nothing had happened. My voice had disappeared somewhere deep in my throat. As if mutu-ally agreed upon, I said nothing and Tommy said nothing. We went grimly on to the dance at the school gym, my heart as hard as a rock.

The gym was decorated with Christmas tree boughs and rib-bons. An inflatable Santa-and-reindeer set hung from the ceiling. A huge fir tree stood in the middle of the floor, lit up and covered with red balls and silver tinsel.

After we'd gotten ourselves settled and I'd managed to swallow some punch, Tommy asked me to dance. We moved stiffly around the floor, nodding to people we knew. "You look very nice," he told me. "You really do."

His touch left me cold inside. I kept my face turned.

We joined Tommy's red-haired friend Paul Malloy and his date, a pale white girl named Lisa from Firelands. Tommy and Paul immediately began whispering together. I made a point of ignor-ing them all, including Lisa, who was feeling ignored by Paul. She kept trying to show off her corsage that seemed to have taken root right there on her wrist.

"So are you and Tommy going together?" she asked.

"No," I told her and turned my head. Monica and Camille appeared then in jovial moods with dates they'd gotten from a Catholic school in Cleveland. They were both dressed and per-fumed and oiled, looking like Cheshire cats.

"How's your health?" asked Monica boldly, with a meaningful look at the clock.

Camille flashed a wicked smile. "Feeling a little sick, Marsha?"

Sitting there with them all, my surroundings melted away and I realized how alone I was, nursing my grief in this empty space. I was seized with panic, afraid I could never dare desire again. Cold terror set in like rigor mortis. In my mind, the door to Calvin's room kept shutting sharply behind me as if forced by a fast wind.

Monica whispered to me that she had a fifth of Wild Turkey in her Rambler. I rose up and followed like a sleepwalker, leaving Lisa and Paul and Tommy sitting there. Outside in the wintry air I shivered in my thin dress. We sat on chilly vinyl car seats, me on one end, Camille on the other. Monica opened the bottle deftly, trying to prove she was practiced. Before us, our lighted school blazed like an alien spaceship that had just landed next to the expanse of football field.

I took several long swallows of fiery liquid.

Monica poked me with her elbow. "Come on, girl, what's bugging you? It's Christmas. Tommy looks go-o-o-d." She urged the bottle on me again.

I swallowed my agony and enough Wild Turkey to fuse my nerves back together. The slow burn rounded off the razor-edge of suffering. Camille took the bottle and shoved it under the front seat. The three of us climbed out and bent, shivering and coatless, into the fury of white.

The fiery pain that seared me comes only once in one's life: it is that first scorch of real grief. It is like losing a limb; surprise and horror join forces at the junction of what should be the impossible. At that moment I would have traded my sight to erase what I had seen in Calvin's room.

When Camille and Monica got up to dance with their dates, I informed Tommy flatly that we had to leave. No explanation. He seemed only mildly surprised. As I gathered my coat and purse, I saw him pause and say something to Paul. When we walked out, Camille and Monica cast knowing glances at me over their dates' shoulders.

In the car, when I put the key in the ignition, I burst into tears and cried for several minutes into the collar of my maxi coat, without explanation. I lowered my head onto the steering wheel while Tommy sat dutifully by.

Finally he said, "Is there anything I can do, Marsha?"

"No," I sobbed.

"It was probably hard for you to see Phil Willis there with someone else."

Phil! I hadn't even noticed.

"I know," said Tommy, "it's always hard to be with the wrong person." Consumed with my grief, I took this is an apology, Tommy's acknowledgment of his failure.

"I'm not ready to go home yet," I told him. I eased the car onto the highway, away from town, and turned directly into the snow. I had no destination, only found satisfaction in the motion of the car. We ended up driving eight miles in the wrong direction, to the edge of Lake Erie, where we sat in my father's car, listening to CKLW from Detroit and staring out at the black frozen space ahead.

As for what happened next, I can't make any excuses for Tommy, except to say that perhaps he was just plain curious about himself and desperate to have an answer.

And as for me, I had grown sleepy from the Wild Turkey and my own grief, and when I closed my eyes I could almost imagine it was Calvin, gathering me against him, then brushing his lips against mine, pressing against my chest, then bearing down on me, lifting my dress, tugging at my orange fishnets.

"Do you really want to do this?" I asked the boy hovering over me, my eyes still tightly closed against the black void. There was no answer, just a purposeful sigh into the hollows of my right ear.

That was all the encouragement I needed to move over the edge. How simple it was to plunge downward when the bottom was no longer in sight! All that foolish, dutiful teetering I had done, adding to the ever-spiraling tension between me and

Calvin—the tortured refusals, the last-minute "I can'ts" whispered breathlessly through our tangled bodies—now gone flat as a bicycle tire. What did it matter? The next thing I knew, strong hands were extended and someone waited below to catch me. Warmth melted my frozen body, and I fell into forgetfulness, floating gently alongside the two joined bodies in the front seat of my father's car. I dropped off to sleep then, and upon opening my eyes later I was surprised, even shocked, to find myself crushed against Tommy Pendleton inside the cold damp car. The side windows had steamed over, the windshield wore a thick coat of snow. Tommy was sitting up straight again, staring out where the lake should have been. He was wearing his black-framed glasses. With one hand, he reached out and gently caressed my hair as if I were a small animal he had just rescued.

After that night, Tommy Pendleton and I still didn't speak much at school. Sometimes in class I'd catch myself looking at the back of his head, trying to connect it with an old longing that never surfaced. As for Calvin, I kept taking him back, a sucker for his inexhaustible excuses, so we were together off and on for the next year or so. He finally admitted he was engaged to a tall black girl named Charmaine from New Jersey. By the time we actually broke things off, it seemed easy. I was already packed for college, a new life ahead.

Over the years I have often compared myself to that anonymous girl, the one in Calvin's bed that night: her sweat-glistening face, her swollen mouth, her big brown legs unwinding themselves from Calvin's back, her breasts rising and falling obscenely, her eyes like flames.

Tommy and I performed nothing like that in the front seat of my father's car. It was something much simpler, much less eventful, and, under the circumstances, quite forgivable. So much so that I maintained I was a virgin until my freshman year of college when I met Nicholas Rush from Chapel Hill, North Carolina.

Now, as I headed back down the green slope toward where Tommy's casket was being lowered into the ground, I was startled to hear my own name. "Marsha! Marsha Hendrickson!" A tall brown woman in dark red, with a black hat, moved from the group of mourners toward me. "Is it really you, Marsha?"

"Mrs. Pendleton!" She saw my tears and approved of them. This was that same woman who had coaxed Tommy and me closer together in her living room some twenty years before, to record a lie that would give her comfort later on.

"Oh, I'm so glad you could come!" she said. "This means ever so much to me. You remember Tommy's brother Joseph? This is his wife Margaret." They were a handsome couple who studied me solemnly. I'd forgotten how much alike Joseph and Tommy looked; it was like seeing double. "This is Marsha Hendrickson, Tommy's high school girlfriend." I let the exaggeration pass.

Joseph and Margaret nodded with mild interest. Mrs. Pendleton clutched my arm. "Betty said you'd be here. She's already back at Tommy's now getting things ready for the potluck. You *will* join us, won't you?"

Before I could respond, she went on, "Praise the Lord, he didn't have to suffer long. The pneumonia came on so quick. He lost his hearing, then his eyesight. In the end, he couldn't remember even simple things. But he wasn't one to complain, not my Tommy. Always kept things to himself."

"That was Tommy," I agreed.

"Yes, Lord love him," she said. She turned to Joseph. "Tommy and Marsha shared an apartment for a while."

She let the innuendo sink in. Then she pulled me against her hip, her hand gripping mine. That was when I knew she knew, that the word "AIDS" would never pass her lips, that she was still trying to make things right. As if we were all off to a party, and not a tear on her face.

"I'm afraid I have to get going," I said. "I have to see students at four." It was a lie, but one that just as carefully matched the conviction of her own sweet deceit.

"Isn't that too bad?" She seemed genuinely disappointed. "It would be so nice . . . so nice to talk again . . ."

Suddenly I was sixteen years old, sitting impatiently on the Pendletons' sofa, thoughts of Calvin having reduced everyone around me to the dispensable. Mrs. Pendleton was removing the corsage from the box, eager to pin me down like a butterfly in someone's collection.

"Oh, please come," she was now insisting, then caught herself. "I'm sorry." She squeezed my waist briefly, eyes lowered. "I'm so sorry it all turned out this way."

I couldn't tell if she was apologizing or blaming me, but in that moment she had come as close as she probably ever would to admitting the truth.

"You take good care, Marsha. It was so nice of you to make it today." She stepped away then, awkwardly, the heels of her dark red pumps catching in the thick green lawn. She clutched Joseph's arm for support. Together they paused at the edge of Tommy's grave and stared down into it. Her face was resigned, and if I hadn't known better I would have thought she was a stranger hesitating out of curiosity, not a mother whose heart was wrung with grief. I wondered then how many times, over the years, she'd studied those photos of Tommy and me, maybe even had one framed for the mantel where it sat like an accomplishment, giving silent testimony. It may have given her much comfort, which was all she was really asking of me now. I turned and walked away. It seemed the only right thing left to do.

ʊʊʊʊʊ *Dianne Nelson*

A Brief History of Male Nudes in America

They step from behind my mother's shower curtain, pose like acrobats and soldiers, they lie bound in the afternoon light of our downstairs bedroom. There are buttons on the floor. Someone's wallet on the dresser. On the back of a chair, a shirt leaves everything to the imagination. The shirt is blue, it is Oxford, it has sweat rings, a pocket, it's a workshirt with the smell of hay still in it, it's khaki, short sleeved, long sleeved, on the back *Sugarloaf Bowl* is machine embroidered with *Del Rio* below it.

I have my eyes open. I see them strut. I see them scurry from the bathroom back to my mother's bed, their big white butts trailing our household like bad winter colds. My mother is divorced and entertains at odd hours.

I get home from school and on the kitchen counter she has a peanut butter sandwich for me or Hostess Snowballs, raisins, applesauce, or a Mars Bar. Under her closed bedroom door there is a crack of light that reminds me of the depths to which we all fall, given time, given enough rope and the disposition for making our own sorrow and then lying in it.

Karl Winckelman's truck is parked out front. My mother's Sheffield bedspread is probably folded back, in thirds, to the end of her bed where it is a silky white margin she tells Karl to keep his feet off. He has undoubtedly come here straight from work. As a construction foreman, Karl sometimes has the option of leaving his job early, and on those occasions he is in my mother's arms by two, the bedspread folded cleanly back by three when I get off the Highland Park High School bus. Karl and my mother move with the scheduled certainty of trains. No sound. The light from beneath my mother's door makes a line of chalk that divides our world—on this side the radio drones and on that side all reason is immediately abandoned. By four they're standing in the kitchen asking me about homework.

"Hey, kiddo," Karl says, pointing at my opened math book. "I have a way of multiplying with my fingers."

For a simple man, Karl confuses me frequently and with great enthusiasm. He goes to work with his fingers, showing seven times six, eight times nine, how you get wild dogs to cross the street, how you get a scaffold to dance down the side of a building.

Karl leans against the refrigerator, and I can see exactly what my mother has had that afternoon: shadow and dark eyes, a square jaw, Noah sleeping with his legs wide apart. In the downstairs bedroom in the afternoon light, Karl stretches out beside my mother and turns white, blank as snow gathering snow, big as a barn, his heart racing on a fool's errand all for my mother.

"I'll tell you one thing," he says, his tanned forehead wrinkling as a prelude to some deep thought. "The day they turn our numbers metric is the day I stop paying union dues. Can you imagine a 2- × 3-meter window? Come on!"

Karl is like a feed bag with a little hole in the corner spilling its contents slowly. Twopenny nails drop from his pockets onto our wood floors or behind the couch cushions. When he walks, his Red Wing boots leave footprints of fine dust picked up from various construction sites.

"Ahhh, look Karl," my mother says, thumbing his tracks caught in sunlight on the newly polished floor.

"What, babe, what?" Karl asks, and there is a real possibility that this man sees nothing, that dust is a given, maybe even the essential ingredient of his world.

"Karl's a darn hard worker," my mother says to me, which is a way of explaining his presence in her bed, though we never talk directly of her bed—a place of sleep and haste and desolation. The expensive Sheffield bedspread cannot change that. Neither can the book she always keeps at her beside, *Egypt in Its Glory*, an oversized photo-journal she ordered from C. C. Bostwick's. My mother gets lost in that book—the beauty of the pyramids, the secrets of papyrus scrolls.

I imagine on their better afternoons that Karl takes my mother somewhere down the Nile, that the waters are soft, that the melon-colored sand eases them from their real lives. Birds stand on one leg. Marble cows low into the ancient moonlight.

Even with his pants down, Karl is all business. My mother has told me this as she sits with a cup of coffee, maybe picking at a cinnamon bun. I know that in the same way Karl creates a building out of rolled-up blueprints he engineers some deep and mysterious pleasure in my mother. I see her walk out of her bedroom with him, and she is flushed, something has been shaken loose, and for a half hour or more she is truly happy. She sits on the kitchen cabinet and eats Fruit Loops out of the box.

My mother doesn't mind discussing her life with me—an only child, a girl already taller than her mother. She explains sex as biology by candlelight. She describes her need and desire as electric impulses that are strong enough to roll a rock uphill. She characterizes her love of men as something that happened to her in the cradle when her mother's back went bad and it was her daddy who held her against his rock chest and in his warm water hands.

She laughs and tells me that Karl likes her on top where he says she is pretty as a cream puff, though I tend to imagine her at that moment as wild-eyed and breathless—something stunned by headlights in a dark night. I don't know why my mother finds no lasting peace.

"Hey, nothing in this life is perfect," she says more times than I can remember. It's meant as the kind of fleshy advice gained through experience, but, in fact, it's a statement my mother repeats so she will believe it. My mother's voice is strong, deep and assuring, but because I am her daughter—conceived on Chinese New Year, she tells me—I can hear the uncertainty. Sometimes when she's talking, if I close my eyes and drift, all I hear is bathwater running.

Karl is not the only one. I see the legs of men and bulls traipsing around our kitchen, looking for something to eat. They work up appetites at our house—man-sized. Cans of tuna, a dozen eggs, a raw red onion sliced thick—I've seen them make sandwiches I couldn't get my hands around.

My mother stands off to the side, sweet in a brocade robe or sexy in a yellow lotto T-shirt, and watches them work her kitchen with the sudden dexterity of hungry men. She points to where the crackers are. She shrugs when she's informed that we are out of milk.

In her way, my mother likes them all. It's not for money that she takes them to her bed, but for lack of words, for something gone wrong with my father that she has no way of explaining. He sometimes calls me from Newark to say hi. He asks me if I'm doing O.K.

"Sure," I say. "Great."

Karl asks me if I've finished my homework. Barry Rivers asks me where I got my green eyes; Tim French, if there are any more clean towels; a one-night Cuban musician, if our dog bites.

I want to tell the musician, "Yeah, he'll take your damn head off," but I answer, "No, never has before."

It's my mother who asks me to help her with Manny Del Rio. Sometime after eleven or twelve she comes into my bedroom and shakes me hard out of sleep. "April," she says, "April, come help me with Manny. I think he's hurt."

It's a Thursday night. This I am sure of because Manny bowls mixed league on Thursdays at Sugarloaf Bowl, then comes by our house for my mother's three-bean soup. Friday mornings he's usually still here. My mother tiptoes out of her room and signals me with one finger to her lips, a sign that has come to mean that all the men of the world are asleep, that they are dear to us in that state, camped out and heavy on our sheets.

In the bottom of our shower that Thursday night, Manny is all flesh — the torso of a grand duke and the short stocky legs of a pipe fitter. He looks up at us out of too much pain to be embarrassed.

"Where does it hurt?" my mother asks him.

Manny cannot decide. He groans, then curses in Spanish. The bar of soap is still under his right foot, the water still beaded across his chest and on his neck.

There is a way to stare politely, and I know how to do it, I've practiced, and I think it's fair to say I'm an expert with my eyes. I give Manny a slow once-over, and I see it all: the broad chest, the narrow hips, wet hair, the story of his life pink and small and lying to the side. I look up at my mother, who hovers over Manny like a dark angel, and maybe it's because I'm still sleepy, but it seems as if we are moving underwater — our hands slow, almost helpless.

"Is it your leg?" I ask Manny, trying to clarify the middle of this crazy night. "Your back? Your arm?"

There is an unbelieving look on his face as my mother and I attempt to pull him out of the shower and onto the cold linoleum floor. "Don't," he tells us. It's as much as he can get out of his mouth at once. Spread, exhausted, Manny lies still and poses for us in our own bathroom, his hip shattered, though none of us will know this until later, after he is picked up by an ambulance and X-rayed at Stormont Vail.

We cover him with a blanket and wait for the paramedics. It seems like a long wait, the three of us in one small room, Manny's hand squeezing the side of the tub in a sad gesture that I can't forget. He is a sweet old-fashioned guy who blushes at a kiss but loves my mother with the force of a bazooka.

We wait forever, which indicates how time passes in this house. My mother flicks her cigarette ashes into the bathroom sink. Realizing that silence is the best alternative here, she stops talking. Her cigarette, then hand, then arm move in one gentle line from knee to mouth and mouth to knee. She exhales with the deepest sigh, one that says life simply cannot be lived this way anymore.

Fat boy cupids, men of stone, athletes, bathers—they kiss and fondle my mother, then give me a sidelong glance. "This is April," she tells them in the way of an introduction. "She's on the honor roll, she's in the choir. You can't slip anything by her, so don't even try. Look at that smile. She's gonna break some hearts in her time, huh?"

Late night or midmorning Judy Garland sings "You made me love you" off one of our old scratchy albums. They are mesmerized. Karl leans his head back in the brown easy chair, closes his eyes, and commits himself to that long languorous kind of beauty. "It's only a song," I tell him. Tim French, in his boxer shorts, does a simple little four-step right there in the living room. He doesn't need a partner. He moves unselfconsciously, and everything moves with him—mind and body, dream and daylight.

At the top of the stairs or in the kitchen doorway, I am where I can see it all: Tim dancing in his own arms, Manny searching for his socks bare-assed, Barry scratching himself as he reads the newspaper. It is a precarious view for a seventeen-year-old. My mother pulls me close to her and says, "You just as well know now." We stand and watch in the doorway together, at the top of the stairs, near the piano, next to her bed, by a chair, by a blanket, by a rug, and in the deepest sense they are beyond us, these men who come visiting.

They step out of their clothes or my mother undresses them, and in the golden light of the Nile they are the bare figures of love and promise. In my mother's care, they see themselves twice their real size, agile, long-limbed, generous, hung like bulls, sweet as new fathers. They are fast to sleep and slow to awaken. She tiptoes out of her room in the mornings and puts her finger to her lips and our world is more quiet than the dark high rafters of a tomb.

I never ask her why, and lately I never ask her who. Karl, Blair, Manny . . . men come and go according to a calendar that only my mother's heart could know.

Laureano, the Cuban musician, drums our coffee table until we have memorized the Latin beat, which he says is the same beat as the heart pumping—da dum, da dum. "That's why you can't ignore Latin music," he tells my mother and me, "because it's the same music as your own body." He taps the left side of his chest where supposedly he has a heart, then winks and stretches out on the couch, dark and suggestive as deep woods. He has grown to love America, he says.

Laureano is a one-nighter, a first and last course all rolled into one. My mother glows for him. She walks across the floor gently, as if it could fall in at any minute. She has filed her fingernails and painted them a soft pastel. She crosses her legs and taps her foot, anxiously pushing the night forward to the moment when she pulls back the bedspread and the air goes thin. My mother will not be satisfied until she has pulled every star from the sky.

Upstairs, in my own bed, I give ten-to-one odds that Laureano will not even show for breakfast.

Mornings are the worst. Everything from the night before has been used up, and it's like starting over. Our lives begin with bare sunlight creeping over the floor, inch by inch. We drink strong black coffee and keep an edgy silence. We are trying not to wake someone, but I can't remember who. Manny? Blair? Tim? They are mostly versions of the same body that scoot from my mother's bed into the bathroom for an early morning pee.

Laureano strolls, and when he looks up and sees me at the end of the hallway he stops short of the bathroom, leans against the wall, and smiles at me with the quick self-assuredness of a lion tamer. I have eyes and I use them. His body is tall and lean—a pen and ink sketch. He moves his left arm slowly up the wall as if he's reaching for something, but nothing is there. He is casual in his nakedness, confident in this small makeshift love scene. I figure it's my hallway, though, so I stare him down. My trick is to stare at the wall just behind him—try to blister the cool white paint. Laureano finally laughs, snaps the spell, and moves with no hurry to the bathroom.

Evenings I sit at a desk in a corner of the living room that my mother insists on calling the study. I open my books and lose myself in homework, in thick black strings of numbers and in the pages of history where fate is swift and lives are not left to sputter and tumble. The yellow pencil in my hand guides me through the night, through the opening and closing of my mother's bedroom door, and through the dull watery sounds of people in the next room.

It's late when she stands over me and says I'm going to ruin my eyes, but she's wrong. I can see every nail hole and scrape on

these walls, I can see the smallest cigarette burn in the sofa, dust
in the corner, a finger-length cobweb in the windowsill. I can see
the storm that has crossed my mother's face and left it soft and
sleepy—obscured as if by the distance of an ocean.

There is a place in me—just under my skin—where everything
and everyone from this house is distinctly remembered.

There are the long muscular arms of David, who sprays our
house for termites in early spring. Under the eaves and around the
baseboards, David has the golden reach of a boxer. He swears we
won't smell a thing. My mother stretches the truth, tells David
that she's seen the signs of termites: a bleached sawdust leaking
where the walls meet. He's standing on a ladder, and she looks up
at him, her hair shining like a new quarter.

I can see Gregory's back and my mother, kissing his vertebrae
one by one, careful and removed as a lady-in-waiting. She won't
let him turn around. He must endure what he is made of.

I remember the strong Norman legs of my grandfather who visits us from Idaho and lounges all day in his robe, pockets full of
Oreos, a milk ring on the table.

I see shoulders without their wings. I remember a bruise as a
place to be kissed. I recall Tony Papineau building a birdhouse in
our backyard so our winter would be crossed with sparrows. My
mother wears a green wool jacket and as his hammer sings she
dances for Tony in the cold.

I love the way that pages in a book feel: smooth and cold, the
edges sharp enough to draw blood. My mother licks her fingers
before she turns the pages of a book. "Easier that way," she says.
She reads about the far-away and long-ago, about primitives ter-
rorized by the moon.

When I open a book I want facts, dates, the pure honesty of

numbers. I want a paragraph faithful enough to draw me away from what's going on in the next room: my mother dragging herself to the bottom, some man thinking it is love.

Blair makes the sound of a wounded duck, which is the combination of a honk and a wheeze. It is not something I would equate with passion, not a sound that I think of in response to my mother's pear-colored skin. In the room next to theirs, I am reading, studying, fighting my way into a book, and that sound goes on forever. The walls of this house aren't thick enough to keep that kind of sadness contained.

I'm sitting at the desk with the English book in my hands, though it just as well be a jellyfish or a brick. The noise goes higher, louder, the duck becomes inconsolable. I strain, but the words on the page are futile hash marks.

Ten steps and I am at the front door, then out into the night, walking as quickly as I can. I live on an old quiet street that's blessed with big trees and where people still use push mowers. The houses are nothing special — bland with red brick, too symmetric with their sidekicker porches. I know some of the names here: Peterson, Barnett, Stanopolous. The only time I've seen the police on this street is the afternoon that Nelda Peterson's eighty-year-old mother fell flat dead in the azaleas and lay there like she was floating until her son-in-law came home that night. That's the only fatality I know of on this street — that is, if you don't count my mother.

When I get to the end of our block, I turn around, and back there is our house — 2431 — and from this distance my mother's lighted bedroom window is no bigger than a postage stamp. My heart is beating recklessly and my hands would be so much better if they had something to hold. I take a breath — the kind that stings the back of your throat — and then I count to ten or twenty or a hundred thousand. Nothing changes. The lights do not flicker. The moon doesn't dip. The sky does not go dark as oil.

I turn around and continue on to the next block and the next, past a row of stores, beyond Ace Hardware, into other neighborhoods where both rambling houses and rattletraps perch at the edge of great lawns, where porchlights shine hot as meteors welcoming somebody home. When finally I don't know where I am anymore, I get smart, as my mother would say. I turn and start back, and at last I'm calm on those sidewalks. I'm limp and light. I watch my feet all the way home, step after step—no melody, no rhythm—until all I know is the beauty of my own shoes.

Winter Money

I've been thinking about Tampa. I'm standing by the window of my room, 203, here at the Hightop Motel in Tomaston, Kentucky, holding the curtain back, watching the sky turn to ash. It's been like this all week. Tomaston has been a bad spot for Amanda and me. I would be surprised now if it didn't rain. Tampa wasn't much of a town for horse racing, but we had it better there.

Amanda doesn't want to go back. She says it would take too much money to rebuild her racing stock, money neither of us has anymore. She wants to take what's left of her horses to Big Chimney Park, a grimy bullring in eastern West Virginia, try to win a race or two there, then unload them. After that she isn't sure what she'll do. Amanda's not a big planner. It's the reason she's never going to get anywhere in this business. It's also the reason she's become pretty good at just getting by.

She told me about West Virginia last week.

"What happens after you get rid of your horses?" I said. She shrugged. It's not as if she would ever think of finding work outside the racetrack. She could find work again back at the track in Tampa, which is what I suggested, but she doesn't want to do that. No more Tampa for Amanda. Tampa is where we met, where we were successful, so I know the problem she has is with me, not some city in Florida where we were happy once.

Something isn't right between us, but I think it's something I can fix if I can show her winter money. Winter money in my pocket means we can go to Florida and rebuild her stock. She can run them when she wants to, not when she has to, and I can find mounts for Grovey on my own time. Amanda and I could get a room back in our old place, the Buccaneer Inn, a motel that's got a little polish to it. Winter money is what we sorely need. I'm not saying Amanda can be bought, but she can be persuaded, and that's one of the things I like about her.

I'm standing here waiting for Grovey to call me back. I've phoned his house three times in the last hour and his girl, Donna, says he's not home. She's lying. She's eighteen years old. When Grovey tells her she's the only girl for him, she believes it. He's probably sitting over in his La-Z-Boy laughing every time she hangs up on me.

Grovey and I have never been friends, but we work well together. He was nearly washed up when I took over his book three years ago. We met in the White City, a cowboy bar in Seward, Nebraska. At the time I was laid up myself, having busted a knee for good when a bull named Monster Man rolled over on me in a rodeo in Great Axe. I needed a job that would let me keep my feet on the ground for a while. He had nothing to lose in getting me for his agent—someone who would talk him up a little with the horsemen. He hired me with a handshake.

Grovey and I went from one track to another, starving a little along the way until we came to Gaspirilla Park in Tampa, which is where I met Amanda. Grovey caught fire there during the winter meet last season. He said I was finally getting him some live mounts. He said the girl must be doing some good. It was a funny thing for him to say.

I was surprised he let me talk him into coming to Old Latonia, the track here in Tomaston. He is forty-four, old for a rider. Most jockeys that age would've been content to finish out their professional days under the sun in Florida. My idea was that we

shouldn't settle for anything just yet. Good riders can hang their
tack anywhere they please, and I saw Grovey taking us right off
this soulless circuit, which is where we seemed to have been since
we started. When I went to talk to Grovey about Old Latonia, he
lit a cigarette, cocked his head, and said, "Why not?" Grovey
wasn't the hard bastard I always thought he was. He still had hope
for the future, which made him different from most journeymen
riders I knew.

Old Latonia is a new racetrack. Why they call it Old Latonia,
I'm not sure. Marketing maybe. I read about the big purses they
were offering for the inaugural meet and figured we'd make twice
as much as we did in Tampa with half the effort.

I had to talk Amanda into coming along then, too. She's been
around horses since she was a kid and didn't seem interested in
improving her outlook, which probably explained more about the
racing business than the *Racing Form* ever could. She'd had a
good meet at Tampa, too, but it only made her want to stay there.
I promised her things about winning and the future and myself. I
don't know what she believed exactly, but when I drove north
with Grovey in the Oldsmobile, she was following behind in her
pickup, pulling a four-horse trailer, singing along with the radio,
smoking cigarettes a mile a minute.

Nothing has gone right since then. The Oldsmobile quit running right before we got to Lexington. It was a car I had barn-
stormed all over the country in, but there it quit on me. It was
four in the morning, and I was driving along with Amanda's lights
just tiny specks in the rearview mirror, and the electricity went
out in my car, but I don't know how. The lights went and the radio
went, and when I tried to ease onto the shoulder I didn't know
where it was, and Grovey and I ended up going down onto a grass
median.

Once we stopped, I tried to make a joke of it. "You should've
been driving, I guess," I said to Grovey.

He wasn't shook up, but he didn't say anything for a minute. Amanda never saw us, drove right by. I guess it was like we disappeared. "Not a good sign," Grovey said. He lit a cigarette.

Amanda said she got concerned after a while when she couldn't see us, but she had no choice but continue driving to Tomaston. There were the horses to consider, she said. I ended up selling the Olds to the guy who towed it, and Grovey and I caught a bus for Tomaston. Amanda already had the stalls bedded down and the horses unloaded by the time Grovey and I got to Old Latonia late that afternoon. I've been borrowing her truck since, and I generally don't like relying on other people for my rides.

Then, as it turns out, the track here was deep and tiring, and Amanda's horses needed more time to get ready for a race, and for a while her patience was thin and she took it out on me. Once she had them fit, they couldn't win. Competition here was tough. A lot more horsemen than I expected had read about Old Latonia.

Grovey started off riding pretty well here, but then that two-year-old flipped in the gate with him, and it laid him up six weeks. He hasn't won a race since he started up again last month. Along with everything else, my money has been running out. I gave Amanda a thousand two weeks ago to keep the feed man off her ass, and it just about left me tapped. The feed man told her he might be able to forget about the bill for a while if she'd let him in her pants. Amanda hadn't exactly made up her mind about what to do about this until I loaned her the money.

An hour ago a man named Kirk called here and told me what we had planned for tomorrow was all set. I need to talk to Grovey, though. That's what Kirk said, "Have you talked to your rider yet?"

"All set," I said. Kirk hung up.

I didn't mind lying to Kirk. All I knew about Kirk was that he was the man setting up this thing tomorrow. He'd called me a few times during the summer offering me a shot at making a small killing at the mutuel windows, if I could get my rider to go along with what Kirk had planned for a certain race. I had always turned him down until this last time.

Grovey must sense what is going on. He's been riding too long not to know how things are, long enough to know panic, which is what he surely must've heard in my voice the last time I talked to him. I'm standing by the window still looking at the sky, occasionally letting my eyes fall to the empty parking lot of this motel.

At a quarter to six the phone rings. It's Donna. "Grovey says he'll see you at seven over here," she says. She laughs. "How was that?" she says away from the mouthpiece.

"I'll be there," I say and hang up. I go to the window again and pull back the curtain. I hope it will go on and rain for a while.

I don't know what Amanda will think about this. She knows that sometimes the result of a race is decided before it is run, and as long as nobody is messing with her horses, I guess she doesn't mind it. Race-fixing is also a kind of habit, something like whiskey, I guess, because there's a point where you start relying on it to get you by. Amanda really doesn't like to rely on anything.

As long as I can show her the money, nothing will matter. We'll forget all about Tomaston and the Hightop. When we first came here, we lingered in our room, made love as often as gifted teenagers, and talked about our plans for the winter. From here we wanted to winter either in Hot Springs or New Orleans. We haven't been to either place. It doesn't feel so bad thinking about it. I'm thirty-three now and don't think much about places I've never been, just places I have, and what went wrong there. So thinking about Hot Springs doesn't hurt so much.

Amanda pulls into the parking lot in her pickup. She gets out and begins to walk this way. I go to the bed and lie down. She doesn't look at me when she comes in. She drops her cloth purse to the floor. I close my eyes as she takes a step towards the bed. In a second I feel the mattress give a little down to the left of my feet.

The springs whine as she shifts momentarily. There is the sound of a boot dropping to the floor, then another whine and shift as the other boot hits the carpet. She seems to take a deep breath. I feel a tug on one of my sneaker laces. I open my eyes. Except for a band atop her forehead, her shiny black hair is tucked under a white bandana with a blue design on it. There are clear pearls of tiny perspiration under her eyes, extending across the bridge of her nose. She stops and looks at me. "I thought of you today," she says.

I lift my head up. "That's a good thing," I say.

She undoes the laces of that shoe and throws it on the floor. "Are you guys riding anything tomorrow?" she says.

I drop my head back to the pillow. "Grovey's got one in the fourth," I say.

She starts on the other shoe. "Should I bet?" she says, pulling off the shoe.

I close my eyes again. "Save your money," I say. She pinches my calf and I open them again. She is looking at me like she sees something she hadn't before. "I'll take care of making us money," I say.

Amanda curls up beside me. "You're up to no good, I know that," she says.

"Let me worry about it."

"It's not going to change anything," she says, dropping her head to my shoulder.

"We'll see," I say.

Donna and Grovey live in a light-blue row house on Cullen Street, about ten blocks from Old Latonia. Grovey hates hotels. He met Donna in the track kitchen, where she was ladling gravy over biscuits. She has a round face and sparkling blue eyes. She's a little on the heavy side, but it doesn't matter to Grovey. He likes young girls.

She opens the door to me. I walk in. "He's in the kitchen," she says. "You missed a button on your shirt." I walk past her. The wood floor is dull and dusty. It smells like they have a dog living in the house, though I don't think that they do.

When I get to the entrance of the kitchen, Grovey is sitting at a small table in the center of the room, his back to me. There's a big box of corn flakes at his elbow. He's sitting on the edge of the chair, his feet barely touching the floor. I walk in and take a chair across from him. The bowl in front of him seems huge. He takes a spoonful and looks at me. His face cracks a little as he chews.

"How's the shoulder?" I say.

He nods and extends his right arm out, wincing as he does it, which I think is for my benefit. The spoon in his hand drips a little milk to the floor. He brings the arm back to his side, pushes the bowl away, then sits back in his chair. "How many mounts did you get for me tomorrow?" he says.

"Just the one," I say. He nods and reaches in his shirt pocket for a cigarette.

"We've seen better days," he says.

"Yes, we have."

He lights the cigarette with a butane lighter which was tucked in the pack. "So, what's the problem?" he says.

"I think everyone thinks you're riding scared," I say. "No agent in the world can talk people out of that."

Grovey shakes his head. "No, I didn't mean that," he says. He looks at me. "And, I'll tell you what, son, I've never rode scared in my life. You ought to know that by now."

I shrug. "I don't know, Grovey, it just seems like you aren't as aggressive, you know. Like you were in Tampa."

"Fuck Tampa," he says. "That's history." He cocks his head to the kitchen door, which is held open by a wood slat, and calls for Donna. He looks at me again. "Why are you here?" he says.

"I need you to do something for me tomorrow."

"What makes you think I'll do anything for you?"

"You owe me one," I say. "I got you on your feet again."

He laughs and looks around the kitchen. "I owe you this," he says. "I owe you this," he says, pointing his lit cigarette at the box of corn flakes.

"Well?" I say.

"I know what it is," he says. "You don't hold your troubles in so good." He faces the kitchen door and calls for Donna again.

"So what's it gonna be, Grovey?"

He leans forward and flicks a cigarette ash in the cereal bowl. "I'll do it," he says. He looks at me. "But you and I are through after tomorrow."

"All right," I say. I didn't expect him to say this. I thought he might want to go back to Tampa, too. "Here's what you do," I say. He holds his hand up. I hear steps coming to the kitchen door.

"Come on in," he says to Donna when she stops in the doorway. She looks at me and walks over to his side. Grovey puts an arm around her behind. "Okay, tell me now," he says. "Say it in front of the girl. She needs to know what a big crooked world it is." Donna looks at me and smiles.

Amanda is up at five-thirty the next morning, without using an alarm. She has a clock in her head where the horses are concerned. I listen to her shuffling around with my eyes closed. She sits up in bed for a minute, then picks up the phone and dials a number. "Time to feed," she says quietly. She hangs up and walks into the bathroom. The shower goes on. Amanda wants her horses fed every morning by six, and she calls her groom, Polly, a girl who Amanda says enjoys a vigorous nightlife, to make sure it gets done on time. The shower goes off. The next thing I know, Amanda is curled up next to me in bed, soaking wet. I don't mind at all.

"I'm leaving the day after tomorrow," she says before she gets up again. After I hear her leave, I fall asleep and don't wake up until ten, when I hear the maid's cart rolling outside the window.

I get up, dress, and head outside. I stop by the front desk to buy a pack of cigarettes. I walk outside, light one, and head across the highway to the Big Boy on the other side of the road. The sky is still gray. It starts raining once I'm inside. I sit in the Big Boy for two hours smoking cigarettes, drinking coffee, watching it rain, trying not to think about anything.

At half-past twelve I walk to the pay phone, flip through the yellow pages, call a Powerline Cab, and stand for twenty minutes in the entrance of the Big Boy waiting for it. When the cab pulls up, the driver honks and I walk out in the rain and get in. The cab is red and white and has a Powerline decal with bolts of lightning shooting out on both sides. The driver is a young black man who says his name is Ted. He has a short Afro and is wearing thick eyeglasses.

When we get to the track, I give him five dollars for valet parking. We pull down to the valet station, and I tell Ted to tell them he is going to wait for me. They wave him to a spot up front. "I'll need a deposit if I'm going to wait for you," Ted says after he turns off the engine. I pull out a twenty and toss it up to the front seat. Ted picks it up and looks at it. "What, do you have something in there you like today?" he says, nodding to the grandstand. I tell him what race and what horses to bet on, but that's all I tell him. He turns off his meter and I get out of the car. He strides up alongside me after a second. "Is this a sure thing?" he says, looking down at me. He has a broad face with a lot of tiny bumps along the jawline.

"Yes," I say. We go inside. There's a tote board hanging right above the entrance. Fourteen minutes to post. Under RACE, it says 4. "I'll meet you under this board after the race," I say. Ted nods.

I head for the farthest end of the grandstand. There's hardly anybody there. Some men are standing together in a half-circle laughing. The air feels damp. I get to the corner of the grandstand and walk a little way out on the landing. The rain has stopped, and now there's a thin mist coming off the blacktop where I stand. A few feet away are an older man and woman sitting in lawn chairs with their legs crossed, staring out over the track.

In a minute the horses are on the track, riders up, for the post parade. Grovey is atop the three horse, a horse he isn't going to let run today. I watch for a minute, then go to a pari-mutuel window and bet all the money I have on the three horses in this race the riders are going to let run. I bet all the perfecta and trifecta combinations I can and end up standing at the window for a few minutes, which is a long time for a gambler to stand in line. It looks suspicious because the people around you know you're betting a lot on something, something you might know that they don't. Kirk told me to spread it around—go to five or six windows—but I don't feel like it. I'm leaving Old Latonia for good. He can answer the questions. I get all my tickets in a stack and put them in my trouser pocket. Ted is standing thirty feet away, leaning against a pole, watching me.

Grovey came through. He had that poor horse all over the track. The others in on it had yanked the run out of their mounts by the time they reached the far turn. The three riders dumb to the fix let their horses roll, and they finished 1-2-3. Just like Kirk said they would. I watched Grovey gallop his horse back to be unsaddled, and he shook his head when the groom said something to him. He dismounted and walked through the mud to the paddock and back to the jock's room. He had his winter money too, now. He told me last night he was going to stay here for a while. He pulled Donna a little closer when he said it.

Ted is smiling broadly when I find him standing under the tote board. "Easy," he says.

"Let's go," I say. He follows me out. There is a woman selling purple flowers wrapped in white paper outside the turnstile. There are women like her who stand outside every track I've ever been to. People who are lucky betting like to spread the winnings around. It's not a well-kept secret. I think about buying a bundle of flowers for Amanda, but that would probably make her suspicious. I don't know if it's this way for everyone, but with people like Amanda and me, doing something extra, like buying flowers, means you've done something wrong or are about to do something wrong.

We get in the cab and drive out. "How much did you make?" I say to Ted. He is smiling in the rearview mirror like he knows something. He's got some money in his pocket. Money will put a man in a good mood. It's the hope of the world.

"Where to?" he says.

"Let's take a drive," I say. "I want to see this town again before I leave. I'm leaving soon, you know."

"I figured that," he says. We head for town, going past the Hightop on the way. We stop at a drive-through and buy a bottle of Jack Daniel's and a six-pack of Olde English 800. Ted drinks the first can with one long bend of his elbow. "That's the thing I love about driving this cab," he says, throwing the can on the floor of the passenger side. "You never know when you're going to find a passenger running over with good luck."

"This is a high time for me," I say. I need to do this, drive around and blow some money, imagining this to be a cab ride that's going to take me someplace important.

"They're building out on the west side," Ted says as we pass one house after another, a small movie theater showing *Fantasy Island*, two blocks of small business shops, then one house after another. "Want to see it?" he says.

"Sure," I say. I lean back and take another drink from the bottle. I imagine Grovey and Donna pushing a shopping cart down an aisle of the Timmon's we pass out on the highway. This place has beat us bad.

We drive to a spot so far out I can barely see the town in the distance when I turn around. Ted pulls onto the shoulder and turns the engine off. We both get out. Ted points to a big blue sign with white letters in the middle of an empty field. FUTURE HOME OF GABRIEL ELECTRONICS, it says.

"They start building here next spring," Ted says. "I'm going to be here for it." He points to a spot in the sky where he imagines something to be. "Me and another guy were out here when they put up the sign. I think I'll try to find work here after it's built."

"There's something," I say, nodding.

"Maybe the next time you're here this won't be just another field with a billboard on it," he says. "There will be men working and plenty for all of us to do."

"It sounds like something worth waiting for," I say.

We don't make it back to the motel until it's dark. "What do I owe you?" I say to Ted as we pull into the parking lot of the Hightop.

"Forget it," he says. He opens his fourth can of Olde English.

"See you," I say. I get out of the cab. He honks the horn and laughs. I shut the door. He heads out. There is a light on in my room as I walk toward it.

There's an open suitcase on the bed when I unlock the door and come inside. Water is running in the bathroom. The television is on, but there's no sound. I take the money out of my trouser pocket, thirty-six hundred and change—"Someone must've smiled on you today," the teller said as he cashed it—and stick the money under a stack of panties in the suitcase. When I stand straight up again, I notice the room smells like perfume. Amanda walks out of the bathroom. She is wearing blue jeans and a white T-shirt with no brassiere underneath. Her hair is in a ponytail.

"Do you remember this?" she says, holding a clear square bottle in the air for me to see. It is nearly full. She sprays a little in my direction. I shake my head. "You bought it for me last winter."

I don't remember. "So why do you have it on now?" I say.

"I found it in the suitcase. I wanted to be special for you tonight."

"What makes tonight any different?"

"Well, I'm leaving in a couple of days and all."

I hold my hand up to her. "Sit down for a second," I say. "Sit down and look in your suitcase there." I point to the stack of panties. She reaches over and tips a corner of them up. She lets go and sits down on the bed.

"Tampa," I say.

She shakes her head. "No," she says. "I can't win there anymore. I think I can in West Virginia."

"It's cold in West Virginia."

She looks at me and blinks. "My horses are going to West Virginia," she says. I turn and take a few steps toward the television set. I try not to think of horses and riders, hotels and cabs.

"I'm going to Tampa," I say, though I know Tampa will not be Tampa without Amanda. This is what I have to show for my plans. A girl in a motel room sitting next to a suitcase.

"I won't go with you," she says.

"I know," I say. It is quiet. Other than meeting some has-been rider in a beer joint out on the prairie, I don't remember how I got involved in horse racing. I think this could be the end of it and I could just take my money and head out into the world to try my hand at something else. Earlier tonight I saw a sign out in a field that seemed to hold some promise for one man. I wonder why I am not like that—I have such little hope for things I can't control. "I guess I sold my soul today," I say.

"At least you got something for it," Amanda says. I turn around. She is lifting the corner of the panties again.

"Maybe," I say. Maybe I would end up being the kind of man who would have to fix a few more races before it was all over with.

She looks at me. "Come with me," she says. "You won't have to make any plans. You can't fail then."

I look at my shoes. "Grovey fired me today."

"You'll find another rider," she says. She lets the panties fall back again. "It won't matter for a while." She crosses her legs and looks up at the ceiling. "That money will last longer in West Virginia than it would most places," she says, looking back at me and smiling.

"That's one way of looking at it," I say. I try to guess how long she and I will last. Maybe as many nights in a cold town in West Virginia as thirty six-hundred dollars will buy. Maybe it will be enough. Amanda pats her hand on an open spot on the bed, and I'm glad nothing will be up to me for a while.

Home and Family

Now, with my wife gone, and my children with her, and my job, I start my day with eggs I buy two dozen at a time on gray cardboard sheets. I germinate bean plants and tomatoes in the little bra-like cups, and I stack the cracked half-shells like bowls in the corner of my kitchen. I toast bread or graham crackers or English muffins in a wire basket over the gas flame of the camp stove until they turn just the color of catalpa husks, and I read a verse out of the New Word Bible. I say a prayer over my plate: God, thank you for this. This day is mine.

I check the sky while hauling out my two-quart Teflon sauce pan that serves as chamber pot, adding a deposit to the growing pile of compost in the southwest corner of my lot, farthest away from the well. I'm interested in seeing just what I might leave behind, just what mark a man might make on the world. I have read that a row of garbage trucks loaded with one year of this country's trash would line up halfway to the moon. I'd like to see that. Or the wall, twelve feet high, we could assemble out of used Styrofoam that would come twisting out of Los Angeles across the Nevada high desert, over the Continental Divide into the corn land of the central plains, through the industry of Ohio and Pennsylvania, onto the avenues and docks of New York. That, too.

We throw away enough paper and cardboard in this country to keep five million people warm for two hundred years, but it would look like Romania, where you can't see now for smoke. There they've accomplished something. They've put their hand to the vein and pinched it off, but instead of the pressure pumping up to burst out in a mighty ejaculation and a cleansing rush of wind, the backside gave out and dribbled everything into the rivers and the Black Sea.

These are the only two man-made things you can see from outer space: the Great Wall of China and disaster.

I try to be unobtrusive.

"Rock," my wife said when she moved out the last of her things, "what's changed?"

"This," I said. She had my youngest daughter hefted in her arms and furniture piled in the street. "Everything."

"You," she said.

The telephone rings without fail by seven-thirty. Connie and Maxine are up already for hours, scratching together work for the employees of the Lend-A-Hand Temporary Agency's light industrial division. I deny any aptitude, take no tests besides the timed one that requires me to screw on wing nuts as fast as I can with both hands. After being caught in the corporate purge of middle management I don't sell, don't wear a tie, don't serve as junior vice president of anything. Connie and Maxine call me to clean a warehouse, pack the belongings of a young officer's family into plywood overseas shipping crates, truck pallets. I am, by virtue of small gifts and little attentions which come at no great cost to me when I am by the office—Connie likes a word about her outfit, Maxine a little pat and harmless flirting—always first on their list. I never refuse the work or the venue. I am reliable.

"Be there by eight?" Connie will always ask. No sense in nine o'clock jobs for me, up already with the morning paper and the milk trucks.

"Sharp," I say. "Thanks, lover," if it's Maxine on the line.

"Promises," she says, "always promises."

"I know somebody for you," she's always saying, too. "Why don't you give it a try?"

This morning it is Connie, checking to make sure I'm still on at Ace Chemical.

"I'm a hit," I say, "they love me."

"Call me when they're finished with you," Connie says.

I am easy to work with, a good man to have working for you. I am a big man, six-and-a-half feet tall and weigh over two hundred and thirty pounds, but I am congenial and a quick hand and study. In the break room over spudnuts, while we wait for the day's roster at Ace Chemical, I keep the ice broken and stirred with mutant jokes. I've stitched a sixth finger onto the side of my Wells Lamont jackass glove.

"I didn't wash my hands," I say. Someone warns one of the younger kids on the crew, newly married and who comes to work tired and propped up on a 32-ounce mug of Coca-Cola and powdered mini-donuts, that caffeine overdose will inhibit his staying power.

"Huh," he says.

The newlywed started as a temp, too, from another agency. Not everybody's looking to get on full time, though. Mostly I work in gangs of men who stoop and stand for five dollars an hour and take no particular pride in their work. I worked with a man moving his family across the country in a beat-up station wagon that breaks down or runs out of gas in front of police stations where they will give him enough money to get him to the next town, off their hands and out of their jurisdiction.

"There's good folks on the road," he said, "people who'll see you a gallon of gas or a sandwich."

"Junky men," my wife would have called them, did call them. "Not like you," she said when I started working with Lend-A-Hand. "Not like you at all."

The newlywed's name is Ethan. His wife's name is Cheryl, and I ask how she's doing while I'm riding on a pallet of empty brown sacks that Ethan drives to the middle of the lot on a forklift. The sacks are heavy and lined with plastic, with the stitched top like pour-it-yourself concrete comes in.

"There's something I don't understand," Ethan says.

"What's that?" I say.

"She keeps leaving," he says. I can see his eyes over the paper surgical mask he wears while we off-load potash from a trailer that came in yesterday five minutes before closing. They are the murky green of pond water in a bottle. I have a mask, too, and we look like doctors over the table.

We talk in between pallets and the noise of the auger. Cheryl leaves, without fail, after the nine o'clock rerun episode of *Knot's Landing*. Three weeks now in a row, and counting.

"She's back by noon the next day," Ethan says, his weak mustache prickled with salt. "She'll call me at lunch. I can't make anything of it." I can't either, though there's nothing in those shows that would lend to a good marriage, nothing to make a man or woman feel adequate. There's all that money and the horses. There are the bodies of women who don't exist in this world.

"Other than that," I say, "how are things?"

Other than that, Ethan talks about hating Rory Lundquist, two weeks his senior on the job. "He just keeps asking for it," Ethan says when Rory drives by on a bigger forklift. "He keeps on riding me."

I could tell Ethan that if he chooses to look at it that way he might be ridden for the rest of his life. But I don't know that. I don't know that any better than I know whether Cheryl might just not come back by noon the next day. There might be an episode that proves to be too much.

You can tell a young man lots of things, though no more than you can tell an old man. The New Word Bible says let all your answers be either yes or no. Beyond this only leads to trouble.

My wife was always the better Christian. She is a good Christian, in fact. It's not a thing she will tell you. She will say, I try and I fail, but there is the grace of God. She didn't believe in divorce. But it came down to her not believing in me even more. A forty-two-year-old Kelly girl. She told me. I didn't ask to be believed in.

She said to me the day she filed, "God is going to have to forgive me for this."

He may have to forgive me, too.

I gave my wife everything without argument to settle. A man who uses up the choicest years of a woman's body, fathers children by her, interrupts her worldly pursuits by virtue of holy promises is a man with debt and obligation. The children went with her by her choice and their own fuzzy instinct.

"I won't take the house, Rock," she said, "It's in your family," which was a final act of love and restraint, rather than pulling down on my head the full weight of the law. "But you'll feed and clothe these children," she said.

"I'll do that," I said.

"You don't owe me anything."

"Not 'I'm sorry'?"

"If you are," she said.

"It's fair," I told her. And she gave me her hand, a formal seeming thing to do, to seal the bargain.

I went on working to keep food on my children's table, clothes on their soft-skinned backs, money in the pockets of piano teachers and soccer coaches and the manager of Cinema 6 and the

roller rink for my thirteen-year-old daughter and the illicit boyfriend she thinks she has hidden there from her mother.

"If I need to step in," I've told my wife.

"They'll need a man in their lives, Rock," she's said. "Girls go
through puberty too soon without a father."

But I've lost my girls.

My oldest calls to ask for favors.

"But your mother has the car, sweetheart," I say.

"She does," my girl says, "but . . ."

"But?" I say.

"How are you getting along?" I ask my youngest, and she says,
"Fine."

I used the phone to turn off the gas first and then the water. I'm
energy conscious about the lights. I've unplugged all my clocks.

"You going on vacation or just moving? Either way, there's
valves inside the house," they said at city water.

"Neither," I said. "I just want it off. And garbage and sewer, all
of it. I don't want any more bills."

"I don't think we can do that," city water told me. The gas
people tried to refer me to their old-age assistance department.

I live by moonlight and cook over the camp stove. I indulge
in a little radio for some news and the bluegrass show on Sunday afternoons, hoping the Lord will look the other way if this is
some infringement of the Sabbath. I provide, most weeks, a hundred and thirty dollars for the care and keeping of my family. I
figure this is thirty-two dollars and fifty cents a child. Giving my
wife a share brings it to twenty-six apiece. Their mother feeds
them casseroles and gets them reduced-priced lunch tickets at
school.

"Every little bit helps, Rock," she says. The kids have jobs. Two
paper routes, a bag boy, one auto parts deliveryman on weekends.

"Keeps them in shoes and pocket change," my wife says. "We're
all right."

Truth be told, my wife's mother, with whom they all now live, would never let the brood starve. She's got pension money squirreled away in half a dozen passbook accounts and forty-year-old Treasury bonds. She calls it her legacy. She claims she'll send every one of my children to college. My wife's mother claims she is very rich and that my children work these jobs because they build character and teach fiscal responsibility. My oldest, Ben, is going to the University of Southern California this fall, he tells me, under his own steam and the old woman's auspices.

"Don't sweat it, Dad," he says to me. "I'm scholarship material." He's come over to work on the truck he has hidden in my garage. I lay my palms out, face up. My son is unrolling an orange extension cord he has plugged into an outdoor socket belonging to my neighbors. The cord runs to a trouble light he has hanging in my garage so he can keep working after dark.

He lays his sockets out according to size on a strip of blue terry cloth. No one has taught him this. He likes things where he can find them. He has a red mechanic's toolbox the size of a baby carriage he straps to the back of his bicycle.

"How about you?" he says. "How are you doing?" This is how my son, the son of my divorced wife and an earlier self of mine, talks to me now. Like an inquiring neighbor. Like a grown-up. "What are you doing these days? Where are you working?"

I can appreciate it.

Still, sometimes when he does this, I take his arm at the wrist and turn it, palm up, to the light. He has a scar down his forearm six inches long and as thick as a coat hanger. The house we lived in when he was a little boy, when his mother and I first married, caught fire from a dry bird's nest and old wiring one night. I ran in for him, upstairs, my undershirt wrapped around my head for smoke and my eyes blurred till I was swimming blind. I pounded on his bed looking for him, but he wasn't in it. I found him underneath, rolled up in a sleeping bag. The fire was in the hall, at the doorway, working up the walls to the ceiling. I left my son in the bag and swung him feet first to smash out the bedroom window. When I dropped him, bag and all, he grabbed at me and slashed his arm on the glass in the windowpane.

I tap the scar with my finger.

"You know how you got this?" I say.

"From love," he says back to me. And then I nod and let his arm go.

I broke an ankle when I jumped out after him. The house was a complete loss.

"It's the pictures I regret, Rock," my wife has said to me, even years later. "We have no record, nothing from the wedding, nothing of Benny as a baby or when he was a little boy, remember, in that red cowboy hat you bought, with his cap gun. Remember?"

I don't remember that picture, to this day.

"Ben," I say to my son, who is rolling back the tarp on his truck, "do you remember a cowboy hat, a red straw one?"

"What hat?" Ben says. "My hat?"

"Your mother says there was a picture of you in it."

"Nah," Ben says. "I don't remember."

"Your mother does."

"She's seeing somebody," Ben says. "She tell you?"

"Her affair," I say.

"You think so?" Ben says, quick to catch an unintended pun. It's not a joke you plan on sharing with your son. Ben hasn't cut his hair in a year and a half; it's thin and hangs straight down his back. He wears his shirts with the sleeves cut off at the shoulder, and his arms are smooth-lined like a girl's. Maybe he's started smoking. I ask him every time he comes over does he need glasses.

"I don't squint," he says.

"You squint," I say. "You look like Clint Eastwood."

"That's not so bad," Ben says.

"You look like Mr. Magoo," I say.

Ben's mother does not know about this truck; it is a confidence between Ben and myself, one thing I keep from her. Ben tells me it is a 1948 Dodge Powerwagon, four-wheel drive. "Clean," he says. "You wouldn't believe it." It is massive; it fills the garage like a whale in a cave. Ben talks to me standing straight up with his arms folded across the hood.

"It's got to be red," he tells me.

"Yellow," I say. "I could see it yellow."

"It'd look like something from a florist," Ben says. "Look." He spreads a plan on the hood and we study over it like architects. He's drawn the wagon to scale, the curved lip of the bed and the arched wheel wells and the bucket headlights. Sketched on the door of the driver's side is *Institute of Archaeology.* "That'll be in blue," Ben tells me, "for a touch of class."

Ben's light draws the mosquitoes and moths, and they swirl around his head like a crown while he is bent over the engine. He comes up for air and says to me, "I tell Mom you're doing all right, lost a little weight, but you're shaved and the house is picked up."

"I tell her the same thing," I say.

"Why don't you let me come live with you over the summer? There's nothing that says I can't, is there?"

"No," I say.

"No which?" Ben says. "No, you can't; or no, nothing?"

"No, nothing," I say. Ben is sitting on the front fender, scratching under his chin where he should have a beard.

"Dad," he says, "what are you doing here? Is this some kind of experiment, or does this prove something?"

"It's what I can afford," I say.

"You got nads, Dad," he says to me. "I'd never say any different."

This, the thought of my sons growing up without me, troubles me. And my daughters. My boys do not have my size. They take after their mother, birds' bones and the tiny bound feet of Chinese royalty. My boys were doll babies, and even now they have too little flesh on their faces. It's unfortunate when this happens, and when girls take their looks from their fathers. My daughters are robust and bovine. They have my extra height and thick legs and heavy arms. My littlest has jowls like a bulldog, and my oldest has uneven skin and at thirteen takes a man's shoe.

I contemplate this standing out on my fence at night while I survey the neighborhood. I know who sleeps and who sits up late and whether or not they watch TV. I stand eight feet in the air on a two-by-four crosspiece, with my shirt open and my hands on my belly like an idol.

I caught a burglar from up here once. I didn't catch him really—I scared him away by shouting, "Go ahead, the old man isn't home and the wife's deaf as a stump." I remember he turned to look at me, three backyards away, like he was considering the advice. I said, "Come here a minute," and he shook his head no, then waved before he slipped off.

Tonight, after Ben, I am convinced that growing up a boy is no easy thing. I'm convinced it's nothing a father teaches you—but only half convinced, and not sure that I couldn't help my boys anyway. I've been alive all this time. Some of it should count for wisdom.

One night a week I spend at the supermarket, where I buy with coupons. Two-for-one is odds I like. And rebate offers, gold mines the average consumer leaves unplundered for the price of a stamp. Potatoes are good. They go with everything. Beans, rice, bread. Staples. In the summers I have my garden. I have a basket on the back of my bicycle, a blue plastic milk crate that says Mountainland Dairies.

Maxine from Lend-A-Hand tells me the grocery store is a fine place to meet women.

Ben will need to learn to shop on his own if he goes away to college. I ask my wife if he knows how to cook.

"He can boil water," she says. "He gets his own breakfast. There's not as much to know these days." She asks me if I've kept up the life insurance.

"The mail goes to you," I say.

Thursday nights are laundry nights. I wash up everything in a tub half full of lukewarm water with a cup of powdered soap while I listen to a ball game or *Mystery Theatre* on the radio. I start first thing when I get home, and everything is out on the line by dark and stiff and dry come morning. In the winter I have clothes draped over banisters and curtain rods all through the house for two days.

Ben doesn't come by on Thursdays. I've told him he's welcome anytime, it doesn't matter.

"I don't want to get in the way, Dad," he says. "You have your life to live."

Maxine gives me her usual line when I come in for my paycheck, "Rock, I've got a hot tip for you."

"I've just finished three days with a local company that manufactures miniature basketball hoops and backstops. We've cleaned and restacked the warehouse and taken inventory. I got a black baseball cap with YELLOW, the name of a big truck manufacturer, stitched on the front from a sales representative. The job let me put in six hours of overtime, which normally is not allowed.

"I don't want a job, sugar," I say.

"It's a woman," Maxine says. "It's a favor, from me to you. You've been separated more than a year, haven't you?"

"Why don't you get me on at Wentzell's again?" I say. "That was good work."

"For me, then," Maxine says.

"What," I say, "are we supposed to do?"

"Get together for a meal, go dancing," Maxine says. "Do what comes naturally."

Maxine's friend is a second cousin who runs a yarn and fabric outlet called Knit-Wit. She's trim and tidy. Her blue print jumper is covered with tiny teapots, and she wears rectangle glasses on a chain around her neck like she's tempting age. Her husband has been MIA in Vietnam for twenty years.

"I lost track of time passing," she says. "Suddenly I'm forty and I wonder what I've missed."

In the end, against all better judgment, she's come to the house. I solved all the obvious problems with a barbecue. I took an extra ten dollars out of the overtime money, out of my children's mouths, and now we sit on the patio eating ribs sticky with honey sauce and ears of new corn. We drink a pitcher of iced tea with a taste of sweet straw, and Sylvia, which is her name, asks me questions about my family.

"Is it OK?" she says. "Do you mind talking about it?" One evidence of her extraordinary politeness. "That's what I missed, having a family."

"What is it you want to know?" I say.

"Oh, anything," she says. "Names, dates, first causes." She offers to take my side in things, defend me, sitting with a napkin in her lap and eating with her fingers.

"I used to play baseball," I say.

"Or we could talk about baseball," she says. "Baseball's fine."

She eats well, heartily. She's making a great pretense of thinking of who else she knows with the name Rock when Ben comes up the driveway.

"Hey, sorry," he says.

"Hello," Sylvia says.

"Ben, Sylvia, and likewise," I tell them. "He's family."

"Come eat, Ben," she says. "What brings you? Or are you living with your dad?"

"For the summer," Ben says. He has a duffel bag with him he tosses in the house. I dish up a plate of ribs and corn.

"It's early, still, for corn," Sylvia says, "but your dad picked a good half dozen ears."

"You'll need to call Mom," Ben tells me. "Let her know I got here." Which means he hasn't moved, just left.

"Are your kids still in town, then, Rock?" Sylvia says. "That's nice for you."

"It works out for Ben," I say.

On the phone, my wife tells me nothing I have to say is any news to her.

"Are you going to keep him, Rock?" she says.

"Do you mean is he going to stay?" I say.

"No, that's not what I mean. I mean, is he going to be up for work and get fed and be ready for school in the fall? Is he going to have clean clothes? Is someone going to keep him from getting arrested?"

"What's he done?" I say.

"Nothing. That's not what I meant."

"He's sixteen years old," I say.

"Seventeen, Rock."

"Seventeen?" I say. "Seventeen."

"Sixteen when we split up, Rock. Seventeen last year. Eighteen and starting college in the fall."

"You keep good track," I say. "You always had that little calendar in your purse."

"I keep track," she says.

"We had a bad marriage, didn't we?" I say. "We must have."

"It got that way," she says.

"But we weren't unfaithful. We weren't unkind to one another."

"I'm seeing somebody, Rock," she says. "Ben's told you."

"Yes," I say.

"It's somebody from church," she says.

"You don't need my permission."

"I would let you know if anything happened," she says. "Why don't you have Ben stay a week or two, see what's what? Is he there now?"

"He's entertaining on the patio," I say.

"Is that what he's been sneaking off for at nights?"

"I've never seen her before," I say. "I think she's older."

"Two weeks, Rock, trial run. Maybe he needs it, I don't know. You might as well know, too, Sissy fell down on the playground. She broke out a front tooth, but it was a baby one. We're going to just let things ride. She has an ugly scab on her lip and doesn't want to go to summer school, though."

"Don't make her," I say.

"We do things in life we don't want to do, Rock," she says.

"That's where I had it wrong all those years," I say.

"Do, do," she says. The closest she'll come to profanity is pretending. "Anything else?"

"Sacco's has some good corn," I say.

"Thanks for the tip," she says and tells me good-bye.

We'll have dusk as late as 9:30 up until the first day of summer, two weeks away. I need no light to get around my house. The streetlamp across the avenue casts a slanted doorway onto the living room floor, and the bulb over the neighbor's carport burns all night right outside the window over the kitchen sink. Upstairs, where the air is hot and stuffy as gauze because I have left the windows closed, you get some light from the moon as well. I open windows on the second floor and dump Ben's bag on the bottom bunk in the north bedroom. Sylvia is laughing out on the patio.

"What did she say?" Ben asks when I come back.

"You're a potential felon. You're in the lockup for two weeks," I say.

"Are you planning a life of crime, Ben?" Sylvia says.

"A life of ease," Ben tells her. He's on his back with his plate on his belly.

"And so young," Sylvia says.

"Seventeen," I say. Ben has the trim waist of a dancer and the wasted arms of an addict—he looks a young seventeen. He's stretched out with his hands over his head like he'll be starting the backstroke.

"Seventeen," Sylvia says. "My brother was working in the coal mines already when he was seventeen."

"I'm a math whiz," Ben says.

"Or he would have been sold like the others," I say.

Sylvia laughs and then asks if she can use the bathroom. This one thing I have overlooked.

"Problem," Ben says. He sits up straight. "The water's off, pipes are bad. That's our first project for the summer."

"Oh," Sylvia says.

"It's awkward," I say, looking at Ben.

"Hey, we'll go for ice cream, my treat, and they'll have a rest room there," Ben says. "Sorry for the trouble."

Sylvia is a sport about it, and Ben has us pile into the big cab of his Powerwagon. I boost Sylvia up and she sits on my side to keep out of the way of the stick. She compliments Ben on his truck. She pats my leg and says look how high up we are. Ben wrestles the wheel around corners like he's steering a tiger by the ears.

"Look at that dash," Ben says. It's spare and functional—speedometer and oil gauge, pull-out knobs for the choke and lights. "Those days are gone."

Sylvia, in the cab, has a scent of soap and rainwater, of new cloth.

"He should paint it yellow," I say. "Yellow the color of cheesecake."

"Maybe you're right," Ben says.

Ben leaves us alone when we get back. He's bought us all double-dip sugar cones, and Sylvia has told him thanks and remembers it's been years since she's had one. They are like the ones she used to get in Virginia, before she left home and moved out West.

"I put your stuff upstairs," I tell him. "I'm gone early in the morning. There's eggs for breakfast."

While I put up the barbecue, Sylvia rocks in a metal patio chair.

"What do you miss most?" she says.

I think about it. "Nickel soda pop," I say. She laughs to oblige me.

"Maxine expects a full report, details, explicit photos," she tells me.

"My sisters used to get together and do that," I say. "I thought maybe it went out with the fifties."

"Girls are girls," Sylvia says. "Maxine's been divorced, twice. Third time's the charm. They've been together six years now."

"She's told me," I say. Ben has made short work of any leftovers. I make two piles of the garbage, wet and dry.

"Anyway, thanks for this," she says. "And you have a nice son."

"I have a couple," I say. "Benny's the oldest, then there's Stephen. Then the girls—Laura, and Sissy's last. She just broke a tooth." The wind starts the chimes while I'm telling her this, the ones with the head of an owl and long wooden tubes of lacquered bamboo. Sylvia comes to me and puts her arms around my waist.

"Here," she says, to offer me a deep kiss and a try at compassion that have both been twenty years in the making.

Sylvia is asleep now on the couch under the light of the street-lamp in the living room. She is frowzy-headed and calm, and she's dropped her earrings into her shoes where she won't forget them. Ben is tossing restless upstairs in his old room, where it's warm even with the windows open until about four in the morning, when you get a crosswind that freezes you in your sheets. The house seems full, like it hasn't for a long time, and out on the fence, far from sleep, I cannot remember which of my children it is that has asthma.

The Writers

WENDY BRENNER was born in Chicago and grew up in Chicago and rural Michigan. She teaches in the creative writing program at the University of North Carolina at Wilmington.

RITA CIRESI has taught on the creative writing faculty at Hollins College and presently teaches at the University of South Florida in Tampa. She is the author of *Blue Italian,* a novel published by Ecco Press in 1996, and a new novel forthcoming from Dell.

HARVEY GROSSINGER was born in the Bronx and grew up there and in Mamaroneck, New York. He now lives in Bethesda, Maryland. He is a professorial lecturer in the Literature Department at American University.

DENNIS HATHAWAY is editor of *Crania,* an on-line literary/arts magazine. A native of Iowa, he has been a newspaper reporter, construction worker, and building contractor. He lives in Venice, California.

HA JIN grew up in China and was for six years a soldier in the People's Liberation Army. He is the author of two books of poetry and a first book of short stories for which he won the PEN/Hemingway Award in 1997. He teaches at Emory University.

CAROL LEE LORENZO lives in Snellville, Georgia, near Atlanta, and teaches fiction in the creative writing program at Emory University and at the Callanwolde Fine Arts Center. She is the author of three novels for young adults.

CHRISTOPHER MCILROY lives in Tucson, where he is program director for the nonprofit corporation ArtsReach, which conducts fiction and poetry workshops in Native American communities. He is a native of New York City.

C. M. MAYO makes her home in Mexico City. She was awarded fellowships at Bread Loaf and the Sewanee Writers' Conference for *Sky Over El Nido*. She is now working on a novel.

ALYCE MILLER lives in Bloomington, Indiana, and teaches in the M.F.A. program at Indiana University. She was born in Switzerland and grew up in Michigan and Ohio. Her novel *Stopping for Green Lights* is forthcoming from Anchor.

DIANNE NELSON was born in Utah and in her early years lived in Kansas. She now makes her home in Salt Lake City, where she devotes her time to writing and her work with the Utah Arts Council.

ANDY PLATTNER works with horses on his farm in Kentucky and writes stories about horse racing. He was born into a racing family (his father managed racetracks in Florida and Kentucky).

PAUL RAWLINS, one of the 1995 Flannery O'Connor Award winners, is senior editor at Aspen Books in Salt Lake City. He is working on a second collection of stories.